T0265650

More praise for *My Darling Boy*

"John Dufresne's *My Darling Boy* is my favorite novel of his—and I love them all. It is actually my favorite novel, replacing my decades-long fascination with *Catcher in the Rye*. *My Darling Boy* is exquisitely painful and wonderfully rendered. It is a novel written as though in a state of grace, a narrator grappling with a son who is grappling with addiction where there are no easy—or hard—answers. Instead of a bookmark, readers, bring a pack of tissues with you."

—Denise Duhamel, author of *Pink Lady*

"In this novel, hard times rewrite the past. But love outlasts death, absence, casual cruelty, rational facts, and late-breaking bad news. It survives betrayals so extreme they're Shakespearean yet astoundingly petty. Love begets hope, and hope changes the future, at lea? for now. *My Darling Boy* is about the fullness of time and is as bit? sweet, beautiful, and consoling as the truth can be."

—Debra Monroe, author of *It Takes a Worried*

"John Dufresne's latest novel tells a story of love and loss, a
to find and rehabilitate his opioid-addicted son when t¹
want to be found or rehabilitated. . . . *My Darling F*
terrible estrangement that shocks so many famili?
the good life sometimes is not good enough. ?
Olney's hope and courage stand out to the re?
is love. There is the chance of a better futur?
only if he continues his quest and does r?
our times."   —Neil Crab?

My Darling Boy

ALSO BY JOHN DUFRESNE

Novels

I Don't Like Where This Is Going

No Regrets, Coyote

Requiem, Mass.

Deep in the Shade of Paradise

Love Warps the Mind a Little

Louisiana Power & Light

Short Story Collections

Johnny Too Bad

The Way That Water Enters Stone

Plays

Trailerville

Screenplays

To Live and Die in Dixie

The Freezer Jesus

[My Darling Boy]

A Novel

JOHN DUFRESNE

W. W. NORTON & COMPANY
Independent Publishers Since 1923

Copyright © 2025 by John Dufresne

For information about permission to reproduce selections from this book, write to Permissions, W. W. Norton & Company, Inc., 500 Fifth Avenue, New York, NY 10110

For information about special discounts for bulk purchases, please contact W. W. Norton Special Sales at specialsales@wwnorton.com or 800-233-4830

Manufacturing by Lakeside Book Company
Book design by Daniel Lagin
Production manager: Gwen Cullen

ISBN 978-1-324-03573-2

W. W. Norton & Company, Inc., 500 Fifth Avenue, New York, NY 10110
www.wwnorton.com

W. W. Norton & Company Ltd., 15 Carlisle Street, London W1D 3BS

10 9 8 7 6 5 4 3 2 1

Always for Cindy

My Darling Boy

(I)

The Bliss of Distance

THE MIST OF A MEMORY

For twenty-six years and five months, Olney Kartheizer worked as a staff writer and copy editor at the Anastasia, Florida, *Daily Sun*. He wrote book reviews until the publisher killed the Book Page. He'd been able to feature local writers who would otherwise have been ignored, like Pen Beeman, whose first book of poems, *My Sudden Angel*, won the Gold Medal in the Florida Book Awards, and Monty Driver, whose *Mosquito County Confidential* became a local bestseller. He wrote travel essays about hidden Florida until the Travel Page folded. He edited *Magnolia*, the Sunday magazine supplement, until the publishers decided that *Parade* would be a better fit for the residents of the Lost Coast. For his last seven years at the paper, Olney wrote obituaries, his favorite assignment, and the occasional human-interest feature. He learned what every necrologist knows—that in the end we're all just stories. A year ago, having no mortgage, no car payments, no outstanding debts, he took a generous buyout from the diminishing daily and retired.

These days he works nine-to-three Monday through Friday at Anastasia Miniature Golf near the Intracoastal. He doesn't need the money; he wants to get out of the house and talk to someone other than himself. Besides his having to capture the occasional rattlesnake in the fountain grass by the water hazard (Veronica Lake), the job's pretty easy, giving him time to write his observations and stories in his notebook: *Yolanda Martini finds a positive pregnancy test on a damp sidewalk on the street where she lives.*

For twenty-nine years and three months, Olney lived as a devoted husband to Kat (née Harvey) and doting dad to Cully. A loving family in a cozy home, all smiles and comfort. Olney told Cully bedtime stories every night, those he made up about the monkey family (the Lemons, Lewis, Victoria, and their boy Spanky) that lived down the block and worked for the circus, and those that he read, like *The Hobbit* and *Fudge-a-Mania*. Cully could juggle three balls by the time he was nine and could do a handful of magic tricks when he was ten: spoon bending, cup through the table, coin levitation, like that. He told jokes like "Q: If you're from England and you're in the bathroom but you're not pooping, what are you? A: European." Cully had a handful of friends from school who dropped by for playdates and went to each other's birthday parties. Cully loved the park, the beach, the mini-golf course. He loved to snuggle on the couch with Mom and Dad and watch cartoons.

He was born with a faint pink birthmark on his left cheek in the shape of a horse's head. His pals at school called him "Pony." The mark faded over the years until it was barely visible by the time Cully was thirteen. He missed it. A friend's older brother worked at Inkslinger's and tattooed a thin black line around Cully's pony. Free for nothing. You could see it then. You can see it now.

Cully's ambidextrous, can write with both hands and at the same time, English with his left hand and Spanish with his right. He never liked Olney calling this ability a gift. He called it a skill. He put his skill to further use on the baseball diamond as a switch-pitcher for the Splendora High Airedales. He pitched righty to right-hand batters and lefty to lefties. Wore a funny-looking ambidextrous glove. He had a seventy-five-mile-an-hour fastball and an erratic knuckleball that no hitter could hit, but no catcher could catch. He pitched the team to the state 5A championship against the Bob Town Burrowing Owls. A no-hitter. Cully was a hero, a local celebrity, picture on the front page of the paper and all that. He was a freshman. He never pitched again. Go out at the top, he said. That made some people angry. Full of himself, they said. Selfish.

He switched to basketball. Played point guard for the Airedales, who had their first winning season in a decade. He ran track, the longer distances, and tried tennis. No backhand needed. Switched hands with the racket as the ball cleared the net. He was singles champ in the districts. So Olney was surprised when his star athlete called it quits. He had other things to do, he told his dad. Olney said, "Weren't you having fun?"

"A blast."

"So?"

"Fun will only get you so far."

When he was fifteen, Cully withdrew from his parents, stayed in his room watching videos on his computer. He slept a lot, skipped meals, nodded out on the La-Z-Boy. He'd get angry when Olney asked about his health and state of mind, offered to take him to a doctor or a therapist, so Olney stopped asking, and maybe that was his first mistake. When Cully was sixteen, Olney caught him smoking pot in the backyard. Cully said it was his first time, but no one gets caught their first time. Olney said he was disappointed. Cully apologized. It was normal enough behavior, Olney figured.

Cully got himself a weekend job working in the kitchen at Jack's

Diner scrambling eggs and slinging hash. The breakfast shift. He settled into a quiet routine of school, homework, and flipping pancakes. One Sunday morning Cully scalded his arm when he somehow spilled a pot of nearly boiling grits on it and ended up in the ER. Olney picked him up. Cully's eyes were squeezed shut and the wound was covered with cling wrap. He'd been given Tylenol and a prescription for something stronger if it was needed. It was. A week later he sliced deeply into his index finger while dicing onions. Back to the ER. And not too long after that, he took a tumble on the stairs at school. Nothing broken, but a drilling pain in his head and a nasty bruise over his left eye.

Kat suspected that these "accidents," if that's what they were, could be attributed to Cully's continued surreptitious drug use. Olney chose not to believe that, saying that Cully was just clumsy like his old man. And then Cully discovered a pain clinic on Blake Street. One-stop shopping. Stand in line at the clinic door, walk in, speak with Dr. Feelgood about the crushing pain in your back (mention the staircase), get your prescription for OxyContin, get it filled on the spot, swallow the tablets whole, do not chew, crush, dissolve, or break, and walk out the door. And then Kat discovered the cache of pills in the empty battery compartment of a flashlight beside Cully's bed and brought them to Olney, who could no longer honestly believe that the injuries were not deliberate and not self-inflicted.

When Cully was eighteen, he and a friend made a suicide pact to die while they were high. They parked the car in the elementary school parking lot, took their pills, drank their vodka, put on a Green Day CD, closed the car windows, turned on the engine, and went to sleep. That was the night Olney realized that Cully had lost control of his drug use and that Olney's failure to insist on a choice of either rehab or the streets had been a profound disservice to his son. That night Olney got a call from another of Cully's pals, Dermid, telling him what was going on. Dermid said he was supposed to be with them but chickened out at the last minute. He cried. Olney called the cops and drove to the school. He found the boys unconscious. He broke the passenger window with a crowbar and dragged Cully out and tried to revive him, only he didn't know what he was doing. Mostly he screamed Cully's name and shook him. Green Day sang something about walking alone. The cops and paramedics arrived. The other boy, Orson, was dead. When Olney called Orson's parents, the Blairs, with the heartbreaking news, Steve Blair choked back tears and said, "At least it's finally over." When Olney took Cully home from the hospital, Cully told his dad he should not have interfered. When Cully fell asleep that night, Kat told Olney, "I can't live like this anymore." When Cully awoke the next afternoon and learned from his dad that Orson had died, he said, "Orson who?" and then he remembered. "How?"

"The car."

"He did?"

"I'm sorry."

Cully closed his eyes and saw Orson as he had seen him last and as he would see him evermore. Orson the outrageous, voted "most likely to exceed" in high school, who could sing like an angel and dance like a dervish, whose dream in life was to be a private investigator because he loved uncovering secrets and wearing a shoulder holster, is sitting behind the wheel of his Celica, pouring vodka on his head and face, lighting a match, and touching the match to his skin when it went out. Cully said, What's the hurry? Several minutes later, Orson's forehead slammed into the steering wheel, and that may have been the second that Orson died. Does it happen in a second?

Cully refused to attend Orson's wake or funeral. Shame, perhaps, Olney thought. Didn't want to face his friends or classmates or Orson's parents. Or guilt, maybe. Olney hoped that this tragedy would scare Cully straight—not everyone gets a second chance. Go ask Orson.

When Olney spoke with friends about Cully's difficulties and wondered out loud what he had done wrong as a dad, the commiserators would respond with comments like: *It's a phase he's going through*; *He'll grow out of it*; *Boys take longer to mature than girls*; *My kid was the same as Cully, a real hot mess, and now he's produce manager at Publix*. Olney asked Anne Matthews, a neurologist at Anastasia College, for her opinion. How do you go from the happiest child in town to the saddest? She said the teenage brain is like a minefield. All the underused gray matter is being pruned away and sometimes too much of the pruning happens in the prefrontal cortex. Then she said a lot of other things about the remodeling of the brain and how the rewire can go haywire, and so on, leaving the impulsive amygdala in charge of decision making. She said, At least Cully's not schizophrenic. Seen that happen too often. Olney said, "One thing I worry about is that Cully's story won't have a happy ending."

Before he went off to college, Cully appeared out of nowhere at his parents' house. He'd been staying with friends in Palatka. Kat was at her volunteer docent job at the art museum. He and Olney sat at the kitchen table. Olney put out a plate of sourdough crispbread and Brie, a bowl of spicy, brine-cured olives, and a ramekin of fish dip. Cully tried the dip and made a face, said he liked his cheese sliced and his olives green and pitted. He told Olney he needed money for a car.

Olney said, "I'm not giving you cash. We've been through this."

"With a car, I can get a decent job."

"Like what?"

"Drive for Uber." Cully wrote a figure down on a piece of notebook paper and slid it over to Olney.

"If I give you money, you'll buy dope. Earn your money like the rest of us. You can work for me."

"Doing what?"

"Research."

"A hundred a day plus expenses."

"Be serious," Olney said. "Ten bucks an hour. I'll have to talk to your mother, of course. She'll be home in an hour."

"I'm on a tight schedule."

"How are you feeling these days?"

"I feel like I'm taking control of my life," Cully said, his convenient optimism surfacing.

"Are you high right now?"

Cully shook his head.

Olney said, "I don't approve of self-medication."

"I didn't ask for your approval."

"You asked for two thousand dollars. What's happening to you, Cully?"

Cully pointed to his head. "Look, you have no idea what's going on up here. You don't have to live in my head. You don't know the pain. I'm so sad. I've got no one. Nothing. I took the pills the shrinks gave me, all of them, Zoloft, Ativan, Wellbutrin, Zyprexa, Paxil, blah, blah, blah. They made me ill or impotent or confused or anxious or suicidal or restless, but not better. How would you like that? When I'm promised that meds will make the pain stop, and it doesn't, only gets worse."

Cully stared at his hands, the hands he clenched and unclenched. "The pain makes me act in ways I'm not proud of. It keeps me inside my miserable self, fighting it off. Look, when I take oxy, I feel euphoric. I have such good intentions and confidence, and superpowers. If I could stay high, I could get somewhere in life. It just doesn't last very long."

"Which superpowers?"

"I can do without food or water or sleep. I can hear sounds only dogs can hear. I can read another person's thoughts sometimes. I can tame wild creatures, slow my metabolism, shut out the world. Things like that. Why would I give it up?"

Olney apologized to Cully for blowing up at him, said he hated to see him waste his talents and wanted him healthy again. Cully asked again for the money. Olney said if Kat agreed, he'd buy the car for him if he had a license. Cully said he needed to leave.

"Cully, please." Olney reached across the table and took Cully's hand. Cully took offense and jerked his hand away like it'd been scalded, stood, punched a hole in the drywall over the counter, and said maybe he should just kill himself. "Why can't you just help me out? You're my father. Who else will?"

"What happened to the voice recorder I loaned you when you were doing the interview with the philosopher for your podcast?"

"I have it."

"I need it for work."

"I have it."

"On you?"

"In Palatka."

"Let's go get it."

"Why are you being such an asshole?"

"Maybe you should leave."

"No. I won't."

Olney wondered if this could really be happening.

Cully smiled and said, "Why don't you call the cops, big man."

( )

THESE DAYS CULLY LIVES A NOMADIC LIFE. ONE DAY HE'S IN, SAY, SEMI-nole Pines, sleeping off a dose of oxycodone in the park; the next day he's in Cypress Springs, then Tampa, then he'll call Olney from Nokomis, saying he needs a loan to get him to Dolphin Island, and from there it's a straight shot to Melancholy, and Melancholy is where he can get back on his feet. Besides his having to sleep under the occasional picnic table and do some dumpster dining, the life's pretty easy, giving him time to contemplate the big questions, like, *Who am I?* and *Who are these other people?* and *What are we all doing here?*

( )

IT'S JUST NOW CIVIL TWILIGHT ON A WARM AND BREEZY SPRING EVE-ning in Anastasia, and Olney is sitting at his kitchen table by the open window—he catches the candied aroma of honeysuckle from the Woodbines' backyard—sitting with a snifter of cognac and a bowl of cashews. He's writing out a hundred-dollar check to Evangelist Rylan Burgess and listening to the Medallions on the Friday night doo-wop show on WHY-AM in Lost Lake. The honeysuckle smells like the tinkling of wind chimes, he decides. He seals the envelope, shuts his eyes, and listens to Vernon Green whispering sweet words of pismotal-ity, and for a minute Olney is sixteen again and sick in love with Betty Ann Truman, and he pictures the two of them at the Splendora High School Junior Prom and remembers how, after the chicken cordon bleu, the three-bean salad, and the banana pudding, they walked outside, she in her mint-green tulle dress, he in his blue batik tux and the rented black tasseled loafers that almost fit, hand in hand, shoulder to shoul-der, across the golf course fairway, as the band inside—the Coyotes—played the Nino Tempo/April Stevens version of "Deep Purple," and Olney leaned toward Betty Ann, inhaled the scent of patchouli from her throat, caught his breath, touched his forehead to hers, and felt awash in a wave of what he believed must have been sublime and abid-ing love, and he stood there transfixed and trembling, and breathing her name with a sigh.

Olney hears the *who-cooks-for-you?* call of a barred owl, and he's summoned back to the kitchen, and Nolan Strong & the Diablos are singing "Mambo of Love." He addresses the envelope to the Wellspring of Joy Ministry, Box 1131, Novelty, Florida, presses a Forever stamp on the corner, and leans the envelope against the cherrywood fruit bowl in which he keeps his keys, his wallet, his several pairs of dollar-store reading glasses, his loose change, a pencil sharpener, a glue stick, and his iPhone.

Earlier this afternoon, Olney asked his doctor if it was possible—"I know this sounds crazy"—for physical pain to occur outside the body, because that's what it felt like to him. Not a constant pain and not intense, like a four on a scale of ten, more of an electric pulse than a throb. He pointed to a spot a half inch above his left ear and a skosh out from his skull. "It's right here, and it's tender, and the pain radiates like a dull drill into my head."

Dr. Abdelnour took off his sunglasses, rubbed his eyes, and said that people once believed that all pain emanated outside the body, and they called it divine retribution. He smiled. "Maybe you should pray."

Samir Abdelnour and Olney go way back to the time when Samir ran a free clinic for the unsheltered and indigent after Hurricane Leo devastated Mosquito County. Olney wrote a feature story for the paper and then volunteered at Samir's makeshift clinic in the parking lot of the Winn-Dixie. They've been pals ever since.

Olney said, "It's like phantom pain, Samir, only I haven't lost anything."

"We've all lost something, Olney."

"Something attached, I mean."

"Perhaps you had a vanishing twin."

"A what?"

"In the womb, maybe there were two of you, but the other died. Got absorbed or expelled."

"Are you serious?"

"It happens, but I think your pain is stress-related."

"You always say that."

"Would you like some Elavil? Paxil?"

"I've got martinis for stress."

Dr. Abdelnour leaned back on his fitness-ball chair, took a red vape pen from his shirt pocket, and asked Olney if he'd like a hit of some Afghani Bullrider.

"No, thanks."

"Settle you right down."

( )

OLNEY IS ESPECIALLY FOND OF REVEREND RYLAN'S CABLE ACCESS SHOW, *The House of Burgess.* The show stars the reverend and his wife Taffi, playing themselves, a handsome, equable, and devout young ministerial couple, and their intractable son, Buddy, played by a freckled ventriloquist's doll with rosy cheeks, sandy hair, and alarmingly eloquent eyebrows. The set is minimal: kitchen table, stove, fridge, sink, and a framed print of Jesus weeping over the city of Jerusalem on the wall above the table.

A typical sketch opens with the family at the table, Buddy on a stool next to his dad. There will be sandwiches on plates and glasses of milk before each of them. Rylan will bow his head and lead the family in grace. During the solemnity of grace, Buddy might raise his lowered eyes, stare into the camera, and lift an insinuative eyebrow, inviting us to share in his skepticism, perhaps, or to collude in his mischief, and then he'll allow his beguilingly pious gaze to fall. The reverend's lips move whenever Buddy speaks. Olney wonders if this lack of labial discipline expresses the reverend's ineluctable obligation not to deceive.

In a recent episode, after an exchange of small talk about school and

Bible camp, Buddy, who's not above asking the impertinent question, responded to his father's inquiry about the upcoming school science fair by asking, "What's so intelligent about God's design, Dad?" And here the parents looked at each other, and Taffi stifled a discerning smile and began to clear the dishes, and Rylan folded his napkin and set it down beside his plate. He explained how God made us in his image and according to his likeness, and Buddy said, "I've got two words for you, Dad: wisdom teeth." And Rylan cocked his head, smiled, and pretended to tousle Buddy's shellacked hair. "Appendix. All it can do is kill us."

Taffi "rinsed" dishes in the waterless sink, pretended to dry them and return them to the cupboard. Rylan held up a finger. "Everything that begins to exist has a cause apart from itself. Are you with me?" A second finger. "The universe began to exist." A third. "Therefore, the universe has a cause apart from itself."

"Infertility," Buddy said, and everything went quiet.

Nobody moved. We could hear the whir of the studio fan, hear the dismayed cameraman clear his phlegmy throat. Taffi turned her back to the table and bowed her head. She wept bitterly. Rylan watched her. Buddy said, "I didn't mean—"

Taffi dried her eyes with a dish towel; Rylan whispered her name, and we presumed this bit of affective and pitiable psychodrama about Taffi's barrenness was unscripted. Buddy looked into the camera, shrugged, and cocked his head toward his dad, as if to say, "My parasite made me do it."

When Taffi gathered herself and turned to her husband, we saw the ferocious sadness in her eyes, the overwhelming grief, and the dreadful recognition that you cannot replace what you've never had. "You had no right," she told Rylan, and Rylan's crestfallen countenance suggested his shame: How could he have allowed Buddy to utter such a ruthless and brutal word? A marriage is not a family, Taffi knows. It is not good for a man and a woman to be alone. Sons are a heritage from the Lord; children are a reward. Happy is the man who has filled his quiver with them. Clearly there was a tear in the fabric of the marriage. And we thought that just maybe Buddy was the mending tape holding this husband and wife together.

Olney is aware that what attracts him to the show is this loving family in a cozy home, all smiles and comfort, and the boy who will not grow up and will never leave. More simple than subtle. Transparent. Easy to see through, he admits. He doesn't believe in God or in the hereafter, not at this point in his life, but he enjoys watching religious programs on TV, especially those that tend toward spectacle and ostentation, and he does wish he could believe in something that transcends our mortal lives, but he just can't.

Olney would like to treat the Burgesses to a night out—say a dinner at Fatboy's Fish Camp in Crocodilopolis: catfish and frog legs and a view of the mouth of Sleepy River. He wants to get to know this brave and heartsick couple. He wants to thank them for their missionary efforts in Mosquito County. He'll tell them he's a believer, if that's what they need to hear. He'll change the subject: "Isn't this fried okra to die for?" Taffi will eat her hush puppies with a fork.

It's dark now and the house lights are on at the Lambs'. Olney can see Althea in her living room chair reading one of her Harlequin romances. She reads five a day. Every day. Her ex-husband, Dewey, is probably out on the front porch rocking, sipping his bourbon, and listening to the trill of the tree frogs. Olney figures he'll join him. He puts a slice of grapefruit cake in a Tupperware container for Althea and grabs a Ziploc bag of pickled walnuts for Dewey. He turns off the radio after listening to the Del-Vikings finish "Come Go with Me." And now the song will be in his head all night. He fills a juice glass with cognac and cuts the kitchen light.

Dewey and Althea's marriage ended after seven years, eight years ago. Their inappreciable erotic fire had banked, but neither saw the divorce as any reason to separate, dedomicile, and make matters even worse. Who needs those legal, emotional, and financial complications? They love each other the way that steadfast siblings might. By then Dewey was sleeping on a cot in what he had hoped might one day be a child's room. Dewey works days at the Wellness Pharmacy out on Plumeria; Althea reads her stories, cleans house, tends to the domestic chores, and cooks supper for the two of them: Meat and two veg. Or meat and three. They go to church services together on Sunday at the spirit-filled Community Church of God and to Publix on Tuesday evenings.

Althea doesn't understand romantic love and has never felt the stirrings of passion that the novels' heroines seem to feel at every explosively conscious moment. She told Olney how when she and Dewey had relations, it seemed like a lot of uncomfortable and ridiculous mucking about, not at all the trembling ecstasy that Sabrina Collins felt when Cash Wilde had his nimble way with her beneath a gibbous moon on the aft deck of his yacht, the *Invincible,* in *She's Gonna Blow.* When Olney asked Althea why she read about what she couldn't feel, she said, "The stories carry me away. I may not can feel the rapture, but I can imagine it."

So Dewey's been celibate for longer than he might care to admit. His passions now run to fishing, specifically bass and crappie fishing on Hidden Lake, and to baseball. He's an Anastasia Brown Bats season-ticket holder. The Brownies play in the Class A Florida State League, and Dewey's optimistic about their playoff chances this season. When Olney once asked him if he was okay with the chaste living situation, Dewey said, "If two be together, they keep warm, but how can one keep warm alone?"

"Think quick!" Olney says, as he lobs the bag of walnuts at Dewey.

Dewey snatches his ball cap off his balding head and makes the catch with it. "You're too kind."

"Be back in a jiff." Olney sets his drink on the plastic side table and heads inside with Althea's cake.

Althea looks up from her book and over her reading glasses. "Hello, stranger!"

Olney holds up the container. "Ruby-red grapefruit cake. Should I put it in the fridge?"

"Set it down right here," she says, and taps her finger on the coffee table.

Olney sees she's reading *Dig Yourself Deep*. "How's the book?"

Althea points to the prodigally handsome pair in the cover photograph. "He's Jonas Grant, a bodyguard hired by the university. She's the brilliant but troubled Dr. Blaze Kaltsas. His mission: keeping the seductive, smart-mouthed lady anthropologist out of trouble with the local warlords. His obstacle: keeping himself out of her." Althea opens the Tupperware, inhales, smiles, and closes her eyes.

"Can I get you a fork?" Olney says.

"What for?"

( )

DEWEY TAKES A NEWSPAPER ARTICLE OUT OF THE BIB POCKET OF HIS overalls and unfolds it on his knee. He tells Olney about little Pebbles Hawthorne, who killed her daddy at her mother's urging. Killed him with a pickaxe to the heart as he slept. Made it look like a break-in. Drove back to Mama's in Daddy's pickup. "You bring them into the world, you give them life, raise them up, nourish them, love them, indulge them, show them the way." Dewey shakes his head and wonders if the child that he and Althea never had would have turned treacherous and lethal like Pebbles did.

( )

LATER, OLNEY'S WALKING THE FEW BLOCKS TO PUBLIX TO PICK UP SOME half-and-half for the morning when he sees a woman, alone, walking toward him. He's remembering when he used to pull Cully to Publix in his red wagon back when they lived in Spanish Blade and Cully was in preschool, twenty-something years ago—little Cully with his dirty blond hair, his bright smile, and his sideways ball cap. Olney crosses the street so as not to frighten the woman, but his strategy may have backfired. She stops and watches him like he's up to something. And then she says, "Hey!"

Olney stops and points to his chest. "Me?"

She says, "Where am I?"

"You're on Amaryllis walking west."

She crosses the street and holds out her hand. She says her name's Mireille, which Olney pictures as *Me, Ray*, and wonders if she thinks he doesn't speak English well.

He says, "Pleased to meet you, Ray," and he wonders if that's short for Rayleen.

She smiles and spells her name for him. "It's French. Born Mireille Marie Bellamy, but now I'm stuck with the ex's surname. Mireille Tighe. You can call me *Ray* if you want. Jack Tighe always did."

"Olney Kartheizer."

"I'm lost, Only Kartheizer."

"Olney," he says. "Where are you going?"

"Home."

"Which is . . . ?

"Lantana and Rose."

"Been walking long?"

Mireille tells Olney how she was just driving along, lost in thought, when she hit something she had not seen in the road and heard a heart-stopping thud. It could be a child, she thought. Or a dog. It turned out to be a green plastic bag full of trash, thank God, but Mireille was so rattled and angry at her dangerous inattention and her persistent distractibility that she left her car where she'd pulled it to the curb and set off to walk home. "I didn't know where I was or how I'd gotten there."

Olney says, "I live down the block. Come with me. I'll drive you to your car or to your home."

"No more driving for me tonight, so you can take me home," she says.

Mireille sits at Olney's kitchen table, her hands folded on her lap. She declines the offer of cashews and cognac, says no to water or lemonade. "But thank you for offering." She's blond, fair, thin as a minute, and brown-eyed.

"A peach?" Olney says.

She smiles and shakes her head. She admires the braided rug in front of the sink. Olney tells her that his grandmother made it for him when he left for college, made it from all his outgrown clothes: T-shirts, pajamas, jeans, dress shirts, khakis. "My whole childhood's lying there on the floor."

He drives. She stares ahead. He asks her what song she's humming. She tells him "Simple Gifts," and she sings:

'Tis the gift to be simple, 'tis the gift to be free
'Tis the gift to come down where we ought to be,
And when we find ourselves at the place just right,
'Twill be in the valley of love and delight.

Mireille's voice is delicate and muted, somewhere between breathy and hoarse, but sweet and melodious at the same time. Olney says, "That was beautiful."

Mireille shrugs and smiles. "I can hold a tune."

He takes a left on Jacaranda. He asks her what she'd been thinking about when she hit the garbage bag. She says she'd been thinking about her sister Lilian—"We called her Lilou"—who died from a massive stroke nineteen years ago.

Olney watches Mireille out the corner of his eye and decides she's adorable. Those dimples, those cheekbones.

She says, "I saw the pair of us sledding down the hill at the asylum. I'm in front steering, and Lilou's holding on to my waist and screaming. And then: Bang!"

"Where did you grow up?"

"Requiem, Mass., the Heart of the Commonwealth."

"And what brought you to Florida?"

"An itch and a Chevy Nova."

"Left or right on Rose?"

"Right. Do you ever wonder what your last thought will be?"

"I'm hoping it's in a dream, because if you die while you're dreaming, the dream never ends."

"Here we are," Mireille says.

Olney pulls up in front of Merriment Manor, an assisted living community. "Before you go, may I ask you a question?"

"Shoot."

"What if I took you out for supper?"

"Are you asking me out on a date?"

"Yes, I am."

"Then yes, I accept. But not out to supper."

"I can cook you a nice pan-roasted chicken at my place."

"I have dysphagia, an illness of the esophagus. It's progressive and irreversible. Right now I can sip liquids and manage small bites of solid food at intervals. Eventually I won't be able to swallow at all. I'm becoming a breatharian. I'll need a feeding tube. And I'm only forty-nine. Okay, fifty. And a half."

She gives Olney her phone number. He says he'll call her tomorrow when he gets off work, and they shake hands good night. He says what about your car. She tells him she'll send a tow truck to fetch it in the morning. He watches her climb the stairs and open the lobby door. She turns and waves.

At home Olney sits with his nightcap and thinks about the surprise and indiscrimination of death and remembers finding his friend Denny Sheehan dead at his desk in the city room at the *Daily Sun*. Denny'd been working on his fiction, a no-no at the office, a short story called "New Happiness." The last unfinished sentence Denny typed was, *The suicide note was in danger of becoming a love lett* and when his forehead hit the keyboard, it typed, *zzxcvv*. Dying because you can't swallow will be neither mercifully sudden nor surprising.

He starts to write a letter to Cully, not knowing where he would send it. He thinks Cully's in Melancholy but doesn't know where in Melancholy. *I had hoped when you went to live near your mom, when you were away from your triggers, you'd clean up your act like you promised. And maybe you have, but your mom doesn't think so. I love you.* He puts down his pen. Yes, Samir, I *have* lost something. My vanishing son. Olney feels his sadness surface, and that provokes his anger and the guilt and the shame that are its consequence.

Olney's been preoccupied with his son since Cully's last phone call. Not surprisingly, Cully wanted money, quite a bit of money, but he'd pay it back and then some ASAP. Promise. What are you laughing at? When Olney reminded Cully that he has never repaid a penny of the thousands of dollars he's borrowed over the years, Cully said, This is different, and it'll be the last time. This is my big chance at an IT job. I just need to get this laptop. Olney said no, terminated the call, and turned off his phone. There has been too much money not spent on rent or food or classes or a wardrobe for that new job that would turn his life around. It all went to pills. Too many rescues, too many betrayals, too many backslides into addiction.

Olney carries a book to bed, William Trevor's *The Old Boys*. He looks at the photo on his dresser of himself and Cully when Cully was four and Olney was the center of his son's life. The two of them are sitting on the couch reading: the *Sunday Daily Sun* and *Calvin and Hobbes*. Kat took the picture. A minute later Cully looked at Olney and said, "How far is Kevin from here?"

"Kevin?"

"Where the dead people go."

"Heaven. It's quite a ways."

"Can we drive there?"

"We'll have to split the driving."

"But I'm just a kid."

When Cully was a preschooler, he never walked when he could run, and his favorite game was being chased by his daddy. Cully ran and laughed, and if he saw a puddle, he jumped in it, and he'd turn and say, "You'll never catch me."

"Oh, yes, I will," Olney would say, his arms outstretched as if to snatch his boy, and Cully would scream and run faster, but he wasn't always looking where he was going—he was having too much fun for that. One evening he ran headlong into the swing set in Turpentine Park, hit the pole with his shoulder, fell, cried for just a second, got back up, and took off running before Olney could comfort him, kiss the bruise, and make it better. Cully yelled back, "Give up yet?"

"Never!" And then Olney would collapse on the grass and yell, "You win!" And Cully would help his daddy up, and they'd walk home. Olney remembers the song they made up: "Cully the K and his Daddy-O /

Listen to songs on the radio / Living the dream / Eating ice cream / Sitting out back on the patio," was how it started. And then something about never seeing the one without the other. But these days it seems to Olney that every time he tries to get close to his son, he drives his son further away. For his part, Cully says he's uncomfortable with constant parental proximity, preferring, himself, the bliss of distance.

PENNY TO MY NAME

This morning, Olney found a photograph beneath a bus stop bench outside the post office. It's a picture of a conspicuously lean young man with a widow's peak, standing, arms akimbo, beside a gold Mercury Cougar in what seems to be a long driveway. The man's gray toy poodle is sitting pretty on its hind legs on the hood of the car. The license tag is partially visible: T-623 and TEXAS 70.

So now Olney's at work, in the hut he calls the pro shop, and he's writing about the photograph in his notebook. Olney studies the photo and decides that little Pierre was a Christmas gift to Buck from his mother, Verna, two years ago. Buck was so happy he cried. This is Nacogdoches, Texas. Verna thinks it's silly that Buck has his own rent house when he could be living right here with her. At home, Buck puts on Sinatra albums and sings along into his microphone. He has tied a red silk scarf to the microphone stand.

"What are you writing, Mr. Kartheizer?" one of the Moore triplets asks him, either Rose, Tulip, or Iris. Olney is startled back to actuality, and he jumps. The girls, who seem to have materialized out of nowhere, get a kick out of that and laugh. Olney puts his hands over his heart and tells them they've scared a month off his span of life.

He's known the eight-year-olds—the S'Moores, he calls them—since their first birthday when he was assigned to write a feature about them. One triplicated egg, three identical sisters—the same reedy voices, the same Egyptian-blue eyes, the same walnut-brown hair, styled in the same fringed bobs, the same turned-up noses. Today they're wearing yellow tank tops, blue cotton shorts, and orange Crocs. The sisters are indistinguishable and, apparently, interchangeable. They like to play a game, they told Olney on their last birthday, where they switch identities. When he asked them if they ever worried about getting confused about who they are, they all said it wouldn't matter. When he asked them if their parents could tell them apart, they each smiled, and one of them said, "They think they can."

Olney hands the girls their clubs, three red balls, a pencil, and a scorecard, and tells them to have fun. He calls Mireille and gets her voice mail. "It's Olney," he says, "from last night," and he tells her to call him when she gets the chance. "Or I'll call you." He calls his friend Julie Fry to see if they are still on for this afternoon. They are. They're meeting for a drink at George's Majestic Lounge in Old Town. Julie's got a five o'clock appointment with a clairvoyant, and she wants Olney along for support. A father and his son, about six or seven, arrive. They are both wearing Brown Bats ball caps and T-shirts that say I'D RATHER BE NOODLING CATFISH. When the boy—his dad calls him "Sugar"—sinks a hole-in-one on the first hole and is shocked speechless, Dad lifts him triumphantly and kisses him on the cheek. The S'Moores, on the fourteenth tee, applaud, and Olney remembers he and Cully, when Cully was Sugar's age, eating messy ice-cream cones on a bench in Turpentine Park during one of their "boys' nights out."

Olney's so often in the past because that's where he left his boy and where he can still find him. Not the actual past exactly but his memory of the past, a past distilled and refined, a past that makes sense, a story not a circumstance. The past, then, is malleable, not fixed. He used to think that maybe if he pursued Cully, he could find him, and if he could find him, maybe he could rescue him, and if he could rescue him, maybe he could redeem them both. But do you keep chasing a person who doesn't want to be caught? He'll wait here by the door, listen for the knock, and when he hears Cully's cry for home, he'll welcome his son back into his life. Or is this *waiting* just another name for *surrender*?

When Kat told him after Cully left home again at nineteen that she might lose her mind if she couldn't find her boy, Olney hired a local detective, Oz Carter, who turned out not to be a wizard. Cully was hard to trace. No address, no credit cards, no bank account, no driver's license, no phone, no social media presence. Oz told Olney he'd probably have to wait till Cully got busted again and called from jail for bail money. Sorry.

Olney had already paid for rehab, sat in on the weekly family meetings, and listened to the users tell the drug counselors what they wanted to hear. One evening after Marla with the gap teeth and the blue hair wept and confessed her shame at her recent relapse, and after Tony with the Yankees ball cap announced that he'd be graduating from Serenity House next week, clean and sober forever, and would miss the place and the people, and after the backslaps and applause, there came a lull in the conversation, and Howard the facilitator, a recovering addict himself, a guy who liked to sit on his hands and glance at the wall clock over the green double doors, a guy who had told Marla just now that her parents' enabling behavior had contributed to her relapse, lifted his arms as an invitation to the forty or so folks in the cafetorium to share, and Olney, who had not spoken a word in the half-dozen meetings he'd attended, let go of Kat's hand and raised his own, and when Howard nodded,

Olney said he wasn't sure what this concept of enabling was all about. He spoke to Howard but looked at Cully, who had chosen to sit across the room in this circle of vinyl stack chairs.

"Go on," Howard said.

He looked at Howard and said he blamed himself for what's happened to Cully, not for what he did, maybe, but for what he didn't do for his son. He wasn't sure how that enabled Cully's fall from grace, however. He understands, he said, that Cully was responsible for his own behavior and needed to take control of his life. "How am I enabling him?"

Howard said, "Are you still bailing him out?"

"Of jail?"

"Of trouble."

"Well, when he showed up a mess at the house, homeless and penniless, we let him move back in. He's our son."

Howard said, "It's your financial support that enables his continuing addictive behavior. He doesn't pay rent, doesn't buy food. He doesn't have a job."

"Not while he's in your program, he doesn't."

"You need to stop supporting him financially."

Olney wanted to say, "Okay, then, give me back my twelve thousand dollars, drop him from rehab, and we'll start with the tough love," but he stopped himself, squeezed Kat's hand.

Howard said, "Let's get the focus back on the people in the room who are struggling."

Olney and Kat also paid for Cully's individual therapy, and Olney volunteered to come along to a session. Maybe this would be the start of the healing. At the session, he confronted Cully about his version of contentious events, and Cully said, maybe we just can't be together.

When Dr. Augusto asked for an explanation of the contentious events, Olney said the drug test, for one. He failed it but justified the failure by saying the test was faulty and then told Olney he didn't fail it. He did fail, and when we confronted him, he screamed.

"Because you called me mentally ill," Cully said.

"But not morally corrupt," Olney said.

"Are you listening to each other?" Dr. Augusto said.

Olney said, "He tossed his Zoloft down the toilet but swallowed his OxyContin."

"You can't make me take them," Cully said.

"I know that."

When the session ended, Dr. Augusto pulled Olney aside at the office door and said to keep in mind what he wants the long-term outcome to be. Work toward that goal.

( )

JULIE MARRIED LONNIE FRY JUST AFTER SHE DELIVERED THEIR FIRST child. She was seventeen. Lonnie's dad, Lane, gave the newlyweds the gas station/home he owned ten miles out of town on a lonely stretch of Novelty Road as a wedding gift just before he died of lung cancer in the infirmary of Florida State Prison in Raiford. Lane had lost his keys one night while he was partying with the Scholten brothers in their trailer. "They didn't just get up and walk away, now, did they, boys?" he said to Tee and Bee. When they both laughed, and Bee said, "Maybe they're up your ass," and Tee said he wasn't joining the search party, Lane walked out to his truck, grabbed the claw hammer out of the bed, walked back inside, and clubbed the two little drunken pissants to death. The keys, it turned out, had been in the ignition the whole time. Lane was so baked at this point that he drove into town for a sobering shot or two of Fighting Cock. When the bartender at Mr. Bluster's saw the blood splattered across Lane's face and arms and T-shirt, she called the cops.

Julie, Lonnie, and the baby, Tallulah Belle, moved into the one-bedroom apartment over the station. Because he could not tolerate the baby's wailing, Lonnie slept on the couch in the living room, his ears stuffed with cigarette filters, or else on a cot in the grimy office downstairs. Julie says she doesn't notice the fumes so much anymore, but she still gets the headaches. The second baby's name is Hedy. The station has one bay and a lift, three pumps. Lonnie can change your battery, patch and air up a leaky tire, adjust your timing, and change your oil or transmission fluid. Inside the station, he sells retread tires, wiper blades, motor oil, soda, salty snacks, candy—and canned beer, if you know enough to ask.

Lonnie is an unmannerly drunk, and a chronic drug abuser, but at least he's not in jail like his three shiftless brothers and six rowdy cousins. They say in Anastasia that nothing goes better with coke than Frys. Julie doesn't hate Lonnie. He doesn't abuse her or the girls. Some folks might think neglect is a form of abuse, but Julie counts it as a blessing. She does, however, sometimes wish that Lonnie were in a for-real prison so that she might escape her own incarceration. With Lonnie locked up, she could cut the lights, shut the door, take her girls, and steal away from Midway Sunoco forever. Lonnie's perhaps too lazy to conduct a proper extramarital affair, but he's not above bartering a little blow for some bedspring poker. Julie is, by now, indifferent to his occasional philandering.

When Olney met Julie, she told him that dead broke and on her own would be better than this gas station life. That was the night her car died for the last time leaving the Winn-Dixie. Olney saw her stranded by the side of the road and stopped. He drove her and her groceries and her two daughters home. When he asked her what it was like living so far from town, she told him she wanted more for her life than staring at the two-lane blacktop and watching travelers come and go. Her husband had all he needed right there, she said. She wanted a change; any change would do. And then she apologized for going on about her discontent. She said, "I should have left long ago." And then, "That's it up ahead." And then, "You could just keep driving if you want to."

Tallulah Belle yelled, "Yay! We're home!" and woke the baby.

Julie had been encouraged to leave Andrew Jackson High School when she became obviously pregnant. She'd be happier with a GED, she was advised. Her adoptive parents, Russ and Gwen Ljungborg (Ljungborg Realty, "Building Bridges between Buyers and Sellers"), turned their resolute backs on her, and she has not spoken to them since the morning they denounced her in front of a reproachful congregation at Abiding Savior Lutheran Church. "You're just like your biological mother," Gwen told Julie. "A loathsome whore!" The Ljungborgs have never met their grandchildren. "They're no blood to us," Gwen tells anyone who'll listen.

( )

"GOODBYE, MR. KARTHEIZER," THE S'MOORES SAY, AND THEY HAND Olney their Saf-T Putters.

"Who won?"

They all smile. "Rose," they say.

"Congratulations, Rose."

"Thank you," they say.

Sugar and his dad are on seventeen, and Sugar is staring into the gaping mouth of a toothy and menacing foam shark. Olney wonders if Sugar's dad ever thinks about the day when all this sweetness will sour.

Olney sees his relief, Craig Dillon, locking his bicycle to the bike rack. Craig's a high school kid who once shot a twenty-one on the course, a world record or close to it.

Craig sets his loose-leaf binder and his notebook computer on the counter beside the box of pencils and the stack of scorecards and asks Olney how he is at math. Olney says he gets lost at long division.

"Well, you're no help," Craig says. He has an Algebra II exam in the morning, and his graduation might depend on passing it. "I'm toast," he says.

"Do they make you show your work?"

"They do."

"Word problems?"

"The worst."

"Surrender!"

"Just give up?"

"Hope is your enemy right now," Olney says. He claps Craig on the shoulder.

( )

JULIE'S WAITING FOR OLNEY AT A SHADED PICNIC TABLE IN THE BEER garden of George's Majestic Lounge. Over the sound system, Django Reinhardt and Stéphane Grappelli are playing "Honeysuckle Rose." Julie's ordered two Bloody Marys. Olney kisses her cheek and sits. He sets his phone on the table. "The kids are with their Fry Daddy," Julie tells him. "He took them fishing out to Bunny's Crappie House."

Today's trip to the clairvoyant has to do with Julie's birth parents, whoever they are. She's used a computer at the public library to place an ad on Craigslist. She shows it to Olney: *I was born on July 29, 1999, at Anastasia General and was put up for adoption. The adoption was arranged by Dr. Klaus Furth and did not go through the usual adoption agencies. I'm told money exchanged hands and no questions were asked. If you think you might be my birth parent, please contact me. I don't want money. I want to know who I am.* Sometimes Julie will see a middle-aged couple behaving tenderly in public, and she'll wonder if they might be her parents. She feels certain that if her parents knew about her dire and disheartening circumstances and about their bright and charming grandchildren, they'd welcome her, welcome them, into their homes, their hearts, and their lives. The clairvoyant, Auralee Fell, will, Julie hopes, tell her if such a reunion is in the cards, or in the crystal ball, or in whatever. Julie thinks if she can just visualize the reconciliation, if that's what it is, and when and where it'll take place, and how, then maybe her will and grit, her emptiness and yearning, can make it happen. Olney checks his phone. A voice mail from Mireille telling him she's out of commission for the day and asking him to call her tomorrow, but not too early. Looking forward to it.

( )

AURALEE HOLDS JULIE'S HANDS IN HERS, TURNS THEM OVER, AND knits her brow. She lifts them as if to determine their heft. Julie and Auralee are sitting across from each other at the small kitchen table. Olney's on a rocker beside the gas range, watching them. Auralee has dyed her silver hair faintly pink and styled it in a pixie cut. Her topaz earrings match her eyes. There is no crystal ball on the table, no deck of tarot cards, no tin of tea leaves, but there is a coffee mug stuffed with crayons and a tablet of drawing paper. There's a framed photo of a toddler with two missing front teeth wearing a safety helmet and straddling her pink bicycle. Olney isn't sure that psychics can even know the present or predict the past, and nothing keeps its secrets like the future.

Auralee asks Julie to give her an item from her purse. Julie fishes around in her cloth bag, puts an eyeglass case and a tissue on the table, and hands Auralee her tarnished house key on an I ♥ Mosquito County key ring. Auralee clutches the key in her fist and shuts her eyes. She runs her thumb along the teeth.

Auralee doesn't see rescue in Julie's future. What Olney and Julie don't know, and what Auralee doesn't know but senses, is that Julie's biological parents do not have the will, the compassion, or the wherewithal to come to her aid. They despise each other, for starters, and want no reminders of their youthful indiscretion. Neither is the least bit curious about the forsaken daughter. The mom, Stacy Clutter, is a reception-desk clerk at the Anastasia Beach Super 8. She's twice divorced and dating a married man, a father of four, Nassim Alfarsi, who owns King Shawarma Falafel Shop over on Buttonwood. Right now Stacy is two miles away from our friends in Auralee's kitchen. She's leaning against the cold drink vending machine outside the motel lobby, smoking a menthol cigarette, and reading a text message from Nassim, apologizing for having to cancel their getaway weekend in Savannah. Stacy snaps her phone shut, stabs the Salem into the sand in the ash 'n' trash receptacle, and gets back to work. Disappointment is the price she pays for romantic sovereignty.

Julie's biological father, Donny Burke, is a cashier at the Palmetto Plaza Kmart and the sole support of his doting but incapable wife, Lyn, and his invalid mother-in-law, Totie, a diabetic who's shy six toes, going on seven. Donny sleeps on a fold-out in the den with his sixteen-year-old Chihuahua, Charo, which is okay because this way he can let the TV drone all night without bothering anyone. Lyn and Totie sleep in the bedroom with the seven long-haired cats. The three of them are on Benadryl.

( )

WHEN OLNEY WALKS JULIE TO HER NEW OLD CAR, SHE REASSURES HIM that she's feeling fine. Today she found out what she should have already known—that it was up to her to secure a happier future for herself and the girls. And for Lonnie, too, if that's what he wants. "I just wish he hadn't been born with a silver socket wrench in his mouth. Wish he'd had to work for the job and the home. He's as happy as a maggot on a honey wagon out there."

Olney asks if she thinks it's possible the Ljungborgs will eventually come to their senses, apologize for their disgraceful behavior, and welcome her back into the family. Julie looks at him like he's on fire and tells him that if she sees those pious motherfuckers on the street, she'll run them down and then back up over them. Olney sees this as a healthy response, actually, and tells her so. And then Olney indulges in a ridiculous fantasy in which he introduces Julie to Cully, and they fall in love, and she straightens him out, and Olney gets the sweetest daughter-in-law and two wonderful grandkids all in one stroke, and everyone wins except maybe Julie, he realizes, and, oh yeah, Lonnie, and then the whole imagined edifice collapses.

( )

OLNEY MAKES HIMSELF SUPPER AS HE LISTENS TO WHY-AM'S TRIBUTE to Doug Sahm. He braises some applewood-smoked bacon and collards and poaches two eggs while the Texas Tornados sing about making guacamole all night long. He thinks about Julie and her kids in their flat and what supper's like over there. He sees a flickering fluorescent light over the table and a TV on in the background. Hedy is whiney, and Tallulah Belle fidgets. Lonnie swigs from his can of beer and burps like a cow, and that gets the kids laughing, and pretty soon the three of them are belching like happy fools while Julie shakes her head and smiles. Olney wonders if someday Julie will look back on these days with fondness, as he does when he remembers his and Kat's first modest rent house on Ticholi Road in Spanish Blade, a beige and hard-water-stained cinder-block cube with a swamp cooler, jalousie windows, gray vinyl tiled floors, and a treeless backyard. They lived there till Cully was nine or ten. Now Cully says he doesn't remember anything about it. Olney eats standing up at the sink, looks out at the backyard, and sees a brassy mockingbird harassing the white-eared squirrel. He remembers Cully waking from a nap all sweaty and smiley and delighted to be lifted from his crib and set down in his high chair with a bowl of dry Cheerios. He ate them one at a time ambidextrously.

Olney washes his plate, glass, pans, and utensils and puts them on the drying rack. They were happy in that house. He makes himself a vodka martini, carries the drink to the kitchen table, opens the Phillies cigar box where he stores his ephemera, and drops in the photo of Buck. He notices a postcard that Kat's parents sent them twelve years ago—a chrome card photo of the Murray Hotel on Mackinac Island, Michigan. *Fudge and manure*, Walter wrote. *Wish you were here.* This was just five years before Walter got his leukemia diagnosis, kept the news to himself, quit his job at Boelyn's Lincoln Ford Mercury, quit the chemo, felt better without it, terminated his relationship with his doctors, and took to his bed. Eight years before Bonnie began her swift decline. Walter never left the house again. Bonnie never allowed another person into the house again, not the health department inspector, not the kids selling cookie dough or magazine subscriptions, not the visiting nurse, not her daughter Kat.

Kat was beyond heartbroken. She was her parents' beloved only child, coddled ("like an egg" she'd joke) and prized. As Bonnie and Walter began their tumble into dementia and decrepitude, they did not prevail upon Kat to care for them, and she resented it. That's what children do, she told Olney—they become the parents of the parents.

On their last visit to Bonnie and Walter's for Walter's seventy-ninth birthday, Kat cooked burgers outside on the grill. Walter ate a jar of Gerber's sweet potatoes, and Bonnie ate the icing off her slice of chocolate cake. Olney cleaned out the fridge and the pantry and threw out all the expired food. As they were leaving, Kat embraced her mother and said they'd be back soon.

Bonnie said, "Give me a call instead."

"I call you three times a week."

"Make it one. We need our privacy."

Kat said, "Now, you listen to me. I'm calling Dr. Dempsey. Dad needs medical attention."

"Dempsey's dead. And all your father needs is a TV remote."

"Well, I'm getting someone out here to look at him."

Bonnie said, "You do what you want," and shut the door.

Back home, Cully, who was taking a gap year after graduating from Splendora High School but was not filling the gap with work or travel or study, and who was failing Kat's random drug tests and who crashed Olney's car every time he borrowed it—swerving to avoid a dog, a deer, a duck—spent most of his days asleep and most of his nights with friends, who knew where, doing who knew what.

"How can we let his behavior go on like this?" Kat said. She sat beside Olney who was working at his desk on an article about pet adoptions. "I can't sleep anymore. I can't eat. My life is shit!"

There was no consoling her. She said she felt like she was under arrest. Ostracized. Locked away from the lives of the people she loves. She picked up the fluted bud vase from the desk and tossed the wilted dahlia into the trash. "Cully lies. Bonnie talks nonsense. Walter doesn't speak."

"And me?" Olney said.

"I try to respect their wishes, but it's killing me."

Olney handed her a tissue.

"I hate my life!" Kat said.

"How do you think that makes me feel?"

"It's not about you!" she yelled, slammed the bud vase on the desk, and it shattered. Her hand was bleeding.

That was the day the food processor jammed, and the sink stopped up, the day she left her phone at the market or the bank or the liquor store. She stood in the kitchen cursing the appliances and screaming at no one or everyone. Olney said he'd go find the phone and left her slumped on the floor.

Walter and Bonnie lived in Hubbard, Florida, on the Gulf Coast. Perhaps Bonnie felt that she was losing everything she cared about, and so she began to save everything that found its way to her—paper and plastic grocery sacks, fast-food containers, newspapers, magazines, egg cartons, jars, unopened mail, bottles, cans, fortune cookie fortunes, jury summonses, calendars, church bulletins, fingernail parings, prescription bottles, burnt-out light bulbs, parking tickets, coupons, useless books of S&H Green Stamps—all of which she boxed and stacked along the walls of the house, and so the living area shrank, and eventually she couldn't put anything else away. There were twelve electric blankets, ten of them still in their unopened boxes, six sets of socket wrenches, five soldering irons, a machete, and in the freezer the leftovers from last Thanksgiving's dinner. When Kat's regular early evening phone calls went unanswered for several days, she made the three-hour drive from Melancholy. She kicked in the front door when no one responded to her furious knocking and bell-ringing. Easier than she thought it would be. She found her mother prostrate on a carpet of soiled clothing and bedraggled blankets on the tile living room floor, dead, Kat was certain. Kat took out her cell phone and took in the bedlam of detritus before her eyes. She knelt beside Bonnie. Bonnie opened an eye and said, "Did you bring water?"

Kat fought her way through the kitchen to the bedroom. She found her naked father on the un-sheeted bed watching a soap opera. The stench of ammonia and human feces was overwhelming. She dialed 911, told the call-taker to tell the cops to bring backup. "We've got an ugly situation here."

( )

HE KNOWS HE SHOULDN'T, BUT OLNEY CALLS KAT. AND WHEN SHE SEES the caller ID, Kat knows she shouldn't, but she answers. She says, "You know El doesn't like you calling me at all hours." El is her husband. Elbert Celoso, a nice enough fellow, owns a small business, into fantasy sports leagues, golf, Italian food, and ZZ Top, but with a boatload of insecurity where Kat is concerned.

Olney says, "Have you seen Cully?"

"You don't call for a month and you don't say hello? That's rude."

"I'm sorry, Kat, but have you? Seen him?"

"Not in a few days, not since he walked out during dinner. The doctor says he's killing me to death. The stress and all."

"How does he look?"

"Better than I do."

"Did you tell him I wanted to talk to him?"

"Yes."

"What did he say?"

"Nothing."

The day that Cully ran away from home the last time, Olney saw Cully pedaling his battered bicycle up Lampkin Road and pulling a rolling suitcase, Olney's suitcase, alongside the bike. Olney honked the horn, waved, slowed down, and pulled to the curb. Cully nodded and rode on. Olney watched in his rearview mirror and saw Cully take a left on Fannin Street by the railroad tracks. He was wearing his droopy khaki cargo pants, a Radiohead T-shirt, and the Doc Martens desert boots Olney and Kat had bought him for Christmas. Kat had told Cully the night before to pack his things and clear out of the house, this after yet another nasty exchange. Cully told his mother to fuck herself after she confronted him about the loaf of green and rancid salami in his sock drawer. He accused her of spying on him, and he shoved her out of his room.

When Olney arrived home after seeing Cully on his bicycle, he discovered just what Cully had been hauling in the suitcase: Olney's laptop and his desktop computer, his Olympus camera, his Bose radio, and who knew what all else.

Olney digs into the cigar box and pulls out one of the dozens of notes Cully has written him over the years.

> Dad, I wish you'd treat me like a human being who has
> feelings. You're behaving like a thug. You don't own me.
> You're no prize. And I don't like being called a disgrace.
> I don't call you an incompetent. Cully.

There would always be time enough to repair the damage and make things work with his son, Olney once thought. But, in truth, there might not be. And what would be the point anyway? So peace is restored. What then? What's the use of harmony without tenderness or affection? Without proximity and engagement? But he has to keep trying. He doesn't need Cully back in the house, just back in his life. Olney reminds himself that he's not going after Cully again but knows he will. But Cully will also have to make a move. No more PIs, no more drives through dicey neighborhoods, no calls to friends, no checking the daily arrest records and obits, no begging, no bargaining, no coercion, no promises, no threats. If Cully doesn't want to change, then nothing can be done. Olney hopes that he and Cully might once again share their lives despite the seasons of turbulence. His love for Cully is undiminished, even if his patience is strained and his trust has come undone. He asks himself if his love is only for the Cully who *was* and not for the Cully who *is*.

Olney's dad, Franklin, was a decent, sober, and affable man with simple needs and humble dreams, a man uncomfortable with displays of emotion. He was never too happy, never too sad, and never ever angry. By the age of twenty-six, Franklin had achieved everything he had set out to do. He had married Glorietta, his chaste sweetheart, in a church ceremony, after an ardent courtship and a felicitous engagement, fathered a male child, bought a comfortable house with a shaded yard in a quiet neighborhood, traded in his Camaro for a late-model Chevrolet sedan, worked at Splendora Hardware. So that was that. Ambitions accomplished. He enjoyed his TV shows, dressed casually, but not offensively so, always a starched oxford shirt, chinos, and polished penny loafers. He kept his financial affairs, his political affiliation, and his metaphysical doubts, if he had any, to himself. He seemed befuddled by irony. He expected people to tell the unvarnished truth but knew they seldom did. And that's why he liked and admired the people on his TV shows. They never changed no matter how many lessons they supposedly learned. When Olney suggested that's because they're shallow, Franklin said, Exactly!

Kat walked out of the marriage not long after Cully had dropped out of college and pedaled off into the sunset up Lampkin Road with the stolen merchandise but before he was arrested for possession of a controlled substance and animal cruelty—he had dipped, if you can believe it, forty-four mice in resin, then sliced them into cubes for a friend's "art project." Cully's defense was they were frozen feeder mice for snakes and reptiles. The charge was dropped. Kat walked into the living room where Olney sat reading "A Good Man Is Hard to Find" and said that she was leaving him tonight for the night and tomorrow for good.

They had both seen this coming. The stress of living together with and then without Cully had been replaced with the strain of living together with and without each other. The quiet house, post-Cully, had now become the silent house. Olney and Kat didn't say much to each other, not even good morning. Kat talked to herself but loud enough so Olney could hear, and when she spoke, it was to call the vac or the slow cooker a son-of-a-bitching whore or to repeat how worthless her life was. She seemed to be enraged and in mourning, Olney in retreat.

They were too distant by now to warm each other and too remote to care. They no longer walked to the beach or drove to the country. They did not make love or whisper to each other. They were, of course, haunted. Olney thought maybe they should forget their undisciplined child, release and absolve him. Isn't that what they say? If you love someone, set him free; if he comes back, he's yours forever, and if he doesn't . . . But he was not about to punish Kat with these thoughts, and anyway, he knew he couldn't forget about his son.

Olney closed the book on his finger and said, "Where will you go?"

"That's your response?"

"Let's talk about this."

"I've met someone."

"Who? Where?"

"Church."

"You're an atheist."

"It's the second-best place to meet someone."

"What's first?"

"Singles night at Winn-Dixie."

That someone was not El, but a fellow named Faye Boekhoff, a landscape architect whose father, as it happens, a minister, had been killed by a congregant whose wife had been intimate with the reverend. The avenging cuckold found the Reverend Cecil Boekhoff in the church hall and battered him with an electric guitar. Olney covered the murder for the *Daily Sun*. Faye, who would turn out to be married, and who claimed to be heartbroken at Kat's decision to move, was still kind enough to drive Kat and her U-Haul to Melancholy in South Florida, where Kat's cousin Kimmie had found her a rent house and a job at the Silver Palace Casino in nearby Eden.

The next afternoon, while Faye was off snagging more boxes from Levi's Liquorland, Kat and Olney took a break from packing her things, sat at the kitchen table with a fifth of bourbon, and talked about what was now coming to a dispirited conclusion—this life they had shared for the past twenty-nine years. What was once an exhilarating adventure had been reduced to a distressing grind of tedium and irritability. The years of battling Cully's addiction and each other had worn them down, left them without the energy or the will to salvage the foundering marriage.

Kat said, "I don't want to be the person I've become when I'm with you. Not anymore. And I don't like who you've become." Kat folded her hands on her lap. She looked at Olney and felt an affection she hadn't experienced in a while. "We're rubbing each other raw. We're bleeding. We deserve better than this."

They'd met at Olney's fifth Splendora High reunion at the VFW Hall. He'd come alone. She'd come with Leo Markarian, former class president and pot dealer, and these days the night manager of a self-storage facility in Puesta del Sol. When Leo and friends stepped outside to burn one, Kat caught Olney's eye and joined him at the bar. He bought her a vodka and tonic; she told him he had a sleepy-time voice, and one thing led to another.

Olney opened the junk drawer, pulled out a Ziploc bag of photographs, and showed Kat a picture of the two of them taken before they were married. They sat on chairs facing each other, their knees touching, his left hand on her right wrist, her long brown hair draping her face.

He says, "We were at your aunt Mel's for Thanksgiving. Uncle Bob took the picture."

"Look at me, hiding behind my hair."

They married at Splendora City Hall, honeymooned in Charleston, settled into the cozy little house in Spanish Blade, and were so happy they sometimes forgot to eat. And then came the pretty little green-eyed baby, and their quiet lives seemed perfect. They would have stopped time if they could have.

Later, after the packing was finished, Faye waited out in his truck with a Happy Meal and a six-pack while Kat and Olney said goodbye. Olney told Kat he'd forward her mail. Said he'd sell the house—their 3/2 on Crestwood Lane. He'd move to Anastasia to be closer to work. "We should get a good price."

Kat said she'd get the divorce ball rolling. "It's best," she said.

"It is."

Kat wiped her eyes with a tissue, kissed Olney on the cheek. "I love you but can't live with you. And I can't be in this house." What she thought but did not say was that with Olney out of the picture, maybe Cully would come to her.

Kat had managed the household and the household finances. She did the banking online and paid the cable, utility, and insurance bills electronically. Olney had not carried his weight, not done his share, not with the fiscal housework, and not with his emotional obligations, he realized, not for a while. Kat left detailed instructions for the banking and billing, but Olney and his computer had an adversarial relationship. So after the house sold, he just canceled everything in anticipation of his move. What's a few days without power? He bought envelopes and a roll of Forever stamps and would write checks the way God had intended bills to be paid. He started out in the new place with the Internet but not the TV. Kat told him that no one anymore has a landline or a radio. He kept the radio and bought the iPhone.

And he wondered what their marriage had been all about. When he watched her drive away with Faye, he felt numb, and then he felt relief, knowing she might be happy away from all this stress and grief. If Cully had not brought chaos into the family, would the marriage have dissolved anyway? Or would they have been happy? Or just settled and relaxed? And what's wrong with that? Was he trying to blame his son for the failure of the marriage? And what's the point of blame?

( )

OLNEY SETS THE ALARM ON HIS IPHONE FOR NINE A.M., FIGURING that's not too early to call Mireille. He cuts the kitchen lights and sees Althea next door in her chair with her book.

Kat's up watching a *Top Chef* episode that she recorded, hoping that her favorite contestant, Kristine from Seattle, is not eliminated, despite the deflated sweet potato soufflé. El's watching a ball game on his iPad.

Faye sits at his desk in the studio over the garage sketching his plans for the Edgertons' intimate backyard. He wants to give them the illusion of comforting and tranquil space. He would like them to feel in that yard what he feels when he listens to Mozart's Piano Concerto No. 21.

Cully's on his sleeping mat, back against the wall, with his Moleskine notebook on his knee. He writes, *Smoked four bowls today. Not high now. Crashed like an hour ago.* The pencil falls from his hand.

Craig's trying to solve for *x*. He's read this word problem at least a dozen times, but it's not making sense. He sips his Red Bull, looks at the time. Christ! He reads in the textbook that for mixture problems like this it's helpful to do a grid. Do what with a grid?

The S'Moores, each asleep in her own bed, share a dream in which they are the heroic Belinsky Girls, leading a battalion of brunette moppets in a war against an invading army of very nasty and unhygienic children from the island of Scomparso in the Sea of the Fallen Angels.

Auralee holds Julie's forgotten eyeglass case in her hand and closes her eyes.

Julie snuggles with her two sleeping daughters and watches a ladybug climb the side of the water glass on the bedside table. The lady climbs, loses purchase, and falls. She rolls herself over, tries again, and fails. She tries again.

Stacy applies a Merle Norman facial mask and smokes a cigarette without moving her lips until the clay hardens. She's watching the news report about the man in Daytona Beach who rose up out of the ocean armed with an assault rifle and opened fire on the sunbathers, shot off fifty rounds, killing eight, including a five-year-old girl, and wounding thirty-one, before a guy driving a cigarette boat sliced him in half.

Donny irons his shirt and slacks for the morning while he watches *Charlie Chan in Paris* for what must be the twentieth time, so when Monsieur Dufresne says, "Be assured we'll help you get to the bottom of this, Mr. Chan," Donny is able to reply, "Must turn up many stones to find hiding place of snake."

Reverend Rylan Burgess sits at the kitchen table with his pencil and sheets of lined paper, writing Sunday's sermon. Buddy's folded on the chair next to him. Taffi's on her knees in prayer in the bedroom, her book, *Jude the Obscure*, by the pillow. Rylan has Olney's check before him on the table. He's so appreciative of the kindness of this man who is not a member of the congregation. He'll write Mr. Kartheizer a note of thanks when he's done with the sermon on men who manifest God's nature. He asks God for guidance, taps the pencil's eraser on the table three times, and writes, *A generous person will prosper, whoever refreshes others will be refreshed.* He hears Buddy stir in his sleep on the chair, moan. "Daddy's right here, hon."

Gwen knows that Russ needs to lose fifty pounds, or she'll lose him, all at once to a heart attack, or piece by piece to diabetes. She's reading *6 Steps to 7 Figures*, and he's asleep next to her breathing through his CPAP machine.

Mireille can't sleep, so she's making a list of *Things That Make the Heart Beat Faster*:

- A phone call in the middle of the night
- Knowing you are loved
- Squealing brakes
- Footsteps behind you on a dark street
- A baby's cry
- A visit to the doctor
- Coffee
- Heights
- Sex
- Running late

Buck doesn't sleep through the night anymore. He naps like a cat—frequently, soundly, and briefly. He makes himself a Sidecar and settles into the La-Z-Boy. Olney notices the framed photo of the gold Cougar with Buck and an eager Pierre on the side table. He wonders what Buck is going to do, and then he hears, and Buck hears, Frank Sinatra singing "Sentimental Journey." Buck smiles, sips, and sings along. And so does Olney.

A BLAZE OF LIGHT IN EVERY WORD

A dying man should die, and a sleeping man should sleep, but Olney would like some assistance. The gentleman behind the reception desk at Merriment Manor has fallen dead asleep in his chair. Olney clears his throat. The sleeper wears a red plaid cotton shirt and brown slacks, and his torso seems to have sunk into his own lap. Olney says, "Excuse me," and the fellow blossoms into semiconsciousness, smiles, and apologizes. He wipes his damp lips with the back of his hand. He has a large mole on his forehead with several coarse hairs growing from it, which means, Olney has read, that it's not cancerous. The man's ears are disconcertingly large and fleshy and set below the level of his rheumy eyes. Olney introduces himself. The man says, "I'm what's left of Bill Tasher," and holds out his hand. They shake. "What can I do you for?"

"I'm here to see Mireille Tighe."

"So you're the one."

Before Olney can ask what that means, Mireille is coming their way across the atrium. She's wearing a sleeveless black jersey, black slacks, white espadrilles, a red silk scarf, and a sporty straw boater with a black and red band like she's ready to go back in time or off to the Henley Regatta. Her metal-framed eyeglasses are tinted a light blue. She's holding a small red clutch bag. She looks so dazzling that Olney can't speak. She takes his arm, nods to what's left of Bill Tasher, and says to Olney, "Shall we?"

What's left of Bill tells them to have a wonderful day. "And don't do anything I can't do."

Olney asks Mireille if she likes baseball. She loves it, she lies.

"I've got two box-seat tickets to opening day. Brown Bats versus the Key West Conches."

"Let's go."

On their way to Godolphin Field, Mireille points out a restaurant she used to waitress at, the Open Boat, built on stilts above Mosquito Bay. Olney knows it. Cully loved the place when he was young because you could feed the fish below you through a small trapdoor beside your table. Cully enjoyed watching the eruption of fish that roiled the water whenever he dropped in a french fry. Mireille says, "There were catfish down there as big as Volkswagens. And all of them with clogged arteries."

While they wait in line at the gate, Mireille gets her picture taken with Brownie, the team's mascot. They watch a flustered mother call ahead to her husband, who's holding the hand of a charming little girl. The mother clutches an infant in her arm like a loaf of bread and pushes a baby in a stroller. She says, "Adam, hurry up! I'm about to start leaking any second." On the way to their seats, Olney and Mireille bump into Dewey and Althea. Olney does the introductions. Dewey's holding a tray of datil pepper puffs and two cups of beer. Althea's holding her novel, *The Virgin Vampiress*, by Finola Wilson. "Paranormal romance is something new for me," she says.

Olney says, "What's it about?"

Althea consults the back cover. "Chalice Beaumont has come to Budapest from New Orleans in search of Attila Erdos, the Magyar prince to whom she was betrothed in 1710 and for whom she has remained chaste these three hundred years. When she finds the dashing young man claiming to be the prince and looking so much like the prince's portrait in the Nemzeti Galéria, she is swept away and goes with him to Simontornya Castle. Every fiery kiss, every heated embrace, every thrust of blistering loins, brings Chalice closer to heaven . . . or is it to hell?" Althea looks up. "I'll stop there."

It's the third inning and the Brownies are up by two. When he asks for her story, Mireille tells Olney she was married for a time to Jack Tighe, a sweet, unassuming, and genial fellow, who liked nothing better than washing and polishing his Chevy in the driveway and then cruising out to Dairy Godmother's for ice cream. "We met at Requiem High in American History class. Jack sat beside me on the first day. He had a severe crew cut and ferocious acne. He was the first boy I ever really spoke to. He showed me a picture of his dog, Mitzy, a Brittany spaniel mix with one floppy ear and one ear standing at attention, handed me a stick of Juicy Fruit gum, and told me he liked my crucifix ring. I was in love. We graduated; we married; we bought a little bungalow; we didn't have the children we were expecting and never thought to find out why not. We stopped trying."

They both worked, he as a history teacher at Robert Benchley Middle School, she as a receptionist at the All Smiles Dental Clinic. She kept a garden; he tinkered in his cellar workshop. Suppers simmered all day in a crockpot or else were picked up at a take-out window. Jack's dream was a retirement cottage in Dennis Port. "We were thirty, for chrissakes!" Mireille says. It was the dusty green artichoke-shaped candle on the TV that finally got to her, that and the chipped paint on the baseboards, and the lingering rancid smell of fish and chips. "I suddenly felt assaulted by insignificance and ugliness. I said to Jack, Is it always going to be like this? He put down his newspaper and said he was doing exactly what he wanted to be doing.

"I said, 'Really?'

" 'I'm happy as a clam at high tide.' "

"We parted on affable terms but never really stayed in touch. A few years later I followed a charming fellow, Gene Tonelli, to Anastasia, a psychologist and Civil War reenactor. We didn't last—he favored the pro-slavery traitors—but I fell in love with the city. I worked seven days a week waitressing and saved my money to buy a B&B in Old Town. And then I started having trouble swallowing, and you know the rest, pretty much. Dysphagia caused by esophageal cancer. My parents are gone. Lilou is gone. I'm the end of the Bellamy line."

With the Brown Bats down one in the bottom of the ninth, rookie shortstop Wyatt Tyler laces a liner to the gap in left, scoring two runners and sealing the victory for the home team. When Olney asks Mireille what she'd like to do now, hoping she doesn't say, "Go home," she suggests a walk through Bayside Resurrection Cemetery. "I want to show you my plot."

When they stand beside Mireille's future grave site, Olney doesn't speak, knowing that anything he says will be foolish. He notes that her eventual adjacent neighbors will be Donald Tyrell, Beloved Father, 1936–1987, and Justine Bendell, 1898–2001, a woman who lived in three centuries. Mireille will have afternoon shade beneath the live oak. Olney then says that he has seldom thought about the deposit of his remains. "And I wrote obits!"

"I have the advantage of knowing when I'm going to die."

"When is that?"

"Soon."

"Maybe not. You don't know."

She raises an eyebrow, cocks her head, and smiles.

He says he has something to show her, and they walk to Pen Bee-man's grave. Olney notices Auralee, the clairvoyant, tending to a grave across the lawn and thinks he knows that the daughter with the pink bicycle is buried there. Olney tells Mireille that Pen was a poet who died too young. There's a poem he wrote, appropriately brief, on his headstone:

In the Beginning God Created the Heaven and the Earth

O
ut
of
for
get
ful
ne
ss
or
in
an
att
em
pt
to
wa
ke

On their walk back to the car, Olney asks Mireille if she likes fishing. She does. He says, "Pick you up at nine."

"I'll have to buy a fishing outfit. I wonder if Orvis delivers overnight."

Olney's famished. He stops at Home Away from Rome for a take-out meal. Rosemary Clooney's belting out "Mambo Italiano" when he walks in, and Patsy Fantasia's singing along behind the deli counter. Patsy says, "Gnocchis and meatballs, my friend?" Olney says he wants to try something different, and he scans the menu on the wall.

Patsy says, "Roast beef sangwich?"

Olney shakes his head and squints harder at the menu.

Patsy says he's got some beautiful toasted ravs. "My mother made them."

"Your mother's been dead for six years."

"She would have made them."

"I think I'll have the Sausage Surprise."

"You got it."

"What's the surprise?"

"No sausage."

"Perfect. And a chocolate milk."

( )

AS OLNEY WASHES THE SUPPER DISH AND PUTS AWAY THE PARMESAN, the red pepper flakes, and the sriracha, he hears a knock at the screen door and, "Hey, Olney, can I come in?"

"You're just in time, Langley."

Langley is eleven and lives across the street with her mother, Jen, who is clinically depressed but is no longer able to afford psychotherapy. Langley's mission is to make her crestfallen mother happy by (1) being sweet; (2) praying; (3) being obedient and dutiful; and (4) telling jokes that she and Olney make up or that Olney remembers.

Olney pours two glasses of lemonade and sets out two bowls of banana pudding and a dish of vanilla wafers. Langley sits, puts her pencil and memo pad on the table, and folds a napkin over the neck of her T-shirt.

Olney says, "How's Mom today?"

"In bed all day with her eyes open."

"Did you tell her our jokes?"

"She didn't think they were funny."

"She didn't think *fifty Teamsters* was funny?"

"She doesn't like light bulb jokes."

Olney cracks the skin on his pudding, tunnels into the mush with his spoon, and pours in a little cream. He passes the cruet of cream to Langley, who does the same. They both eat the pudding proper first and save the skin for last.

Olney says, "Is she taking her Zoloft?"

"Yes."

Olney says, "Knock, knock."

"Who's there?"

"Polish burglar."

"Polish burglar who?"

"No, that's the joke. Get it?"

"That's insensitive, Olney."

"But hilarious, right?"

"Not."

"Okay." Olney sits back, drums his fingers on the table. "Okay, ready?"

"Go!"

"How was the little girl able to send her mother a letter while riding her Schwinn?"

"How?"

"It was a stationery bike."

Langley licks her spoon, puts her elbow on the table, and rests her head in her hand. "Do you think she'll ever get better?"

"Of course she will. Take her a bowl of this pudding. It'll pick her right up."

( )

NOW MANY YEARS LATER, AS HE LIES IN BED AND FACES THE DISSOLU-tion of his hopes, Olney remembers that distant afternoon when his first-grade son took him to discover, not ice, but ant lions. At the beach, he and Cully knelt beside a slanting funnel in the sand and watched a solitary ghost ant step on the crest of the pit and slide down the slope into the jaws of the waiting predator. Olney said he had never seen this in his life. Cully said it's a scary world out here. "I could get lost, lose my way back from school or something."

"I'd find you."

"Or you could get lost. Or Mom."

"Yes, it can be scary," Olney said, and he hugged his boy.

Cully said, "Better watch your step! You never know what's under your bed. Might be a clown."

The barred owl on the telephone wire has a field mouse in her beak. She looks through the window at Olney tossing in his sleep. She calls out and listens for a response. She takes the mouse in her talon and tears off a piece of pink flesh.

SO TIRED OF ON-MY-OWN

"Call me Bunny," Bunny says when Olney introduces her to Mireille. She shakes Mireille's slender hand, leans back in her swivel chair, opens her cash box, and tells her excitable blue heelers, Alice and Ralph, to behave themselves. The dogs dutifully lower their heads and whimper, but keep their tails wagging a mile a minute. Bunny snaps open a can of beer and says, "Welcome to the Crappie House!"

Bunny's Crappie House is an unprepossessing rusted sheet metal structure, an enclosed floating dock, tucked into Wistful Cove on Hidden Lake. The house is roofed with corrugated galvanized steel and windowed with plexiglass. The six-foot-wide plywood deck surrounds a ten-by-fifteen-foot opening into the lake. The lake here is twenty feet deep. Bunny's got a portable TV on a tobacco-brown end table next to the red plaid sofa that she shares with the dogs. She keeps the TV tuned to the TLC Channel—hoarders and the morbidly obese. Next to the sofa is the swivel chair she salvaged from an Office Depot dumpster and repaired with duct tape and WD-40, and next to that is a small banquet table on which she keeps her cooler of Keystone Light, her carton of Newports, a bowl of peeled hard-boiled eggs, and several plastic gallon jugs of tap water.

Bunny lights up a cigarette, shakes the flame from the match, and flicks the smoking matchstick into the lake, where a taillight shiner rises to fuss with it. She tells Mireille, "What you catch here mostly are black crappie and the occasional channel cat. Lots of folks in Florida call them speckled perch or specks, but I call them black crappie because that's what they are. *Pomoxis nigromaculatus.*"

Alice has her snout in the water, and she's attracted the attention of a juvenile banded water snake. She snaps at it. Olney asks Bunny how they're hitting today, and she tells him about like the Brown Bats hit last season. "But it's early yet." The sign on the wall over the banquet table reads NO CUSSING. NO GLASS CONTAINERS. NO RUNNING. NO HOOKS ON THE FLOOR. GOT TO PEE: TAKE IT OUTSIDE. Bunny says, "All you need to feed your family is a cane pole, a Missouri minnow, a number-four hook, a split shot, and a spoonful of patience. Best-tasting fish there is—sweet, delicate, white, flaky meat. You can pan-, oven-, shallow-, deep-, or stir-fry it. You can broil it, poach it, bake it, stuff it, grill it, or barbecue it. You can make a Parmesan crusted crappie casserole. I hope you like fish, hon."

Olney pays her for two all-day passes, and Bunny says, "Where else on earth can you have so much fun for six bucks?"

Wendell Mattress walks in with a Pocket Fisherman, a bucket of minnows, and a stadium cushion: GO 'SKEETERS! Olney doesn't say anything about there needing to be a comma after GO. Wendell's just shy of five feet and weighs in at ninety pounds, give or take. He works nights for Intrepid Industries cleaning supermarkets. Drives a ride-on single-brush floor scrubber, a linoleum Zamboni, he calls it. He supplements his income by cleaning fish at Bunny's. sits on his cushion at the edge of the deck, his feet not quite touching the water. He unfolds his little rod, works a minnow onto a hook, and drops the bait into the drink. He says to Olney, "I see you caught yourself a keeper," and Mireille blushes. "How's Cully these days?"

"He's living down south near his mom," Olney says. "In Melancholy."

"Tell him hey."

( )

AND IN MELANCHOLY AT JUST THIS MOMENT, CULLY IS WALKING UP Main on his way to work. He's a sign spinner at Sophie's Golden Touch, a jewelry store/pawnshop on the corner of Main and Dixie Boulevard. Cully likes to think of himself as a performer. His official job title is Human Directional: "Stand on the street corner in front of the business and hold/twirl our sign. Get jiggy with it." He can do the Propeller with his WE BUY GOLD arrow, can catch the sign on his back and flip it with his heel, and he's working on the Wind-Up Toy and Street Tornado. He's approaching the Dixiewood Motel when he catches sight of Lip O'Brien walking toward him, just a little too late to do anything about it. Lip was Cully's sponsor at AA and still would be if Cully bothered to go to meetings anymore.

Lip holds out his fist, and Cully responds with a dispassionate bump. Lip says, "We miss you, man. How's it going?"

"Working."

"Clean?"

"Eight days, no oxy."

It has, in fact, been nineteen hours.

Lip's been clean and sober for eight years. He wears a black T-shirt, khaki chinos, and black Chucks—his uniform. His wavy white hair has a slight yellow tint to it. His eyes are weak and his prescription old, so he tilts his head back a bit when he talks to you. He jiggles the coins in his pocket and says, "Pot?"

Cully says, "Pot's not my problem, Lip. You know that. Pot keeps me sane."

"There's a meeting in fifteen minutes at St. Luke's."

"I'm on my way to work."

"I'll walk with you," Lip says, and they head up Main. "What time do you get off? Work, I mean."

"Meetings aren't for everyone."

"Work for me."

"There's no higher power, Lip, no power greater than ourselves."

"Gravity is a greater power. Try that."

A kneeling bus squeals to a stop just ahead of them, lowers its front end, and releases a passenger on an electric wheelchair. The passenger, an elderly woman in a blue wig, unfurls her parasol and drives toward the Dollar Tree.

Lip says, "What do you want for yourself?"

"To be happy."

"That's what you always say."

"Tranquility, then."

"Not love?"

"If I want love, I'll get a dog."

"Cats are better. They'll leave you alone when you're blue."

"So you're a dog, then?"

( )

MIREILLE SAYS, "WHAT DOES CULLY DO IN MELANCHOLY?"

"Treads water." Olney smiles and lifts his pole to check the bait. Wendell pulls in a ten-inch crappie, and Bunny rings the ship's bell mounted by the door.

"Have you spoken with Cully about your concerns?"

"He's hard to talk to." Olney explains how Cully has come to rely on stock gestures and clipped responses—the irritable, mirthless laugh, the two-note murmured affirmation, *Un-huh*, the cocked head and furrowed brow, feigning interest, enabling him to acknowledge without actually responding, to engage the world through disengagement.

"You're a big boy, Olney. You can ignore his theatrics and move on, right? Patience is called for. And perseverance."

"I'm behaving like a petulant child, right?"

"Which works in his favor, doesn't it? Don't let him sabotage himself."

The bell rings again, and Olney wonders if he just said all that out loud to Mireille or simply thought it. Mireille feels a nibble, and Olney tells her to give the pole a yank, and she does, and she loses the fish and the bait. "Just as well," she says.

Trophy Tivnan's sipping a wild berry wine cooler when he walks into Bunny's with his son Tiger. Bunny salutes him with her beer can. Tiger's nasty cough sounds loose and juicy, and Bunny tells him he ought to have it looked at. Wendell says, "That's got to keep you up at night, bud." Tiger laughs until his unchecked mirth erupts into a croupy convulsion and then dissolves into a prolonged wheeze. Tiger's seventy-five and is the spit and image of his ninety-four-year-old father—the pendulous earlobes, the icy blue and bloodshot eyes, the fleshy nose, the impuissant chin. Tiger's never taken a medication of any kind and has never seen a doctor in his life. And for those reasons he considers himself sound as a bell, fit as a fiddle, strong as an ox. Trophy unfolds his camp chair and sits. He spits into the lake for good luck. He says of his son, "Been contrary all his life."

Tiger says, "You mean *vigorous* all my life."

Trophy says, "You just wait, mister. I'll bury you like I buried your sisters; God bless their unsullied souls."

Tiger remembers he left the bait in the truck. When he walks outside, Trophy says, "You never stop worrying about the little shits."

Olney marvels at this father and son who have been together, have lived together, for seventy-five years, and who are still not sick of each other. Trophy's wife, Tiger's mom, Rosealma, died twenty or so years ago, and since then, they've taken care of each other. They finish each other's sentences; they share their meager wardrobe; Tiger cooks; Trophy cleans. They have no TV. In the evening, Tiger reads to Trophy in the living room. The *Daily Sun*, *Field & Stream*, and the stories of Jack London. Tiger's read "To Build a Fire" so often he can recite it by heart. Surely they must have rubbed each other the wrong way on occasion, but if they did, they left no abrasions. Even Trophy's exasperation is played for laughs.

Trophy lets out a whoop and reels in a sleek and gleaming fifteen-inch channel cat. Tiger claps him on the back. Wendell takes his fillet knife and pliers, picks up the flapping cat, and carries it to the fish station. A knife to the brain settles the cat right down.

Olney says, "When Cully was little, he and I went to that miniature golf course I work at on our boys' nights out. Eighteen holes and then ice cream at Sherbet Hoover's." And when he says this, he pictures Cully at seven wearing sneakers with flashing red lights in the soles and a khaki *Ghostbusters* jumpsuit, asking him why the moon doesn't fall to earth like everything else, and the memory is so sweet that Olney wants to cry.

Wendell says, "It's a damn eel, that's what," when Trophy hauls up a three-foot long brown wiggly something-or-other. "A marbled eel, if I'm not mistaken."

Alice and Ralph are beside themselves, barking and trembling on the sofa and trying to hide behind the cushions. Bunny swats Ralph's muzzle, Alice licks Ralph's face, and they hush.

Tiger disagrees. "A swamp eel."

Wendell severs the head with his machete and tosses it back into the lake, where a catfish with a mouth like an open bread box swallows it in one gulp. "Eels is good eating," Wendell says. "Sweetish and mild."

"Like Ingrid Bergman," Tiger says.

"Not *Swedish*," Wendell says.

Trophy tells Wendell he's got no use for the eel, so Wendell decides to keep it, have it for supper, fry it up in olive oil with chilis and capers and umami sauce. The eel, however, is not an eel, but an eel-like fish, an invasive Asian species, *Monopterus albus*, confusingly known as the swamp eel, and it is host to a foodborne zoonosis, *Gnathostoma spinigerum*, which, when consumed by humans, may cause fever, rash, vomiting, pruritic swelling, stabbing intestinal pain, and in dire cases when the parasite enters the central nervous system, meningitis and encephalitis. Wendell's liver was long ago compromised during a bout of hepatitis A, making him particularly susceptible to the ravages of the larval invasion. When he splits open the swamp eel to gut it, Wendell finds it infested with thousands of milky white, translucent, inch-long worms. He gags and then sweeps the entire repulsive mess into a paper grocery sack, fills the sack with rags, douses the rags with lighter fluid, takes the sack outside, and lights the whole infernal rubbish on fire.

Olney sees the book in Mireille's backpack and asks her what she's reading. She pulls the novel from the pack to show him. "*The Appassionata*. I just started it." She opens to the bookmarked page. "Oboist falls for the first violinist in the Boston Symphony. Sublime music and passionate love."

Olney apologizes for the lack of angling action. Mireille says that's what makes for a perfect day of fishing. Wendell, meanwhile, is back on his Anastasia College cushion, and he's furious that the kind of ooky and depraved obscenity such as they had just witnessed, that maggot-infested rope of slime, could exist in this wonderful world. He doesn't think he'll sleep for weeks.

When Mireille has trouble swallowing air, Olney puts his arm on her shoulder and pulls her close. "Will I need to take you back for a treatment?"

She shakes her head. "There is no treatment."

"I don't know how you do it."

"You do what you have to do."

"I'd be feeling sorry for myself twenty-four seven."

"Self-pity's a waste of time. As the Buddhists say, pain's inevitable; suffering's optional." Mireille slips the novel into her backpack. It's a bit of a doorstop, she acknowledges, and she hopes she has time to finish it. She says, "So what are your intentions, Mr. Kartheizer?"

Olney's taken aback. He furrows his brow and smiles. "The usual?"

"You'll find that I'm not the usual kind of woman."

"I see that."

"Well?"

"I intend to get to know you."

"Better hurry up." She smiles and turns her head to glance Bunny's way. When she turns back, her smile is diminished, and her eyes are damp.

( )

WHEN CULLY IS ALMOST SIDESWIPED BY AN SUV PULLING INTO THE parking lot of Sophie's Golden Touch, he thinks that if he just once let one of these text-and-drive morons hit him, it would mean a weekend staycation at Everglades General, clean sheets, three squares, and heavenly medication. The driver, a bottle blonde with trout pout and saddlebags, steps out of her big rig and examines the fender where Cully's arrow sign brushed the metal when he jumped out of her way. She tells him he's damn lucky there was no damage, and he thinks she must be joking and says he could try harder next time. She takes his photo with her iPhone and says her husband's in law enforcement. Cully says, "Rent-a-cop at Sam's Club?" but not loud enough for her to hear it. No use rattling Sophie's cage on payday. He wants to tell the driver that if she owned a Hyundai Sonata and not a Cadillac aircraft carrier, and maybe if she lightened up on the face filler and the peroxide, then she might not have to be here selling her daughter's tennis bracelet, a daughter named Serenity that he just made up.

He pivots and turns toward the passing cars on Main. He lifts his sign and spins it while doing an admittedly graceless moonwalk. He thinks, What if Serenity is dead, and Mom is only trying to divest herself of painful mementos? That's the thing about life—you shouldn't go judging people until you have all the facts, because nothing is ever as it seems, not even the facts.

( )

CULLY HEARS THE DOUBLE HONK OF A WHEEZY HORN WHEN HE WALKS out of the check-cashing store and sees Shane Autry in his piece-of-shit 1989 Dodge Aries, which he bought because he, too, is a dodgy, 1989 Aries, an April Fools baby, and it tickled him. He waves Cully over. Cully leans his elbow on the car's rusted roof and says, "What?"

"Get in."

"We ain't leaving the parking lot, I hope."

"We're leaving the planet."

Cully says, "Your car's a death trap, Shane," but he figures, what the hell, Shane's always generous with his party favors. He shakes his head and walks around the front of the car, which Shane bought from the Scobies, a family of copiously chinned, bounteously obese, cigarette smoking men, women, and children, who live in a cluster of sorry looking double-wides at the Mar-Vel Trailer Park, which neighbors refer to as the Scobieville Compound, and so the car's seats, front and back, bucket and bench, are worn to the springs. In fact, the whole faded red interior looks exhausted, including the headliner that's come loose and is held up with hundreds of silver thumbtacks.

Cully opens the back door, slips in, shuts it, and climbs over the seat to the front where the passenger door is welded shut. Shane drives with expired tags, a busted windshield, and a two-tray tackle box of pharmaceutical drugs behind the driver's seat. He's had the Dodge for seven years but no amount of Febreze and Dakota Odor Bomb has been able to rid the cabin, as Shane calls it, of the astringent funk of the malodorous Scobies.

Cully says, "I don't have your money if that's what this is about."

"You need to start planning ahead, friend, pretending, at least, that you have a future."

"I don't like the future."

"Why?"

"That's where I die. Anyway, my rent's due."

"I can't believe those two scumbags charge you to sleep on the floor of their closet."

Shane takes a joint from his shirt pocket and holds it up. "Attitude adjustment time." He drives west on Cypress Avenue, turns the radio dial to FM 108, Trenchtown Rock, and sings along with Desmond Dekker. When they pass the Tequesta Reservation at State Road 15, Cully stares at the clutch of white guys loitering outside Tribal Smokes in their paintball head wraps and chest protectors, and it crosses his mind that just maybe Shane's driving him out to the Everglades for dispatch and disposal. But he hasn't seen a pistol in the car. He looks at Shane, who has his eyes closed and is tapping the steering wheel with the heel of his hand to keep the beat. Cully thinks, Bad weed, and taps Shane's shoulder and hands him the doobie, and Shane manages to swerve the car just before he would have clipped the terrified newspaper vendor on the traffic island.

Cully owes Shane $218. He owes Paul Skopetski and Tee Quitadamo, each of them, twice that, and you don't see those boys all bent out of shape. He thinks he should maybe get his huevos out of Rancheros, start over somewhere else with a clean slate. Maybe visit his old man up in Anastasia. And then he thinks, Start what over? He says, "Where are we going?"

"To see Jasmine."

"She's got a restraining order on you."

"She's also got my son."

"Daughter. You don't have a son."

"My baby. Whatever."

"I thought she lived in Melancholy."

"She works at the Pollo Tropical on Blue Heron."

"She has your daughter because you're an unfit father. She got the restraining order because you beat her up."

"People change, Cully. People learn from their mistakes."

"You're asking for trouble here. We should turn around."

"She takes the bus home, a forty-five-minute ride. It's raining. We were in the neighborhood. We offer to drive her."

"It's not raining."

"It's not? Shit! My eyes are doing that thing again."

"I told you to see a doctor."

"All I want from her is a picture of the baby I can put in my wallet. A guy's baby picture is an aphrodisiac for the ladies." Shane pulls into the Pollo Tropical parking lot and backs into a space facing the window so they can admire Jasmine behind the counter. He says, "I love that woman with all my heart."

"No, you don't."

"You'll be driving. I need to sit with Jasmine in the backseat and explain the way things are to her."

"I don't have a license."

"Neither do I."

Shane tells Cully he'll be driving them to the banyan tree across from the junkyard on the Melancholy Cutoff Canal because that's where he and Jasmine used to go fishing and whatnot. "Scoot over here," Shane says. "I'm going to fetch her."

Cully says, "She ain't getting in the car," but when she does, Cully says, "You smell like Caribbean ribs, Jasmine."

She says, "Thank you." And then says to Shane, "Don't try any of your nasty shit. 'Kay?"

Cully watches as Shane lowers his untrimmed unibrow, cocks his head, looks at Jasmine, and pouts. Cully thinks his sidekick might be overselling the damage done to his delicate feelings, but Jasmine buys it. She touches Shane's hand and apologizes. Shane brings her hand to his cheek and shuts his eyes, and Cully wants to gag or laugh or blurt out his disbelief, but he starts up the car, turns off the radio, pulls out of the lot, and drives east on Cypress.

Shane tells Jasmine how much he misses her and the baby.

Jasmine says, "What's her name?"

"What's her what?"

"Name."

"What's her name?"

"I asked you first."

"I'm not good at pop quizzes. You know that."

"Her name's Lilias."

"Is what?"

"Middle name's Sidra."

"Lilias Sidra Autry."

"Last name's Saavedra. Like mine."

At the red light, Shane bites his lip. Cully stares at Shane's snaggled, chipped, and discolored teeth in the rearview mirror, and he is offended. And it's not just aesthetic umbrage he's taken. The way Cully sees it, once your teeth go, and you can't chew, and you can't get your daily allowance of protein, then it's all downhill, and pronto. Teeth are the sentinels of good health and a robust constitution. And that's why Cully visits the free clinic at Everglades Dental College every six months, and he'd go whether they gave him nitrous oxide or not.

Jasmine says, "So you're going to sulk now?"

Shane tells her to fuck herself, and Cully says, "If I have to stop this car, you'll both be sorry," but nobody laughs. He hears Shane say, "Yes, I do a little ice from time to time. What's the big deal?" And the car goes silent except for the grinding of the wheel bearings and the squeal of the brakes. Cully sees a tweaker leaning against the wall of the Sunset Motel. The girl looks fifteen going on fifty and is so obviously spun she's got a busy hand down her Daisy Dukes and only the whites of her fluttering eyes are visible.

Jasmine asks Cully why he's taking a left. "I live on Avila."

Shane answers. "I want to go someplace we can talk. Neutral ground. Not my place, not your granny's."

"I have nothing to say to you."

"Well, then, you can listen."

"You are such an asswipe."

"I was hoping that maybe we could work things out. Be a family."

"Are you insane?"

Cully says, "He wants a photo of the kid for his wallet."

Jasmine says, "I'm seeing someone."

Cully pulls off the street and onto the swale by the canal, and parks.

He cuts the headlights and kills the engine. He hears what must be a mullet splash into the water, and then another. Barracuda hunting for a meal.

Shane says, "Who?"

Jasmine says, "No one you know."

"We know the same goddam people."

"My world is not so small as yours. And besides, all of your friends are jerk-offs. No offense, Cully."

Shane insists that he needs to know the name of the other dude, and when Jasmine won't tell him, he slaps her face.

Cully says, "That's enough."

Shane says, "Shut. Up. This is personal business." He tells Cully to get out and go for a swim.

"I can't swim," Cully lies, but he does get out of the car. He leans his butt against the fender, crosses his arms, looks up at the sky, and everywhere he looks he sees another Big Dipper. There's only supposed to be one, right?

Shane reaches down and pulls a fully loaded crack pipe from his tackle box, tells Jasmine it's time to bake the cake, and lights up.

She says, "None for me."

He laughs and says, "I think you're being disingenuine, sweetie. I know that you know that I know that you are craving a taste. Bad."

"I have a child now, retard."

"And so do I. And I don't think our little what's-her-face is going to know what Mommy and Daddy are up to." When he holds the pipe to Jasmine's lips, she swipes it away, out of his hand and onto the floor, which infuriates Shane, and he punches her. Aims for the jaw but strikes the forehead.

Jasmine screams for Cully to please please please help her. Please!

Shane says, "Start walking, Cully. And if you don't, I'll knock every one of Buttercup's tiny gray teeth down her throat."

"I won't let you do that."

"How you going to stop me?"

Cully takes the keys from the ignition. "For starters, I'll toss the keys into the canal."

"I need five minutes," Shane says. "That's all." He whispers into Jasmine's ear.

She says, "Cully, wait across the street. If I scream, come running."

Cully takes a step back, lowers his arms, steadies himself, and walks across Cypress Avenue. He briefly imagines himself a knight errant back at the car with his hands through the window and around Shane's throat. But he can't imagine what happens next. He sits on the sidewalk, back up against an olive tree. He shuts his eyes and puts his head in his hands. And then he laments, not for the first time, his descent into wretchedness. He's stolen from friends, family, and strangers, some of those strangers were no more than slices of comatoast, passed out on the sidewalk.

He does not see Jasmine bolt from the car. He does not see Shane run Jasmine down and drag her back to the car, but he does hear her scream and looks up. He runs to the car and opens the trunk, grabs the tire iron, and opens the back door. Jasmine is on her back, and Shane is pulling down her pants. He tells Cully to fuck off. Cully slams the tire iron into Shane's teeth, and Shane screams. Cully hands Jasmine the tire iron, takes her phone, calls 911, and hands the phone back to her. He can't stay here. He tells her to meet him at the corner after she reports the assault.

As he nears the corner of Edison, he hears the whoop-whoop, the chirp, and the intermittent warble of the approaching police sirens and sees the flashing red lights of the squad cars—three of them—as they make the turn at the Edison Avenue light and run hot down Cypress. He puts his hands in his pockets and lowers his head as they speed by.

Seven blocks east, Jasmine's abuela has fallen asleep in her rocking chair by the kitchen window, her amber rosary beads wrapped around her arthritic fingers. She dozed off during the Fifth Sorrowful Mystery. "My God, my God, why hast thou forsaken me?" She snores. In the crib in Jasmine's bedroom, the colicky baby cries herself back to sleep at last.

When the lead deputy arrests Shane, and as the paramedics are lifting a battered and barely conscious Jasmine onto the gurney and into the ambulance, and as the two other deputies are cataloguing the drugs in Shane's tackle box, and while Shane is spitting out broken teeth, he tells them that what happened here was all an accident and a misunderstanding, but they can't understand a word he's blubbering through his swollen and bleeding lips. He tries to say he loves Jasmine with all his heart and is super-sorry for her injuries, and he was just about to carry her over to Everglades General when you gentlemen arrived.

Once upon a time, but not so long ago, after leaving Splendora High, Cully was a philosophy major at UNF with a 3.5 GPA, well on his way to a career in academia and an idyllic life of intellectual stimulation; bright, shiny faces on eager, nimble-witted, and grateful students; amusing, if occasionally vicious, departmental intrigue, and ample time to write his monographs on moral reason and epistemic humility. But he and philosophy had a falling out at about the time he began his love affair with heroin and convinced himself that philosophy was so much pretentious nonsense, a parlor game played by smug sophists.

On Main, Cully sees the blind octogenarian Silpher twins up ahead, Agnes and Maude, born and orphaned in Barbados, brought to the States by a grandmother, walking toward the Dixiewood and home, both tapping their folding canes on the sidewalk and holding hands. When they speak in unison, they speak in prefect tight harmony, as only siblings can. Agnes speaks in a high soprano and Maude handles the bottom register. They say, "Good evening, Cully."

He says, "Ladies," and asks how they know who he is.

Maude says, "We each have a distinctive aromatic signature."

When he gets home to Critter and Lardo's apartment, there's a party going on, if you can call unmelodious songs about killing people blasting from the bookshelf speakers and a half-dozen wasted stoners passed out on sofas and chairs a party. He takes a serviceable cigarette butt out of an empty Chinese take-out box, tears off the lipstick-stained filter, and lights up. He opens a fortune cookie he finds on the floor and reads, THE CURE FOR GRIEF IS MOVEMENT. Nothing in the fridge but two limp stalks of celery, a half-empty bottle of blue Gatorade, and an opened jar of queso—the cheese now stiffened to a paste so thick you'd have to spread it with a spackling knife. He steps into his closet and shuts the door behind him. He hangs up his shirt and jeans, stuffs tissues into his ears, lies on his foam mat, and tries to put the horror of Shane and Jasmine out of his mind. He's asleep in no time. He's in physics class and hears the professor say that every place is the center of the universe or no place is, and he is comforted. And then the professor solves for x, puts down his chalk, wipes his hands of the dust, steps back from the board to admire his equation, turns to the class, and says, "Proof that something can come from nothing."

( )

OLNEY CRAWLS BACK INTO BED AFTER A VISIT TO THE BATHROOM. HE punches his pillow, slides his arm under his head, and enjoys the simple bliss of stretching his legs as tightly as he can and for as long as possible, and soon he's asleep and back to the vexing dream he'd been hoping to avoid, a dream of a predacious ichthyosaur, as black and shiny as a gum boot.

Across the yard, Althea, at her window, considers the last line of *Naked Brunch*. "He tasted of Chantilly cream and cognac, and she knew nothing bad could ever happen to her again." Althea considers it wanting. She puts out the light on her end table. On the front porch, Dewey sits in the dark and sings, "Why Have My Loved Ones Gone?" so softly that only the barred owl in the live oak can hear him. "Why am I left alone while all their troubles here are done?"

LET'S GET LOST

When you eat a pineapple, the pineapple is eating you back. Olney has arrived early for his six o'clock dinner date with the Burgesses at Fatboy's Fish Camp, and he's been reading about fruit on an iPhone cooking app. Pineapple has a flesh-eating enzyme, bromelain, that devours protein, and that's why your tongue may bleed when you eat one. He takes a screenshot of the page. And now he's thinking about Buck at seventy-five, alone in that cluttered house, eating canned pineapple slices and getting around with a walker because his right leg won't listen to him anymore. His only friend is a friend since grade school, a man whose first name is a verb and surname, an adverb: Trace Lightly. A half-dozen men in ball caps are slouched at the bar drinking pints of beer and watching the local Fox News station on the several TVs around the room. Breaking news about a Florida politician. Olney pulls up a stool and orders a Forever Amber ale. When the photo of a stunning young woman appears on the screen, the man two seats from Olney leans back, folds his arms across his chest, and says, "I'd hit that." When the photo of a reasonably distinguished-looking septuagenarian appears beside her on a split screen, the man says, "Bubba's gonna need a pinch hitter." According to the report, a retired state senator from Palmetto Beach has recently discovered that he unknowingly married his granddaughter. Imagine his shock and dismay. Imagine her bewilderment and shame.

Olney checks the hostess station, checks his watch. Maybe he said six-thirty, not six. Every inch of the ceiling over the bar is stapled with inscribed dollar bills. The man two seats away has lost interest in the senator's story. He's talking to the empty seat between them. He shakes his head, gesticulates like he's trying to persuade whoever he thinks is sitting there that it was all a fluke, a mistake, and it will never happen again. Scout's honor!

Olney's perusing the autographed celebrity photos along the wall—Anita Bryant, Bobby Bowden, Mel Tillis, who spelled his name with a graphic stutter, and Vanilla Ice planting a kiss on a twenty-pound bass—when he hears his name being paged. He walks to the hostess station and introduces himself to Rylan and Taffi.

They take a table on the patio overlooking the Sleepy River. From here they can watch the sun set over the pines in Emma Hinton State Park. A pontoon party boat, an airboat, and several bass boats are tied up at the dock. When Rylan orders an all-you-can-eat catfish dinner, Olney compares it to the miracle of the loaves and fishes but doesn't get the pastoral chuckles he was expecting. Taffi orders fried oysters, Olney frog legs and gator tail. They'll share the deep-fried swamp onion. Sweet tea all around.

Rylan thanks Olney for his generous donation to the ministry. Olney says, "How old is Buddy?"

"Nine."

"That's a great age."

"You have children, Mr. Kartheiser?" Taffi says.

"I have a son. Grown and gone."

When the food arrives, they join hands, bow their heads, and say grace. Taffi eats her hush puppies with a knife and fork. She declines Olney's offer of frog legs. Olney sees that her blue eyes have darkened. Rylan and Taffi grew up in rural Indiana, Rylan as an only child in the town where his daddy was a backsliding but charismatic preacher, and Taffi on a farm where she was the youngest of six girls. "Girls on a farm, tits on a bull," her daddy was fond of saying. When he was ten, Rylan learned to throw his voice from an Edgar Bergen correspondence course. Then all his imaginary friends could talk to him. Rylan's mom was a rock, reliable and indomitable, but silent, lusterless, and hard. He loved his daddy. "What I admire more than anything is a person who gives in but doesn't give up."

Rylan and Taffi met at a sock hop at their tiny high school where every life was an open book. They married. Rylan went into the family business, and Taffi prepared herself to raise a brood of babies. They tried and tried. Rylan doesn't say this to Olney, but the hardest thing he ever did in his life was to spill his seed into the collection cup at the fertility clinic. Taffi says, "When I realized I could not and would not conceive, well, I wondered what was the point of going on."

"To praise His name," Rylan says.

"And that's when Buddy came into our lives."

A band is setting up on the small patio stage. Olney has seen them around town, a John Denver tribute trio called Almost Heaven. Taffi asks their waitress, Dana, for a doggie bag and a slice of key lime pie to go—she smiles at Olney—for you-know-who. Olney pays the bill and answers his phone call from Merriment Manor. What's left of Bill Tasher tells him Mireille's been taken to Anastasia General. Lump in the esophagus and possible lung infection. Olney explains the situation to the Burgesses and excuses himself. Taffi bows her head and prays. Rylan puts his hand on Olney's arm. "If there's anything we can do . . ."

Before he leaves, Olney gives the Burgesses a gift-wrapped bow tie he's been carrying in his pocket. For Buddy. It's red just like the one Jerry Mahoney wore. He tells them he's off to the hospital, and they say they'll pray for Mireille, and he thanks them for their kindness. We'll do this again, he says.

Olney squirts sanitizer on his hands from the dispenser outside Mireille's room and rubs briskly. It doesn't quite eliminate the fried food odor on his fingers, but may have, he hopes, killed any contaminates from the deep fryer. The corridor itself smells of a heady disinfectant. He walks into the room and sees that Mireille is, or seems to be, asleep. She's hooked up to a heart monitor and an IV drip. The walls of the room are the color of sliced turkey breast. Olney wants to dim the lights but thinks maybe he's not supposed to. A framed Rothko-inspired abstract expressionist print hangs on the wall by the bed. Three horizontal rectangular fields of color: an ecru sky above a hazy purple horizon, above a green expanse of what could be imagined as bamboo or asparagus.

Olney squeezes Mireille's cool forearm and kisses her forehead. He sits in the recliner beside the bed and picks up the novel she's been reading. He's intrigued by the cover photo—a tattoo of musical notes tumbling down a woman's violin-shaped back—but he's not in the mood to read. He sets the book back down on the bedside cabinet. On the wall beneath the TV is a whiteboard, on which someone has written the date in red marker and the names of the on-duty nurse, ETTA, and the aide, JAMES. What are the chances? Olney smiles and thinks his love has come at last and his lonely days are over. He decides he'll play Etta's *Blues to the Bone* CD when he gets home. Crying skies, crawling snakes, and smokestack lightning.

A call on the intercom for "Dr. Dallah, Dr. Mandeep Dallah" does not wake Mireille. A woman with wild gray hair, a blotchy face, and a stuffed toy puppy on her lap shoots Olney a withering look as she wheels past the room. Olney walks to the window when he hears approaching sirens. He pulls back the curtain and looks down at the ER entrance. Nurses are scrambling to assist the paramedics with what must be accident victims. Three of them. Mireille stirs, opens her eyes, looks around the unfamiliar room, and smiles when she sees Olney. He takes her hand. "How do you feel?"

She nods and then points to her mouth and shakes her head. Can't talk.

"Shall I read to you?"

She nods again.

He picks up the book. "*The Appassionata* by Kaime Brandelyn." Valentine Damato falls desperately in love with Martine Juneau. He reads from the opening *Allegro* movement and sees that Mireille may have nodded off, or maybe she's just listening intently. He continues but doesn't get beyond the moment when the principals' eyes first meet during a rehearsal for a Roll Over Beethoven concert on the Esplanade. He sets the book down and whispers good night. She opens her eyes. He says, "Let's get married." She squints and smirks. He says, "Let's get lost." She smiles.

Olney sees Samir waiting at the valet podium outside the hospital's main entrance. He's wearing an Everton soccer jersey, number 77, and a hinged knee brace. Olney taps his shoulder.

"Olney, my friend."

"Imagine finding you at the hospital. Are you sick?"

"I learned today that I'm too old to try a bicycle kick. Hyperextended the knee, the medial collateral ligament."

Olney tells Samir about Mireille's dysphagia.

"That's a tough one."

"A slow fast."

"Can I give you something for your stress?"

"I'll be okay."

"Any word from Cully?"

"Not a peep."

( )

WHEN HE WAS A BOY, OLNEY SOMETIMES WORE HIS SCHOOL CLOTHES to bed, so when he woke in the morning he was already dressed and only had to brush his teeth, or pretend to, and run a damp washcloth through his crew cut to be prepared for the day. Lately he's decided to wear only white T-shirts and white pajama shorts to bed, his slumber ensemble. And that's what he's wearing at the kitchen table. The window is open. The sweet scent of ozone tells him it's going to rain. He looks over at Althea sitting in her reading chair and feels comforted. He's just ordered flowers online to be delivered to Mireille first thing in the morning. Bright and cheery daisies. Etta's singing about the man she loves who loves another woman.

Olney opens his notebook and writes down a couple of intriguing lines he's heard today. "I got the Glock. Now I need to get a sidepiece," and "Oh yeah, the pancreas is a big deal." He opens the cigar box and takes out the photo of Buck and Pierre and writes about Buck's seventy-fifth birthday. You write about a person, and you begin to feel close to him and to feel cheered by his presence, saddened by his absence.

Trace knocks on the front door and lets himself in. He steps around the piles of clothing and the boxes of books, tchotchkes, hardware, and whatnot. Since Buck can't get upstairs any longer, he's had everything from the second floor and the attic brought downstairs. He hired his cousin Emerson's sweet but simple-minded twins, Crosley and Victor, to do the job. Trace says, "Happy birthday to you," and sets a sugar-free truffle cake and a bottle of Blanton's Special Reserve on the card table

MY DARLING BOY

beside the scrambled thousand jigsawed pieces of Bosch's *Temptation of St. Anthony* puzzle. Trace pours three fingers of bourbon into the two juice glasses, and they toast to another seventy-five.

Trace squeezes himself onto the sofa beside Buck, and when he expresses his concern about the clutter, about the dust and the mold, about Buck's maybe tripping over the debris and falling and not being able to get back up or call for help, Buck says as soon as he can sift through the mess to save what is dear to him, then he's going to call the twins and have them haul the rest of it to the dump. He lifts his arms and spreads them to take in the whole room. "Behold, this is my life, Trace Lightly."

Buck tells Trace that he came across an old photo of himself and Pierre taken one Easter morning before church out in the driveway. Found it in that old shoebox there on the hutch. And he also found his old, rusted Radio Flyer wagon. "I'm keeping that and having it restored. I loved that red wagon."

So did Cully. When he was five or so, he'd roam the neighborhood in Spanish Blade with his wagon and return in time for lunch with his found treasures: rocks, empty cans and bottles, the occasional discarded phone bill or supermarket circular, and often the Melroses' calico cat, Tangerine. Olney recalls Cully now on one of his infrequent visits to the house, sitting there across the table, drinking Red Bulls, one after the other, tearing up napkins into little squares, and lighting them on fire in his dessert plate. He'd stopped by to tell Olney he was changing his major to theater and had never been so excited about school ever. He'd already written a one-act play, "A Man Walks into a Marriage," about a dying man whose family gathers at his bedside. One of his boys is a priest, and the dad wants to confess that he cheated on his wife, their mom, for years. And he wants forgiveness and absolution.

"Love it," Olney said.

And he was already working on a full-length screenplay—that's where the money is— about a man in a fugue state who has forgotten who he is and wakes up as someone else in Uncertain, Texas. And then Cully said he was taking the semester off and was heading to Key West to finish the play and could use some money to see him through. "An investment in my future."

"I can drive you."

"No, that's okay."

Olney said, "You didn't flunk out, did you?"

"No."

"Are you okay?"

"I'm fine."

"I'll buy you a bus ticket, but you should stay the night. I'll take you dinner, drop you back at school tomorrow. You can show me the draft."

"I got to run."

When Cully was a toddler, Olney loved to watch him sleep in his little bed, his damp hair pasted to his forehead, his eyes moving beneath his lids, lost in dreamland. Olney would watch until Cully awoke, opened his eyes, saw his daddy, and smiled. Olney would say, "What did you dream about?"

Cully might say, "Colors."

"Which colors?"

"All of them."

Or, "My friends."

"Which friends?"

"I don't know."

Olney wonders what Cully's dreaming about tonight and wishes he could shake Cully's shoulder and say, "Wake up, honey bunny," like he used to.

( )

CULLY STRETCHES AND STIFFENS EVERY MUSCLE IN HIS BODY, HOLDS himself rigid like that for several seconds, and then relaxes. That release from tension and inflexibility is as good as he'll feel all day, and it only happens upon awakening. Before he opens his eyes, he tries to remember what day it is, even though all his days, these days, are identical: Wake. Wash. Rinse. Look for food. Get high. Sleep. Wake. Wash. Rinse. Repeat. He's sick of feeling adrift, hollow, and bewildered. Euphoria is not what it used to be. He needs to stop what he's doing and live. One day at a time, like Lip says. But that Day One is just so punishing and dissuasive.

He tries to make sense of the annoying dream he was having that he won't remember five minutes after getting up. He was a red chili pepper with sunglasses, a thin mustache, and a wide-brimmed hat. He had two arms and two hands but no legs and an open mouth in the shape of a stealth bomber. He wore white gloves and had a lot to say about the importance of reducing one's carbon footprint. If he talked, he remained upright. When he paused, he fell over. The closet door is cracked enough that he can see that it's morning. He hears water in the pipes and knows that someone is in the bathroom, and he'll have to pee in the backyard. He's got one more OP 40 time bomb in his shirt pocket but doesn't have enough saliva to swallow it. He looks up at the closet ceiling and sees the familiar stain in the shape of a flounder and remembers his archaeology professor holding up an Eocene-era fossilized fish, *Cockerellites* something or other, and saying, "In order to survive, you have to tell a story."

( )

WHEN HE WAS A BOY, CULLY OFTEN WORE HIS SHIRTS BACKWARD, slipped them on over his head, buttons up the back. And when he did, he might walk backward into the future and into the furniture and the walls and into a tree. Said he'd rather know where he'd been than see where he was going. One morning Olney was shaving at the bathroom sink. Cully sat on the hamper watching him. Cully told Olney that the boy in the mirror wasn't himself.

Olney said, "It's your reflection."

"It's my friend Lucky."

Cully and Lucky point at their chins. They tell Olney, "You cut yourself."

Olney dabbed at the nick with a styptic pencil. "Does Lucky live in the neighborhood?"

"When he's not in the mirror, he's nowhere."

"Do you miss him when he's not around?"

"I know where to find him."

Olney's at his kitchen table staring at a picture of ten-year-old Cully and writing all this down, letting one memory carry him to the next, letting one detail provoke another. He's writing about Cully and happiness as therapy, and it's working. He feels hopeful for the first time in a while. And he feels a nettling sadness, too.

For a few years until he was seven, Cully shared his bedroom with his Time Pony that no one else could see, a pinto named Powerhouse. At night, they rode off into the past, back to preschool, back to the olden days before computers when the world was black-and-white. They rode into the future, which Cully said was quieter than it was now, and there weren't many people around. Olney sat on the edge of Cully's bed, his finger tucked into the *Grimms' Fairy Tales*, saving the page. He said, "Where are you two going tonight?"

"To 2015."

"Do you talk to anyone in the future?"

"It's not allowed."

Because there is no happiness in Cully's present, at least no happiness that Olney knows of, he decides to imagine Cully's future ten years from now—after detox, after rehab, after a thousand addiction meetings, after struggle and reconciliation. Olney imagines he's sitting right here then, at the kitchen table, writing an obituary for his website, *The Dead Beat*, where he memorializes the folks that the *Daily Sun* deems unworthy of black ink and white space. This morning it's a eulogy for Bunny, who was found dead on her sofa in the Crappie House by Wendell Mattress. Her arthritic and gray-muzzled blue heelers, Alice and Ralph, were asleep beside her. Wendell removed the burned-out Newport from between her fingers, grabbed himself a can of Keystone Light, sat on the floor, dangled his feet in the water, and dialed Addie Morin, undertaker.

There's a knock at Olney's door. It's Cully and Cully's three-year-old son Leslie. Leslie? No. Morley? No. Skylar. Better. Sky is the light of Olney's life. Olney babysits for Sky every Monday, Wednesday, and Friday from nine to one while Cully teaches his classes at Anastasia College. Cully's wife, Amy, is the executive assistant to the AC president. Cully kisses Sky goodbye and thanks his father for watching the rascal. He tells Olney Sky didn't eat his breakfast. Olney tells Sky he has the Hot Wheels tracks set up in the living room. Of course he does; he never takes them down. Sky says he's hungry and heads for the carbo cabinet. Olney watches him and understands that Sky is his shot at redemption.

(II)

Striking Distance

WHEEL IN THE MIDDLE OF A WHEEL

The unidentified female victim's severed head was found Tuesday in a crab trap pulled from the Indian River near Turtle Harbor by a local fisherman. According to police reports, a frayed silk bow was still tied to her hair, and six blue crabs were eating her lips, having already devoured her eyes.

A cell phone left behind in a taxi in Jacksonville displayed a video of what appeared to be the execution of a blindfolded and hog-tied couple outside a popular Atlantic Beach nightspot.

A prostitute was found dead in her room at the Siesta Motel on A1A in McDermott. The Gideon bible lay open to the Book of Ezekiel on her pillow. She had been strangled with a priest's red tasseled cincture.

Mireille is reading the newspaper to Olney as they drive down I-95. She's been out of the hospital a week and feels strong enough to resume the search. They're already outside Melbourne and making good time. The billboard south of town features a bikini-clad woman holding an AK-47. SHOOT AN ASSAULT WEAPON AT MACHINE GUN AMERICA. NEXT EXIT THEN RIGHT. Mireille says, "Did you know there's a Christian health spa in Splendora called Pontius Pilates?"

"You're making these things up, aren't you?"

She smiles. "Here's the ad right here," she says, and holds up the paper.

The previous evening, Olney and Mireille joined his neighbors in a search for Mrs. Woodbine's dad, who lives with them, suffers from dementia, and had wandered off when Mr. Woodbine forgot to lock the back door and set the safety alarm. When Mr. Woodbine woke from a nap to an empty house, he called his wife and alerted the neighbors. The search ended a half hour later when Dewey called Olney and told him that Mr. Nick had just walked into his house, collapsed on the couch, and asked for a glass of water.

On the drive back to Merriment Manor, Mireille said, "We found Mr. Nick; now let's find Cully."

Olney said, "I wish."

Mireille said, "I thought you wanted him back."

"I do."

"If you want him back you have to find him first. Do you know where he is?"

"He could be anywhere in Everglades County."

"What's that—a four-hour drive?"

"Give or take."

"We'll be back by bedtime. I love a road trip."

"Are you sure you're up to it?"

"I've always wanted to be a detective. We'll pack lunch in a cooler. Apple juice and tuna sandwich for you. MiraLAX for me. And when we find him, we'll convince him to get into rehab or see a therapist. Or we could do an intervention. Me, you, Kat, her husband."

"An intervention could get bloody."

"What?"

"Kidding. It's a fine plan, but it's doomed. I've been here before."

"The stress you're under is going to kill you."

"I'm at a loss with the boy."

"When you don't know what to do, do something!"

"All right, we'll go, but don't get too hopeful."

( )

AND SO THEY DRIVE PAST THE THIRTY-FOOT-LONG CONDOM ON A BILL-board, PREVENTS ZIKA TRANSMISSION, and on to Melancholy. Mireille puts her bare feet up on the dashboard, wiggles her toes, and asks Olney if he likes the color of her toenails. He does. "It's called 'I'm Not Your Waitress.'" She asks him if he has any idea where Cully might be, and she takes out a memo pad and gel pen from her tiny purse.

He says, "I've got nine of his most recent phone calls and his last three addresses. Maybe he's still at one of them."

Mireille calls the nine numbers on Olney's phone. Four are out of service. One is Frying Nemo's Fish & Chips. She listens to requests to leave voice-mail messages from Henry, Don, Selena, and A-1 AC Duct Cleaners. "The phone numbers don't look promising." She checks the addresses on Google Maps and sees they're all within two blocks of Main. She says, "What are you going to say to Cully when we find him?"

"I always say the wrong thing."

"Pretend I'm Cully. You find me in a bar. Your lovely girlfriend is sitting outside in the shade at a picnic bench, reading her novel. You take the stool beside Cully—I'm Cully. I say, 'What are you doing here?'"

"I came to see you," Olney says.

"And now you've seen me."

"I'm worried about you."

"Stop. You should tell him you love him. Lead with that."

"I love you."

"I love you, too, Dad."

This billboard features a fetus saying 18 DAYS AFTER CONCEPTION MY HEART STARTED BEATING. Olney's cell phone dings. Mireille opens the notification. "Another mass shooting."

"Where?"

"Family planning clinic in Delaware. Eight women killed in the waiting room. Doctor and nurse wounded. Critically." Mireille stares out the window. "What happened to our country?"

"We bought the lie that the country was founded on the principles of life, liberty, and the pursuit of happiness. The truth is, that it was founded on genocide, slavery, and the pursuit of wealth."

"And the right to bear arms and use them with impunity."

The next billboard reads YOU CAN'T HOLD HANDS WITH GOD WHEN YOU'RE MASTURBATING.

( )

KAT WELCOMES OLNEY AND MIREILLE INTO HER LIVING ROOM.

"Kat, Mireille."

They shake hands. "Sit," Kat says as she opens the vertical blinds. Light floods the room. She tells Alexa to stop, and Chet Baker's trumpet goes quiet. Olney and Mireille sit on the leather couch and Kat on the matching chair across the coffee table from them.

"You just missed Elbert," Kat says. "Just as well, I suppose. These days if he's not bitchin' about Cully, he's delivering lectures about Flex Seal. He swears by it." She looks at Mireille and says, "Olney always did have good taste in women."

Olney asks Kat if she knows where Cully's at.

"No," she says. "He comes and goes."

"I thought you moved here to get away from him."

"And you."

"Ouch."

"He followed me. And he doesn't live with us. He eats with us."

"We tried the addresses I had for him."

"Have you tried the Motel Amour?"

"Is that a joke?"

"We have a very literal-minded netherworld here in Melancholy.
A no-irony zip code. Rooms are rented by the hour. Corner of Main
and Dahlia."

Mireille has been studying a framed oil painting on the wall over
Kat's head, a portrait of an otherwise undistinguished woman with
three eyes, wearing a milkmaid's bonnet. "Is that a Julie Speed?"

"Love her. Got this one for a song at an estate sale in Naples. The
guy was okay with the praying mantis on the gal's forehead but couldn't
handle the redundant eye."

Mireille walks to the bookcase and picks up a framed photo of baby
Cully. Cully's shirtless, wearing large sunglasses, and is stuffing a fist-
ful of cake into his mouth.

"His second birthday," Kat says. "I miss that little boy."

Kat tells Olney that Cully doesn't want to see him. He says he
knows that. She says he had been working at a pawnshop.

"Where?"

"Just up Main. Left at the corner, right, left, and up five blocks. On
your left."

Mireille asks Kat if she works in the art world.

"Blackjack dealer at the Silver Palace." Kat slaps her hands on her
knees. "I've been so rude. Wine and cheese?"

Olney says, "We've got to get going. Need to be back tonight."

"You haven't told me how you're doing, Olney. You okay? I mean
besides Cully."

"We're doing okay," he says. He takes Kat's hand. "May I?" He gives her a peck on the cheek.

She says, "Cully's a poor little lamb who lost his way."

( )

OLNEY PARKS ON MANGO COURT OFF MAIN NEXT TO THE DIXIEWOOD, a motel without a parking lot. He sees a man standing on one foot, waving his arms over his head, and wiggling his fingers. The man's wearing a large wooden cross around his neck, and he's chanting something about ten shimmering circles of light. And beyond the chanting man, a young woman in a blue swimsuit is walking across the motel lawn on her hands. And she seems to be in a hurry. When he and Mireille stop to check his iPhone's GPS for the directions to Sophie's Golden Touch, which Mireille says sounds more like a massage parlor than a pawnshop, a passerby asks if he can help them out. Olney tells him what they're looking for and says that's where his son works.

"Cully?"

"You know Cully?"

"I'm his sponsor at AA. I'm Lip, by the way. Lip O'Brien."

"Olney, and this is Mireille. Have you seen him around?"

"Not in a few days."

"Is he okay?"

"Not okay, but not KO'd, either. He's a lovable guy, but he doesn't believe it."

And Olney thinks, What did I do to that boy? Did I make him feel unlovable somehow?

"Sophie's is at the corner next to the UPS Store. Best of luck. If you find him, remind him there's a meeting at the church at six."

( )

SOPHIE SANDERS GREEN SHAKES OLNEY'S HAND AND NODS TO MIREILLE. She tells them that she had to let Cully go. Her hair is limp, slate-black, and falls to her shoulders like a chapel veil. Her left eye is higher than her right eye, and the right eye moves more slowly than the left. She's wearing a string of pearls and a crystal seahorse brooch on the lapel of her blue blazer.

Mireille says, "Do you have any idea where he might be?"

She doesn't, but she does hope they find him.

Cully is not in the Wayfarers' Inn, not in the Lamplighter Lounge, and not in Walsh's Pub. "We scratched that boy a long time ago," the bartender tells them. "Try the Drydock up the block. They'll let anyone in." But he isn't there, either.

Olney and Mireille sit on a bus bench and watch the pedestrian traffic for a while. They walk five blocks north, return, and then five blocks south, then decide it's probably time to go. When they turn off Main, they see an old Dodge being towed away. No tags, broken windshield. Late eighties Aries, Olney figures. Mireille says, "I know we're close. I can feel it. He's around here somewhere." But they turn in circles, and he's not.

Cully's across the street in the Peruvian diner next to the Dollar Tree, eating a meal of veal hearts and fried corn, bought with the last ten dollars of his final paycheck. Another benefit of Percocet is you can swallow a spoonful of the Peruvian salsa verde without screaming. At first he doesn't recognize his father out the window and out of context and with a strange woman, but then he does recognize the maroon Scion xB with the faded and peeling paint. He doesn't think; he just stares at his old man. Surprising him like this! He feels his hollow bones humming and feels like his whole body is idling at a red light. Maybe one pill would have been enough. He can't focus his eyes. His fingers tingle. He can't stop smiling. He kind of misses the old dude. They'll have one of their upbeat chats like they used to. Not about what I've done but about what I'll do to become the man he'll be proud of. The light turns green, and he runs out the diner only to see the Scion turn on Main and drive away. His body goes suddenly slack. He's slouchy, limp, and unable to move. A rattlebag. The old man probably came to confirm his conviction that I'm a disaster.

( )

MIREILLE CLOSES HER NOVEL AND RUBS HER EYES. "WHERE ARE WE?"

"Approaching Daytona. So how are Valentine and Martine?"

"She's called off the affair. Did I tell you that?"

"You did. Music's more important than romance."

"Valentine is inconsolable. He's thinking of quitting the orchestra. He's dating a brass player." Mireille closes her eyes and leans her head against the window, and she feels the vibration of the car in her skull, in her teeth, and in her hollow, growling stomach. She says, "Do you ever think about death, Olney?"

"That was my job as an obit writer. Thought about it day and night. Still do, I guess."

"When you know death is imminent and inescapable, it loses its power to frighten you. When you abandon hope, you are free." She takes a dysphagia cup from the cooler and sips a bit of thickened water.

Olney says, "I still think we should get married."

"We're already together."

"Here's the plan. You move into my house. I hire nurses twenty-four seven, get you a proper hospital bed, and all that. I've talked with the social worker at Merriment about it."

"And what did Sandy say?"

"Said it was doable."

"And?"

"She would advise against it."

"Case closed."

"I don't want you to be alone."

"I won't be."

This billboard advertises vasectomies. No needle. No scalpel.

Mireille says, "Instead of marriage, buy me a pair of tap pants?"

"Pair of what?"

"Tap pants. I've wanted a pair ever since I saw Ginger Rogers wear them in *Professional Sweetheart*."

"Do you tap-dance?"

"Not without tap pants. Gold if they have them. Silk. Down to here."

"What are they exactly?"

"They're like silky boxers. Ruffles would be good. Maybe a lacy camisole to match."

"Tap shoes?"

"I won't be wearing shoes."

Olney smiles.

"Or standing up."

It's dusk, and they can see the earth's shadow rising on the horizon. Mireille begins to hum. She snaps her fingers and sings.

> Ezekiel saw a wheel. Way up in the middle of the air
> Ezekiel saw a wheel. Way up in the middle of the air.
> Big wheel run by faith.
> Little wheel run by the grace of God.

She says, "You're the *big* wheel, Olney. You know that, right?"

A STORM FRONT COMING

Two days later, on Sunday, at Mireille's insistence, and despite the Merriment Manor nursing staff's concerns and Olney's anxiety, Mireille and Olney are back on the road to Melancholy to find Cully. This time they'll stay until they track him down, or until Mireille grows weak, tired, or ill, or until Thursday, when Olney has to be back in Anastasia to relieve Craig Dillon, who will be covering Olney's shifts at the course, because on Friday night at the Los Lonely Boys concert in Orlando he's going to give his sweetheart, Ashley Greenwood, an engagement ring, making their mutual commitment to love and to each other public and official.

While Olney drives, Mireille sings along with Billy Joel about a force-nine gale blowing on the Beaufort scale. She's reading a beginner's guide to private investigating and highlighting salient passages. They pass a billboard that reads BIG BANG THEORY, YOU'VE GOT TO BE KIDDING—GOD. Olney points out that it's like God's talking to the theory, and Mireille says that grammar might not be a big deal at Bible school. Beyond the billboard, off to the west, smoke rises from the piney woods. Forest fire, Mireille thinks. She says, "Where are we?"

"Frostproof."

"Well, Frostproof's not fireproof." She points to the smoke.

Kat has gotten them a not-quite-comped, but reasonably discounted suite at the Silver Palace Casino in her name. If they do locate Cully, he'll have a room of his own.

"It'll be fun playing private eye." Mireille closes the book and sings "Private Eyes." When she's done and Olney stops applauding, she says, "We can be Private Investigators Hall & Oates. We'll need business cards and headshots for our web page. I'm Hall," she says.

( )

ANOTHER STEAMY DAY IN MELANCHOLY. OLNEY PARKS ON A FAMILIAR side street beside the Dixiewood Motel. Two boat-tailed grackles tumble out of a gumbo limbo tree and face off on the sidewalk, hopping, croaking, and squeaking. Olney calls Kat to tell her they have arrived, and Mireille watches a man holding a three-foot-long iguana by the tail cross the motel lawn and walk into his room. She doesn't want to think about any possible in-room scenarios, so she opens the PI guide and reads. Olney tells Kat they've got an hour before they can check in at the Silver Palace. She says she's working her shift at the table tonight, so she'll come out early, and they can have a drink before she deals. She'll ask Kimmie to join them.

Mireille reads to Olney. " 'There may come a time when you will have trouble locating someone. And that will be the time to set a trap, a time to outfox the fox, as it were, to lure the viper from its hiding place.' We'll need some items for our stakeout. Water, snacks, flashlight, cell phone, pee bottle." And then she tells Olney they need to purchase that pee bottle pronto. Olney says it'll be easier to locate a nearby restroom. "Unless, of course, you really have your heart set on the bottle."

They walk to Main and see a café down the block. Olney orders a coffee while Mireille uses the women's room. At the condiment bar, he lightens his coffee with half-and-half and watches a man in a guayabera empty four packets of sugar into his coffee. The man looks at Olney, smiles, and says, "Don't judge me." He tastes his coffee, smacks his lips, and says, "Más azúcar," and empties another packet of sugar into his paper cup.

Olney hears, "You're back," and turns to see Lip O'Brien with a colada in his hand. Olney says, "Nice to see you again."

"Cully told me he saw you the other day driving away from town. Said he was disappointed, wanted to talk to you."

"He did?"

"I think he wants to make amends. Step nine."

"We'll find him this time, have that talk."

"He got tossed out of the closet he was living in. Didn't say why."

"Where should we look?"

"In this heat, I'd say the beach would be a good place to start. Give me your number and I'll text you if I see him."

( )

OUTSIDE THE SILVER PALACE, OLNEY SAYS, "SMELL THAT?"

Mireille says, "Smell what?"

Olney sniffs the air. "Someone nearby has a smoker going, and the smell of pork is drifting our way."

They follow the scent to the outdoor food court and find the source—Ribs-Я-Us. Mireille says, "You should get some."

"I'm kind of excited to get up to our room."

"Me, too." She wraps her arms around Olney.

He says, "Shall we dance?"

( )

MIREILLE PUTS ON HER V-NECK BURGUNDY TUNIC DRESS THAT SHE calls her summer shift. She and Olney are meeting the two Ks at the outdoor Banyan Tree Lounge. They take the elevator to the lobby and walk through the casino amid the ringing and beeping, the laughter, the clanging of coins on metal, and the wailing of sirens. Mireille says she'd like to play the slots later, and when Olney raises his incredulous eyebrow, she says, "Life's a gamble."

Kat and Kimmie are wearing identical starched white shirts, red brocade vests, black slacks, and black athletic shoes—they'll be on their feet for the next several hours. Olney kisses them both and introduces Kimmie to Mireille. The cousins are sharing a carafe of cabernet and have ordered a martini for Olney that's on the table waiting for him.

"So," Kimmie says, "you're here to find the un-get-at-able Cully." She lifts her wine glass. "Here's to a successful search."

"You haven't seen him, have you?" Olney says.

Kimmie shakes her head. "The last time I saw him was, I don't know, two, three months ago over at Palmetto Park. He was on the playground swings pumping his crazy ass higher and higher trying to wrap the swing and himself around the top bar. I made him stop. He leaped off the swing in midair, landed on his butt, rolled over, and stood. He couldn't walk straight. Said he was dizzy from the swing. He couldn't focus his eyes. Made me sad. I gave him twenty bucks and my phone number. He hasn't called."

Mireille says, "Olney tells me you're Cully's godmother."

"I am. And my ex is his godfather. Turns out the ex was not the man he said he was. He wasn't actually a lawyer, but he played one in real life."

"He was clever like that," Kat says.

"And his name was not Chase Oliver; it was Johnny DiBenedetto.

And he wasn't from Manhattan, and he didn't go to Harvard. But he did have another wife out West."

"California?"

"Tampa. And any number of kids, which is why, I figure, he never wanted kids with me."

"Is he with that other wife now?"

"Johnny ran a Ponzi scheme and screwed people out of several billion dollars. And he finally got caught."

"He was kind of a genius," Olney says. "He kept hundreds of clients' portfolios in his head." Olney taps his forehead.

Kimmie says, "But he Ponzi'd the wrong people, some very bad, vindictive sociopaths, so he chose to spend the next fifty years in protective custody in a federal prison under an alias."

A light breeze whispers through the ficus leaves above and lifts Kimmie's feathery blond bangs. Mireille closes her eyes and tries to remember the song about restless wind. Olney and the Ks reminisce about the time they took the four-year-old Cully to Disney, and he melted down. Hated the place, said he would never ever go back. He held his hands over his ears and wailed the whole time.

"Well, it is a frightening place," Olney says. "And so depressing."

Kat slaps his hand. "Don't be ridiculous." And then she tells him that she and El will join the search in late morning tomorrow, do a drive-about past all of Cully's usual haunts.

"And we'll cover the beach and stay in touch with Lip, who'll be downtown."

Kimmie checks her watch, and she and Kat take out their compact mirrors and check their teeth for wine stains. Mireille says she wants to gamble for a bit and would blackjack be a good choice.

Kat says, "The house always wins."

"I can count to twenty-one, and I don't mind losing."

"You wouldn't be able to play at our tables—friends and all."

"The Wayward Wind," Mireille thinks.

( )

AT THE BEACH, MIREILLE SAYS, "I CAN WALK THIS MORNING, BUT NOT far and not fast." It's ten and already the heat is sizzling. So after she and Olney walk a dozen blocks or so along the Broadwalk, past restaurants, bars, and souvenir shops, they find a shaded bench by a bicycle rental business, and Mireille sits. She'll keep a lookout for Cully and maybe read what she can of her novel while Olney walks the half mile to Surf Road and the mile beyond that to the pier. Olney kisses Mireille on the cheek, and off he goes.

Surf Road is a narrow pedestrian walkway with a bicycle lane, separated from the beach by twenty yards of sea grapes draped with Virginia creeper, a haven for feral cats. At every block or so, there's a sandy path to the water. Olney sees the occasional roller skater or cyclist, a kid on a motorized scooter, a slender woman bouncing along on her jump shoes, and a guy walking along and shaving with an electric razor, but no Cully. He stops at the Little Free Library near the Marine Education Center and finds a row of religious books in Haitian Creole and a pile of illustrated children's books in Spanish. He sees a book by an author he doesn't know that might be interesting. He opens it and reads the first line: "A man with a five-inch lockback knife buried to its heel in his chest stumbles into Café Olé on Dixie, settles into a chair, and leans his shoulder against the wall." He decides, yes, he would read the next sentence.

He walks back along the beach, making his way through the sunbathers. He hears a woman tell her friend that they're leaving Daddy's armoire behind. The friend tells her that she really needs the keys to the Saab. Farther along, he hears a woman tell the man in the adjacent chaise longue, "Start drinking the whole bottle without breathing."

A short man with oval sunglasses, smoking a cigarette, wearing a green plaid golfer's hat, a teal Speedo, black socks, and sandals steps in front of Olney and blurts out, "My husband has a new boyfriend." Before Olney can say he's sorry to hear that, the man says, "He's an oncologist from Belgium named Florenz, the boyfriend is. And he's flying in tonight from London." Before Olney can say he's sorry, the man, who's now crying, says, "It's a blessing. My husband has stage-four pancreatic cancer, and I'm tired of taking care of him twenty-four seven." And before Olney can say what he can't think of to say, the man walks away.

Olney takes a call from Kat, who tells him she and El are driving to and through every park in and around Melancholy. Nothing yet. "See you guys for dinner."

( )

AT A PICNIC TABLE OUTSIDE RIBS-Я-US, MIREILLE SIPS HER THICKENED apple juice and watches Olney eat his plate of pulled pork. "Happy?" she says. He is. She tells him that during her nap, she dreamed that they found Cully.

A breeze lifts the leaves of the buttonwood, and Mireille notices the lighter shade of green beneath. "Tomorrow," she says, "we'll bring Cully's photo and hit all the stores in town." She's having trouble swallowing her saliva. She sips the juice and is able to clear the passage. "Yes, I'm okay."

"How did you do at slots?"

"I won sixty-four dollars."

"Great."

"Then I lost eighty-five."

"Learned your lesson?"

"Do you think Cully doesn't want to be found?"

"He doesn't think he's lost. He came here to Melancholy to be near his mom. Kat loves that boy to death. He was always her life. Everything she did, she did for him, and she couldn't do enough. When he showed up here with no place to go, she took him in until she couldn't take him anymore."

The myna bird on the red plastic lid of the concrete trash can clenches a french fry in its beak but still manages to chatter and croak before flying off unto the coinvines.

Mireille says, "Do you want him back more or want him better?"

"Better. And that might not include being home with me."

Olney wonders, once again, how Mireille can go on like nothing terrifying is happening, like every day is okay. Maybe being afraid of death is like being afraid of the moon like she says. What would be the point? Or maybe she's terrified. The thought of death is so distressing to most of us that we concoct fantasies about a future that cannot be.

When Cully was two, Olney found him trembling and sobbing in a corner of his room, and said, What are you afraid of, hon? The dark. When Cully was three, he was afraid of loud noises—fireworks, thunder, the crash of falling objects, screeching brakes. At four, he was afraid of being alone, especially being alone in bed in the dark during a thunderstorm. He was then variously afraid of water, spiders, blood, and heights. And now Olney knows what he'll ask Cully when next they meet.

( )

KAT LEADS MIREILLE AND OLNEY THROUGH THE HOUSE AND OUT THE glass doors to the backyard patio, where El is at his Hasty Bake grilling corn, asparagus, tortillas, and shrimp for the tacos. "Fifteen minutes," El says.

"We finally meet," Olney says.

El puts down his tongs, wipes his hand on his apron, and shakes Olney's hand. He points the tongs at the wet bar and says, "You could make yourself handy by mixing the drinks."

"My pleasure."

"Kat and I will have Manhattans."

"Three Manhattans it is."

When they're all seated at the dining table in their cushioned bistro chairs, they raise their cocktail glasses, Mireille her cup of thickened juice, and they toast to a happy ending in the search for Cully. Kat wonders out loud what Cully might be eating, wherever he might be. And then she and Olney talk about Cully's peculiar eating habits when he was a child. Kat says he ate so many jars of Gerber strained carrots that his face turned orange. And then for a while he would only eat red food: tomatoes, cherries, watermelon, apples.

Mireille asks El to tell her about himself. Kat smiles, lifts her eyebrows, and sits back. El grew up in Atlanta, married a Georgia peach named Mary Jo, moved with her to South Florida to work construction after a hurricane, and never left. He had a daughter they named Jolene. Jolene went to live with her mother in Islamorada after the divorce. And then she died. Kat holds up her hand and suggests that before we get the rest of the story, she'll refresh the drinks. And while she does, and after Mireille and Olney express their condolences, Mireille looks up at the small trees swaying in the fresh breeze. Olney's thinking about the many ways to lose a child, and of all the things there are to lose—your money, your dignity, your mind, your home, your way, your health, your freedom—a child is the worst.

El sips his drink. "You won't believe this, but it happened." He reaches for Kat's hand and holds it. He tells them that Jolene had been drinking with a friend at a bar in Marathon when she decided to visit her boyfriend, Dusty. Dusty lived on Stock Island. Jolene's friend asked her if she was okay to drive. And then she said that maybe Jolene should call Dusty to see if he was even home. Nope. She wanted to surprise him, she said. She jumped into her Corolla and took off down U.S. 1. El takes another sip, sets his glass down, and says, "What she didn't know was that Dusty was on his way to surprise her at her place in Layton. They met head-on in Cudjoe Key at Mile Marker 22 when Jolene's car crossed the highway into Dusty's lane and into Dusty's motorcycle. Both died at the scene. What are the goddamn odds of that?"

"Jesus Christ! What a horrible coincidence!" Olney says.

"Providence," El says. "That's what Mary Jo calls it. There's no room for coincidence if God's running the show."

"So the crash was the Lord's way of keeping the young lovers together for eternity," Kat says.

Mireille asks El what he does for a living. He installs high-impact windows for work and mines Bitcoins for a living.

"What's a Bitcoin?" she says.

"Cryptocurrency."

"Can I see one?"

"It's more like the idea of currency than currency."

Olney says, "It's computer code, right?"

"So how do you mine it?" Mireille says.

"By solving math problems," El says. "Well, not you solving them, but your computers doing it for you."

El tops off Olney's and his drinks and explains that he and his buddy Tripp Dixon own a cluster of one-bedroom cinder-block houses up in Mullet Junction where they do the mining. "Takes an awful lot of power to run those machines twenty-four seven, three-six-five."

Olney looks up at the half-moon rising over the trees and at the faint stars beginning to appear in the darkening sky. Most days he doesn't know what phase the moon is in. Why doesn't he? he wonders.

In the driveway Kat says she'd like to join Olney and Mireille in the morning for the search. El has to finish a window job out in Westonzuela. She's got an afternoon shift at the casino. They agree to meet right here at eight-thirty.

El says, "You sure you're okay to drive?"

( )

ON THE DRIVE BACK TO THE SILVER PALACE, MIREILLE WATCHES THE fronds on the palms along the median turn away from the wind. She checks the weather app on Olney's phone and tells him there's a rip current alert out for tomorrow. "Says we can expect intermittent storms throughout the day."

"So we may not be able to walk store to store with Cully's photo."

"But we can still drive around."

"It's not likely he'll be out and about in the rain. We'll check the library. And the churches."

"Churches are all locked up."

"When did they start that? How do you make a visit? Do the stations of the cross?" Olney waits for the light and pulls into the casino parking lot.

Mireille says, "I hate to think of Cully out there alone."

Olney enters the hotel garage and heads up the ramp. "Addiction is a solitary existence. And I don't think he can recover in reclusion. If that's even a word." They drive to the roof to find an empty parking space.

"Here comes the rain," Mireille says.

( )

THEY EACH HAVE AN UMBRELLA. KAT'S IN THE BACKSEAT, OLNEY AND Mireille up front. They check the library. They check Dunkin' and Lee's Diner. They check the St. Vincent de Paul thrift store and the Goodwill thrift store. They check both Publix supermarkets, the Winn-Dixie, and the Ideal Food Basket. They check the Family Dollar, Dollar General, and the Dollar Tree. They check Las Americas Bakery and the European Deli. They check the lobbies of the Super 8, the Motel 6, and the Sleep Inn. And now they are driving by the picnic shelters at Mizell Park. The rain is no longer driving but is softly falling.

Mireille says she can't get Jolene's horrific accident out of her head. Kept her up much of the night. She asks if anything so unlikely ever happened to him. Olney says nothing remarkable, although he once took a flight to Columbus and sat next to a guy who had been a friend in middle school. Didn't recognize him at first. Cosmo Dadis. It was surprising but not so unusual.

Kat had one perplexing encounter like that. She ran into an old friend from her high school debate team on a street corner in Jacksonville. They exchanged pleasantries, and when he opened his wallet to give her a business card, she saw her own laminated class photo inside.

"Yikes," Mireille says. "What did you do?"

"I bolted."

Mireille tells them that she once took a pottery class at the Requiem Craft Center, and a week after the class ended, she was in Paris with Jack at Sacré-Coeur. They were looking out over the city when she heard a familiar voice and looked at a group of women about twenty yards away. They were laughing and talking, and she recognized her pottery teacher, Cyndi. "How improbable is that? Anyway, I decided not to approach Cyndi or say anything, so it was a jarring coincidence for me, just another sunny day in Paris for her."

( )

"WE NEED A PLAN, OLNEY," MIREILLE SAYS. THERE'S A FLASH OF LIGHT-ning in the distance, a gust of wind snapping the branches of the crape myrtle, but for now the rain is holding off. They're parked on Main near the Dixiewood. Olney's watching a bearded fellow in a wheelchair at the bus stop. Plastic bags are tied to the arms and back of the chair. The bag in his lap reads Wok This Way. His head is down, his hands are folded in his lap.

Mireille says, "Let's make a list of what Cully needs." Food. Money. Shelter. A shower. A toilet.

"Let's start with money," she says. "Maybe he's panhandling."

They decide to check the exit ramps on I-95.

Mireille consults the map app and says, "There's two exits, eight ramps. Let's go."

As they drive west on Calathea, Olney calls Lip and asks about possible shelters for homeless guys in the area. There's a mission on Freedom just east of 441, he says. But when he was a derelict, Lip says, he found any convenient public restroom, locked himself inside, and slept.

They don't see Cully at an exit. They do see a petite blonde holding a cardboard sign reading Hungry Homeless and wearing a T-shirt that reads Girls Bite Back. Olney rolls down the window, hands her a dollar, and asks if she might know Cully. She looks at Olney like he's going to explode and steps back.

She says, "I don't know no Curry."

"Cully."

"Not him neither."

They don't try the public restrooms, figuring if the door is locked, anyone could be in there. People need their privacy.

Mireille says, "What does Cully like to eat?"

"Everything fried and pizza, the last I knew."

"Let's stake out a restaurant."

"But he has no money that we know of."

"A restaurant dumpster, then." And she tells him when she was a girl, she got lettuce for her guinea pigs every night from the dumpster behind the Stop & Shop.

Olney drives up Main. Popeyes? Not there. Yes, he had a pet, a dog who followed him home one day and moved right in, a dog he named Shep, part German shepherd, docile and sweet, liked to rest his head in Olney's lap. Chick-fil-A? Nope. "And then one day Shep saw the paperboy walk by the house with a dog, and he followed them. He turned back when I called him, looked at me, blinked, and kept going. I cried for days. My dad said Shep was a hobo, and he would be okay. And maybe he'll come home. I can't forget that final look of his or how easily I was displaced." Olney pulls into the lot at Melancholy Subs and parks. "What the hell is that? There on the dumpster."

"Looks like a monkey eating a tomato."

"That's crazy!"

"That's him."

"Who?"

"Cully."

"Where?"

"Standing in front of Wok This Way."

And that's when lightning flashes, thunder claps, and the sky opens up. Cully leans into the wind and runs down the side street. "Let's go before we lose him," Mireille says.

()

OLNEY PULLS THE CAR TO THE SIDE OF PINEAPPLE TERRACE, OPENS the door, and yells for Cully to jump in, and he does, looking like a drowned ferret. He pulls back his hood and shakes his hair.

Olney tells Cully to take off his hoodie and put on the raincoat there on the seat. "And there's a towel in the wayback to dry yourself off. And say hello to Mireille."

Mireille says, "It's so nice to finally meet you." They bump fists.

A force-nine gale drives the rain in furious sheets down on them. It's too loud to hear a person speak. So Olney shouts. "It's so great to see you again." When Cully doesn't respond, Olney shouts, "How are you doing?"

"Doing okay." And he nods his head, well, his whole upper body, for emphasis. "Hanging in there."

They watch a blue tarp on a previously damaged home lift from the roof and blow across the road. And then the rain lets up.

Olney says, "Where are you staying?"

"With friends."

"We'll drive you to your friends' so you can get some dry clothes, and you can come stay with us. We've got a room for you at the Silver Palace."

"Wow. Thanks, but we'll need to do it later. You caught me on the way to a meeting. I promised Lip."

"Where?"

"Take the first left."

Olney drives a block, turns left on Poinciana and a right on Main. He tells Cully, "You'll have a warm and comfortable bed, a big meal tonight and breakfast in the morning, and then we'll talk."

"That sounds amazing. Sure I won't be imposing?"

"Of course not."

"Two blocks on your right. St. Luke's. Okay, here we are." Cully thanks them for the ride and hops out.

Olney says they'll wait right here in the parking lot.

"Should be about an hour."

They watch Cully open the side door to what must be the church hall, wave to them, and enter.

"He's skin and bones," Olney says. "And he could use a haircut."

"He's a handsome boy."

A half hour later, a man steps out of the side door, opens his umbrella, lights a cigarette, smokes it, flips the butt into a puddle, and goes back inside.

"I'm worried," Olney says.

First one guy, then three and four guys, then a dozen or more guys exit St. Luke's. They're all lighting up, shielding their smokes with cupped hands. And here comes Lip, who stops and locks the door behind him. Olney flashes his headlights and steps out of the car. Lip says Cully was a no-show.

"We saw him walk in."

"And out the other side door, no doubt. I'm sorry."

"We'll drive you home."

"I'm meeting a guy I sponsor around the corner for a coffee."

Back in the car, Olney says, "Fooled again."

Mireille says, "Well, at least we know he's okay. Kind of."

( )

LIP CALLS OLNEY'S CELL AT EIGHT. "IF YOU WANT TO CATCH CULLY, HE'S having his morning coffee on the patio at Mug Shots right now. He hasn't seen me yet. I'll keep my eye on him till you get here." And he gives Olney the address, says he's happy to help.

Mireille wakes when she hears Olney getting dressed. He tells her what's going on, and she says to call her with any news. She gives him a goodbye kiss and a good-luck wish. In twenty minutes, Olney's outside Mug Shots. He sees Cully slumped in a chair, his back to the street. He sees Lip across the street and gives him a thumbs-up and holds up crossed fingers. Lip waves, turns, and walks back toward Main.

Olney tells himself to smile, one of those smiles that involves the eyes and the cheeks, but wonders if such extravagance would seem fake. Maybe a reassuring, dimple-triggering smile would be better, one that's gentle and symmetrical. By the time he reaches Cully, he drops the idea of a smile. He says, "What happened last night?"

"Something came up."

Olney takes a cell phone out of his pocket and slides it to Cully.

"What's this?"

"It's yours. I got you a burner and a sixty-minute plan. I worry when I can't reach you."

"Thanks."

"Maybe it'll make your life a little easier."

"It will. I appreciate it. Really."

"You look exhausted."

"Kinda."

"The offer's still good. Come back with me now and you can crash in your own room. We'll stop at Target and get you some dry clothes."

"I love you, Dad. I want your respect, and I feel bad that I let you down so often. You're the most important person in my life. I stay away because it hurts to see the disappointment in your eyes."

"I love you, Cully. We're going to get through this."

"Where's your girlfriend?"

"Back at the suite."

"Is she going to be my stepmom?"

( )

CULLY SLEEPS THE SLEEP OF THE JUST WHILE OLNEY AND MIREILLE whisper about the best way to approach Cully when he wakes. Olney peeks in on Cully, walks to the bedside, and checks his breathing.

Back on the sofa, Olney puts his hand on Mireille's knee and kisses her cheek. She asks him what he plans to say to Cully.

"That I'll help him to change his life."

"Let him tell his story."

"He'll talk about how depressed he is. He says that's why he uses, but sometimes I think depression's his excuse, not the cause. Or it's the result. A good day for Cully is a yellow pill and oblivion. No wonder he's depressed. Who would choose that life?"

"Don't give in to your cynicism." Mireille says she'll leave them alone to talk. She could use a nap herself. She takes her head off Olney's shoulder and sits up on the sofa. She rocks her body and pushes on the cushion to stand. She gets herself a cup of thickened juice from the fridge. She kisses Olney and reminds him to be calm with Cully. "The more emotional you are, the easier you are to manipulate."

Cully stumbles out of his bedroom, says hi, and wipes the sleep from his eyes. He asks if there's any Red Bull in the minibar. He checks. There isn't.

Mireille says she's off for her nap and picks up her novel from the side table. She looks at Cully and says, "I may not see you again, and I may not see you get well, but you will get well."

When she closes the bedroom door, Cully says, "She's sentimental."

Olney taps the sofa cushion beside him and asks Cully to sit.

Cully says, "Are you going to ask me what I want from my life?"

"Well, now I don't have to."

"I want running water, clean sheets, AC, someone to talk sensibly with, a future that's not more of the same. It might not be much, but it won't be easy."

"Come home, Cully. A room of your own. Three squares. Proper health care. Dr. Abdelnour's always asking about you. You can enroll at AC and finish your degree."

"Thanks. That's kind of you, but I'm not ready to go back to school. I can learn as much on my own."

"But you don't get the degree."

"Yeah, that makes it harder. I know."

"So what are you reading?"

"I'm not reading. I'm watching films. I'm writing a book on doppelgängers in movies."

"That's great."

Jekyll and Hyde, Vertigo, Strangers on a Train. Like that. All the way back to German expressionism."

"Where do you see these movies?"

"Library."

"If you lived with me, you could watch them at home."

"We all have a double, someone out there somewhere exactly like us. We're never alone."

"I wish that were true. Have you met your double?"

"If you meet your double, you die. That's the folklore."

"Lucky was your double."

"Who?"

"Your friend in the mirror."

"I forgot about him."

"You don't have to stay with me. We'll find you an apartment."

"That might be better. We'll be out of each other's hair."

"After you get some treatment."

"No treatment. I can stop if I want."

"So why don't you?"

"I will when I'm ready."

"You may be dead by then."

"Dad, stop!"

"So what are your plans?"

"Plans don't work for me."

"So your plan is doing nothing?" The minute he says it, he regrets it.

"I'm an optimist. I know that the right situation will come my way."

"Nothing changes until you do *some*thing." He can't stop himself now.

Cully says, "There are things you don't know about me."

"Like what?"

"Like sometimes I don't know who I am. I have to concentrate to remember. Or where I am. I lie down in one place and wake up in another. When I'm alone I can imagine having a friend. When I'm with people, I'm disconnected. I think everyone's all the time lying to me."

Cully picks the petals off the gerbera daisies in the glass vase on the table and drops them to the floor. Olney asks him why he's doing that. "People try to help you, and you push them away."

"Just you and Mom."

"Your mother loves you. What you're doing is killing her."

"You went from advocate to judge pretty quickly."

"What happened to us?

Cully plucks a daisy petal. "She loves me not."

"What did I do to drive you away?"

"You gave up on me as soon as I had a mind of my own. You didn't want a son who talked back or disagreed."

Olney folds his arms across his chest and leans back. "Sorry. I love you, Cully. I won't tell you what to do anymore."

"Look, I'm a big boy. I can take care of myself. I'm twenty-six."

"You're twenty-seven."

Cully stands. "I'm done here." He zips his pants, buttons his shirt, and ties his shoes.

"Where are you going?"

"The casino. I'll be back. I've got a key."

When Cully steps out the door, Mireille steps into the room and sits beside Olney. "Didn't go so well. I heard. Sorry."

"I was just trying to talk some sense."

"A lot of resentment between you," Mireille says. "Resentment is like sticking your hand in a flame and waiting for the other person to burn."

( )

IT'S EIGHT A.M. AND OLNEY AND MIREILLE ARE PACKING FOR THE drive home. Olney says, "He's probably still downstairs at the casino. Kat called after you were asleep to tell me she'd just bought him dinner, and she was heading home. I called. He's not answering his phone."

Olney can't find his keys. He looks under the bed, checks all his pockets, under the sofa cushions. He says he thinks he's got early-onset Alzheimer's. Mireille says not knowing *where* your keys are is normal, not knowing *what* your keys are is Alzheimer's. He finds the keys in a soap dish between the two master bathroom sinks. Now he can't find his reading glasses because he's wearing them on his head.

Mireille says, "You don't think anything happened to him, do you?"

"I hope he hasn't run off." Olney pours himself one last cup of coffee and sits at the table. "We'll know he's high if he comes in and is pleasant and reasonable and wants to talk about his bright future and how I'll be so proud of him. He puts on the show because he's high and feels alive, and he wants to tell me what I want to hear, wants to lift my flagging spirits, and I believe this eventful future *is* what he wants. This is a guy who needs a victory, so he can start to believe in himself. But then he's not high anymore and his clarity is replaced with obscurity. He relies on my wanting to believe his lies are true."

And then Cully walks through the door. Olney says, "Are you okay?"

"I'm okay."

"Will you come home?"

"No."

"We'll start over."

Mireille squeezes Olney's elbow. They tell Cully they're leaving. Checkout's at eleven. Olney asks for a hug. He steps up to Cully, who responds to the embrace by pulling his head away from Olney's.

"You have my number," Olney says, "if you change your mind or just want to talk."

Cully says, "I'm leaving, too."

At the elevator, Cully says he's going to take the stairs. When the elevator doors close, he walks back to the room and lets himself in. He dumps the daisies and the few inches of water out of the vase and onto the floor. He throws the glass vase against the round accent mirror above the sofa. The mirror shatters. He lays his phone on the table and strikes it with the vase until they're both in pieces and his right arm is bleeding. He's watching himself do this, and he's both alarmed and puzzled. He's never done anything like this before. (He *has*, actually, but he doesn't remember the night at the Bel Air Motel in Sugar Creek when the two girls he was with, the girls from the migrant labor camp, the girls who were going to show him a good time, took off with the fentanyl and the Molly and drove away while he was in the bathroom.) He doesn't like what he's doing, but he can't stop himself. He opens the minibar and puts all the liquor into the complimentary Silver Palace tote bag. He breaks the stemware against the master bath's tiled walls. He picks up the tote bag, and leaves.

OVER TIME

Olney's mom, Glorietta (née Dolan), had what she called prescriptions for a well-ordered life written on index cards that she kept in several recipe file boxes on the kitchen counter next to the chrome toaster, guidelines, rules for dealing with many of life's untoward eventualities, and she was ever eager to share them with her only child. As a result, Olney knows how to move across a dance floor, remove a splinter, splint a broken leg, and break a nasty habit. He knows what constitutes the perfect picnic lunch: pan-fried chicken, corn salad, buttermilk biscuits, and sweet tea. He knows how to behave in church, at work, and on the road, how to clean a house, how to deep-clean a "clean" house, how to be the life of the party, how to order at a sitdown restaurant, and how to take control of a hotel room. He knows to shield his lemon and not to show up empty-handed. He can make a dry martini and a wet burrito. He knows the difference between ignorable misbehaviors and unimaginable improprieties, between acceptable pets and unspeakable monstrosities, between what matters (e.g., family) and what does not (e.g., rumors). He knows which words, people, shortcuts, and motels to avoid. He knows the eight characteristics of civilized people (#4: They fear lies like the plague), the nine easy steps to tie a full Windsor knot (#1: Stand facing the mirror), and the ten steps to better health and well-being (#7: Drink a lot of water and avoid margarine and charred meats). He knows how to make friends. But not how to keep them. Glorietta apparently believed that friends were for life and that the engine of friendship would not require periodic maintenance. No protocol, then, for enduring harmony. And no protocol for dealing with her early-onset Alzheimer's. She was absent long before she was gone, and when she went, Franklin made the call to Olney, walked to the closed garage, started up the old Chevy, gave it some gas, and went to sleep. They never got to meet their grandchild. Would their love have made some difference?

Olney's picking snails off the third fairway with chopsticks and dropping them into a Tupperware rice keeper and thinking about Cully when he was in Sunshine Academy preschool and was best friends with Anthony DeMarchi. Cully wrote, *I love Anthony*, in his Mead primary journal every day. When he and Anthony weren't in school together, they were at each other's houses playing Hot Wheels or dinosaurs. Never an argument; never a tear. When Olney learned from Anthony's father that the family was moving to Savannah, he kept the news from Cully. When Cully told Olney that Anthony would be his friend forever, Olney hugged his son and said, Yes, he will. And then, two days after preschool graduation, the DeMarchis stopped by on their way out of town to say goodbye. The last thing that Cully said to Anthony was, Let's play cars on Saturday. When Kat said that Cully would get over the loss, Olney said, He may get on, but he won't get over. This was Cully's first betrayal. Kat said, It won't be his last. On Saturday, Cully sat at the living room window and wept. And now Olney wonders if Cully keeps his distance from others because you can't be abandoned if you disconnect first.

Before coming to work, Olney drove to the hospital to see Mireille, who had experienced excessive regurgitation a day after their return from Melancholy, and found her asleep, propped up on the raised hospital bed. On the tray in front of her were untouched cups of thickened lemon water and iced tea. He opened the novel on the bedside table and read a paragraph about a lunch date at Jacob Wirth. Valentine is clearly head-over-heels in love and is lavish in his praise of the food. Martine moves the schnitzel around her plate but doesn't eat. She's guarded. She tells Valentine that she needs to get home to practice the Bartók sonata. No, it can't wait. I'll call an Uber. Olney closed the book and thought about the nexus of food and love and nourishment and the irony of Mireille's vacuitous hunger. He wrote a note with the stubby golf pencil in his pocket on the back of the menu slip. *Sweet dreams. Back after work.*

When Olney sees the flash of lightning over the Intracoastal, he waits for the crash of thunder and counts to five-Mississippi, dumps the snails over the fence and into a pile of mulch, closes the course, and takes shelter in his hut. Who are his friends who are now family? Julie, Samir, Kat, Mireille, Dewey, Althea. He thinks about his cousin Woodrow Kartheizer, his best friend throughout his childhood. Inseparable. Olney was best man at Woodrow's first wedding; Woodrow was best man at his. But it's been twenty years at least since they were together and a dozen or so years since they've spoken.

The wind is driving the rain in sheets across A1A. The course is littered with fallen palm fronds. Olney checks his TV-38 weather app, and it does not look like it'll be clearing up anytime soon. He'll give it twenty minutes, and if the rain doesn't let up, he'll lock the hut, make a dash for the car, and drive back to the hospital. He's got the radio on and hears that the Brown Bats game with the Hialeah Cubans has been postponed. Olney turns off the radio and calls Kat to ask if she's seen Cully.

"I'm looking at him," she says.

"He's at your house?"

"Chowing down. He stops by on occasion."

Cully bites into his garlic naan.

"Let me talk to him."

Kat holds the phone out for Cully, tells him his father would like to speak with him. Cully shakes his head, dips his naan into a puddle of mayonnaise. She says, "Your father wants to know if you remember Anthony from preschool."

Cully flicks the toothbrush he wears on a lanyard around his neck. "I don't remember preschool."

Elbert joins them at the table, smiles at Kat, cracks his knuckles one by one, and asks Cully if he needs a ride anywhere. He doesn't. Cully studies the painting on the wall over the gas range—horses and men in chains, a Purvis Young, acrylic on distressed wood, that has to be worth a bundle.

"Anywhere at all," Elbert says.

Kat says, "El, be good."

Now that Goldie is dead, Kat has filled the fishbowl with loose tropical-flavored Skittles. Cully reaches in, takes one, and pops it in his mouth. He says, "Why do you keep them on the table?"

Elbert reaches into the bowl and grabs a handful. "So I can do this."

"You're going to get diabetes," Cully says.

"I'm a risk-taker."

Kat studies Cully's face, trying to see that pretty little green-eyed baby she once held in her arms.

Kat believes that Cully can only be saved by the love of a smart, strong woman, because, let's face it, men without women are dopes, self-absorbed schlubs, happy to live in squalor and disorder just as long as they're not bothered. Kat says, "Your father wants to know if you're seeing anyone." She holds out the phone so Olney can listen.

Cully says, "I've got a girlfriend."

Elbert says, "What's she like?"

"She's short."

"How short?"

"Shorter than a novel."

"What's her name?"

"Novella."

"You're a funny guy."

( )

THE GIRLFRIEND'S ACTUAL NAME IS PIXIE SMITH. WELL, IT'S PAMELA Smith. Pamela Ellen Smith, and she glows in the dark. That's how Cully found her that night at the beach. She walked out of the surf, naked and dripping with bioluminescent algae. He couldn't take his eyes off her. He had several hits of MDMA in a baggie in his pocket, and she stayed for the party. She pointed at his face, said, What's the pony's name? Fury, he said. She told him all she ever wanted in her life was boobs and a fireplace. He said, You're halfway there. Her eyes were gold, her cheeks were dimpled, and she moved so fast she gave off heat. He showed her his empty hand, reached behind her ear, pulled a quarter out of nowhere. He said, I can snatch money out of thin air. She said, Snatch more.

That night, Cully said, "Where have you been all my life?"

Pixie said, "Waiting for you to notice me."

"You're funny."

"I love you."

"I'm a loser."

"That's why I do."

( )

KAT SAYS, "NO, HE WON'T TELL ME WHERE HE LIVES," AND SHE LOOKS at Cully. "Will you?"

Elbert says, "How about a lift to work?"

Kat says goodbye to Olney and ends the call. She tells Cully he looks tired.

"I can't sleep at night."

Elbert says, "If you got up before noon, you might feel tired at night."

Kat says, "Okay, boys, let's not start."

"I'm just saying," Elbert says. He looks at Cully's drifting eyes. "You need to stop that shit you're doing, take a shower, apply deodorant, pull up your pants, and join the rest of us in the real world."

Kat says, "Please," but Elbert won't stop.

"How's that arrow-spinning job treating you?"

Cully says, "It's part-time; there are no benefits; the pay sucks, and I just got fired, but it's not the worst job I've ever had."

For most of two weeks last summer Cully was a living statue. The job description seemed irresistible: "Do as little as possible." He spray-painted himself bronze and sat on a pedestal outside the Burlington Coat Factory at the Paradise Place Mall. He was Rodin's *The Thinker*, but a more discreet *Thinker* in a bronze bathing suit. Paid to sit and think. What could go wrong? Well, it was sweltering in the sun in that paint, and he couldn't keep himself from blinking and scratching, and the little kids fucked with him mercilessly, pelting him with coins they took from his tip bucket. So when he dope-slapped an eight-year-old and the little shit ran off howling to find his father in the PGA Superstore, Cully bailed.

The bus driver refused to let him board, said he was not going by the nuthouse. The Uber driver shook her head and took his photo with her smartphone. So he walked the three miles barefoot, burning the soles of his feet on the concrete, to Leo Wondolowski's condo, let himself in, showered, put on shorts and a T-shirt, crawled into Wolfie's storage closet—they call Leo Wolf because of his silver eyes—lay down on the yoga mat, and tried to sleep.

The hard part is not falling asleep but staying asleep. When his dreams ebb and he wakes, regrets surface—like that slap to the young boy's face today, like his failure to protect Jasmine. His big regret, always, is the loss of his family, a regret so intense and debilitating, it prevents him from struggling to heal that fractured family. There is no sleeping when he confronts this failure. He hears the smoke alarm in the kitchen chirp and beep, and he rolls over onto his good ear.

( )

AT THE RED LIGHT ON RIVER STREET, OLNEY'S BEHIND A CAR WITH A garland of faded blue plastic flowers in the back window and a BE AN ORGAN DONOR—GIVE YOUR HEART TO JESUS bumper sticker. The flowers are a good idea. He stops at Sherwood Florist on Minorca and buys a bouquet of roses and lilies.

At the hospital's front desk, the receptionist, Caroline, tells him that Ms. Tighe has been transferred to the ICU, and since he is not in her immediate family, he can't visit.

"What happened to her? Will she be all right?"

"I don't know."

"Is there someone I could talk to who would know?"

"HIPAA." Caroline lifts her brow, cocks her head, and smiles. "You could try Merriment Manor. They will be monitoring her status."

"I've got these flowers."

"I'll see that she gets them."

On his way to Merriment Manor, Olney calls Samir and explains Mireille's situation. Any chance he could find out more?

"I see my last patient at four, and then I'll head to the hospital. Meet you at George's Majestic at seven, seven-thirty."

"You think you can get access to her records?"

"I'm a doctor, I can do anything."

"Can you levitate?"

"Not *every* anything."

"How's your knee?"

"Giving myself a cortisone shot as we speak."

What's left of Bill Tasher is awake and sitting at the reception desk at Merriment Manor. He tells Olney they don't know anything about Mireille's status, but he knows that she has had pneumonia twice before, and that's likely the culprit now. Bill's wearing a plastic bib and is eating yogurt from a cup. There's a magnifying glass lying on an opened notebook on the desk in front of him.

"What are you writing, Bill?"

"My memoirs. Just getting started."

"What brought this on?"

"The dark at the end of the tunnel." Bill puts down his spoon and picks up the magnifying glass. "I can write without this, but I can't read without it, and it turns out writing is a lot of reading. Been writing about Mother's discipline. Woman had a short fuse and a big charge. Was just me and her. Daddy ran off with Mother's twin sister when I was three, and we never heard from them again. They were indistinguishable, Mother and Aunt Dot. Go figure. I imagine the betrayal's what got Mother all crosswise to begin with."

"So what did your mother do to you?"

"She would punish my behavishness by fetching the radio cord she kept in the shed. She'd soak it, plug and all, in the kitchen sink, then run it through the sandbox, and lay it over the block of ice in the icebox. She'd draw me a cold bath and force me to sit in it. When I stepped out, she'd whip my naked ass with that cord. My ass, my legs, my back."

"Jesus Christ!"

"I suspect we both knew who she was punishing, but that didn't ease the pain any."

"I'm so sorry, Bill. That was barbaric."

What's left of Bill shrugs. "Oh, I turned out all right."

( )

THE BAND OF THUNDERSTORMS HAS PASSED, AND THE SKY HAS cleared, but the third and seventh holes at the miniature golf course are under several inches of water. Olney puts up the umbrella-shaped CLOSED TODAY sign, texts Craig, and tells him to enjoy his day off. He drives to Wright's Books and picks up three used romance novels for Althea and an acceptable copy of Aldo Leopold's *A Sand County Almanac* for himself. It is a book he loved as a sanguine young man and is hoping to regain some of his youthful buoyancy with a reread. At the checkout counter, he talks with Manasha about an article in *In These Times* on mountaintop removal mining in West Virginia. Manasha says, "We live in a heartless country," shakes his head, and slips the books into a paper sack.

Althea tells Olney to take a load off his mind and sit. Dewey's at work. She takes a bottle of John Jameson out of the cabinet and sets it on the kitchen table. She takes two glasses from the drying rack and pours. It turns out that Althea hasn't read *Surgeon on Horseback*, *The Coolest Game*, or *Cotswold Wedding*, but she has read twenty-seven other books by *Cotswold Wedding* author Tegan Brae. Althea examines the book jackets, decides she'll read *The Coolest Game* first, and reads from the back cover. "Zandra Loveless has never been a puck bunny, but now she can't keep her eyes or her mind off the Ice Cats' rookie defenseman, Nikita Petrov, the Moscow Mule, Baryshnikov on skates, a man with flowing hair, broad shoulders, and thighs of steel, a man about to get butt-checked by fate. The coolest game is about to get red hot." They raise their glasses to love on ice.

( )

SAMIR SITS, DROPS HIS KEYS ON THE TABLE, AND SIGNALS TO EUSTIS, the bartender, that they would like two—what are we drinking?—two gin and tonics. Boodles and Schweppes.

Olney says, "What did you find out?"

"Nothing definitive and nothing promising. They're awaiting test results." He takes out his iPhone and opens his notes. "Her liver seems to be failing. They did a CT scan which showed no liver lesions."

"So that's good."

"Liver metastases doesn't always show up on a CT scan, or on an MRI, for that matter. They're doing lymph node and liver biopsies. I think they'll find distant recurrent cancer. In the liver. And she's too weak for chemo and wouldn't survive surgery if that were even possible."

"Shit."

"I'm sorry, Olney."

Eustis signals that the drinks are ready, and Samir limps to the bar. Olney becomes aware that Van Morrison is singing over the sound system about being lifted up to higher ground.

When Samir returns with the drinks, Olney says, "So is there any hope?"

"We can't live without it."

"Then I'll hope."

"But don't confuse what you want with what is possible." He squeezes lime into the drink and sips.

"And the expectations are?"

"She'll go into hospice care at Merriment Manor."

"Death Row."

"No. Comfort and compassion."

( )

OLNEY'S AT THE KITCHEN TABLE SIPPING COGNAC AND WRITING IN HIS notebook. He hears the distant rumble of thunder, sees Althea's reading lamp go dark. He's written Mireille's name at the top of the page. He briefly entertains a fantasy where he sneaks Mireille out of hospice, and they go to the beach. He doesn't write that down.

He turns the page and writes Cully's name at the top, Cully whose birthday approaches. What do you get a man who has nothing? A future? Not the future, Olney thinks, but the past. That would be a gift worth having—Cully himself when he was the happiest boy in Spanish Blade. The future's messy; the past is tidy. He wants to tell Cully it's not too late to be the person he wants to be.

Cully told him once, right here at the kitchen table, that he did not want to die, but he couldn't take the pain anymore. I'm tired. Depression doesn't ever end. I'm stuck. It's dark in here, Dad. And that was the first true thing that Cully had said to Olney in ages. Olney wanted to reach across the table and touch his son but was afraid Cully would startle and flee. How terrifying it must be to think that every day will be like this day, that nothing will ever change, and nothing, not love, not kindness, not family, has meaning, and you will always be at the mercy of your intractable thoughts and immobilizing emotions. Cully refused therapy, refused medications, was too old to be forced into rehab without consent. How did this happen? Where did Cully's future go? And how can Olney help him get it back?

These days, Olney worries that he will eventually, inevitably, stop thinking about Cully, just to maintain his own sanity, stop caring, and that's why he keeps a photo on the fridge of Cully dancing in the yard at his fifth or sixth birthday party. That night Cully and Olney walked to Turpentine Park with Cully's Red Flyer wagon to look for treasures, and Cully fell asleep in Olney's lap on the bench where they usually sat to eat ice cream. Olney pulled his sleeping boy home in the wagon. But now this joyous memory is rendered unbearably sad by the wretched present. It is the present that determines the past. Olney is angry at Cully, he realizes, because Cully took that little boy away from him. Olney caps his pen, shuts his notebook. He knows he has to stop thinking like this, like there are two Cullys when there is only one, and that beautiful boy needs to be found so that he can then find himself. Olney pours himself another two fingers of Hennessy, turns on the radio, shuts his eyes, and listens to Lucinda and Willie sing "Overtime."

THE FAMILY'S UNOWNED BOY

A lie is not a deception to Cully. It's a defensive weapon that keeps the wolf of consequence from the door. That's how Olney sees it, anyway. When he says he'll do something—call you at six, let's say, get his ass to a meeting—he does intend to follow through, Olney guesses, but as we all know, so much can happen between now and then to change a mind.

( )

OLNEY PULLS INTO THE MIDWAY SUNOCO STATION AND SEES THAT Lonnie's holding Hedy in his arms. Olney's come to take Julie and the girls shopping at Auralee's consignment shop in town. Olney's installed two child seats in his Scion. He gets out of his car and shakes Lonnie's hand. Lonnie apologizes for the grease and wipes his hand on his jeans. Olney says, "What do you know, Lonnie?"

And Lonnie says he knows about the secret NASA slave colony on Mars where the government sends kidnapped children.

Julie helps Tallulah Belle into her seat and secures the belt. She says, "Don't listen to him, Olney."

Lonnie kisses Hedy on the cheek and hands her to Julie. "You can see mechanical wreckage all over that little red planet."

Olney says, "You've got better eyes than I do."

Lonnie smiles. "Sources inside the CIA have leaked proof, put the images up on the Internet. Do your research."

Hedy arches her back despite her mother's coaxing. So there's no way to fold her into the seat. This will take a cherry lollipop to remedy, and, fortunately, Lonnie has one in his pocket.

On the drive to town, Hedy falls right to sleep, and Tallulah Belle tells her doll, Gina, a story about the bear who went over the mountain to see what she could see. First, she gets lost, then she gets found, then she gets to the top of the mountain, and guess what she could see, Gina? No. Nope. No. Give up? She sees Daddy!

Julie asks Olney about Cully.

"He's been in touch with his mother, not with me."

"Are you okay with radio silence?"

"I may have to get used to the idea that we'll coexist at a distance. And that will be okay as long as he recovers."

They pass a BLIND CHILD IN AREA road sign, a mailbox, a Ljungborg Realty FOR SALE sign, but see no house. Julie says, "Can I be frank?"

"You can."

"You did what the support group people told you to do—you put him out and let him go. That didn't work out so well for him. You told me he always comes back home to you, even if briefly, even if he has ulterior motives. Now you should go to him. Fight for your boy. You've got nothing to lose."

"You're reading my mind."

"That's Auralee's job."

Olney smiles, says, "I talk like a tough guy sometimes, but I know what I have to do. Cully's got no one but Kat and me."

( )

THE RACKS OF CHILDREN'S CLOTHING AT WEECYCLE ARE ARRANGED BY gender, by size, and by color. Burl Ives is singing about Mr. Rabbit over the sound system. Auralee asks Olney if he's found Cully or heard from him. He doesn't remember telling her Cully's name or mentioning his troubles. Olney tells her he's seen Cully briefly and heard more about him from Kat, but he remains elusive and reluctant to return home.

Auralee takes Olney's right hand in her hands. "May I?" She stares at his palm and then into his eyes. She smiles. "You're going to find him."

"Will he be all right?"

"He will."

"I don't know if I believe in palm reading."

"You don't have to."

"We saw you, Mireille and I, at the cemetery."

"I'm there most days."

"If you don't mind my asking, how did your daughter die?"

"Zoë stopped breathing. She was cold as ice when I checked on her before I went to bed. No known cause. They call it SUDC, sudden unexplained death in childhood."

"I'm so sorry."

"Thank you." Auralee hears Hedy screaming and goes to the rescue.

Taffi Burgess is in the boys' section looking through the blazers. Olney says, "Buddy?"

Taffi holds a blazer up to Olney's face. "Green is not your color."

"I loved Sunday's show. I'm a sucker for father-son stories."

"Abraham and Isaac."

"Even if the father is insane."

"Obedient."

"Especially liked when Buddy rolled his eyes and said, 'He told Abraham to do *what* to *whom*?'"

"I'll tell the boys you said hello."

Tallulah Belle bought herself a violet tutu and a pair of blue tights. Hedy bought a black beret, which she rubbed against her cheek but refused to put on her head.

( )

SAMIR TELLS OLNEY HE'S WORRIED ABOUT HEALTH CARE IN THIS country. "It's never about wellness with us; it's always about the bottom line." They're sitting in the McDonald's inside the lobby of Anastasia General, sipping coffee. They watch a patient with a shaved head and a deep scar over his left ear dip fries into a paper cruet of ketchup. Finds his target half the time. "This place, the KFC across the way, the Taco Bell—they're all here because the hospital makes money selling saturated fat, sugar, and sodium to sick people." He shakes his head. "Don't get me started."

"You're a self-starter."

"This hospital district has been systematically defrauding patients and the government for years now. The district was just fined seventy million dollars, but it will only have to pay six million. Why? you ask."

"I knew I didn't have to."

"Because our senator, the former governor, feels the district's pain. Before he was elected, Senator Batboy oversaw the largest medical fraud scheme in U.S. history when he was CEO of a health care system, and his company, his criminal empire, had to pay a one-point-seven-billion-dollar fine."

Olney says, "Mireille?"

"It won't be long."

"Weeks? Months?"

"Days."

"Is she in pain?"

"Some. She's under heavy sedation. She's losing strength. Her kidneys are failing."

"There's no coming back from this?"

"Do you believe in miracles?"

"No."

"There's your answer."

( )

MIREILLE'S IN HOSPICE AND HER EYES ARE OPENED, BUT SHE CAN'T SEE, at least not as far as Olney can tell. He passes a hand over her face. Nothing. He sits in the chair beside the bed, checks the heart monitor. A nurse comes in, a woman Olney recognizes. Faby's here to check vitals.

"Is she in a coma?" Olney says.

"I'd say she's somewhere between sleeping and waking."

"What happened to all the tubes that were attached to her yesterday?"

"We're in hospice mode now."

"Do you think she can hear me?"

"Yes, I think she can."

When Faby leaves, Olney opens the bedside cabinet's drawer and takes out *The Appassionata*. He opens the novel to the bookmarked page, but before he can read, his eyes close. When he walked into the room a few minutes ago, he was wide awake. Now he's exhausted. They must be pumping melatonin through the AC ducts. He dreams of a lake, at first calm, glassy, still, and then rippled and choppy, and he realizes he can see the passing wind by the surface of the water it has disturbed, and he thinks he's discovered a way to see that which can't be seen.

He looks at Mireille. Her eyes are closed. He opens the book and reads Chapter 22 aloud. Martine arrives at Valentine's apartment and tells him that she's calling off their separation. He's more important to her than music, and she wants to spend the rest of her life with him. Valentine tells her that he has been seeing Alicia the French horn player. We're engaged. Martine wants to know how he could do this to her. He says, You left me. She says, I'm back.

Valentine's wedding day approaches—he's marrying into a wealthy family. House in the Back Bay, cottage on the Vineyard. But he and Martine can't stay away from each other. They are deliriously happy and dolorously miserable. What do we do now, darling? Martine says.

"What happens next?" Mireille says, and a startled Olney drops the book.

He says, "Holy shit! Here you are!" He stands and leans in to give her a kiss, inhales the sweet herbal scent of lavender from the stem bouquet on the side table, catches his breath, kisses her cheek, and touches his forehead to hers.

"Tell me," she says. "Read me the rest." Her voice is hoarse and barely audible.

Olney knows he doesn't have the time to read the last fifty or so pages while she's awake. He tells her that this is one of those choose-your-own-ending love stories. And when she frowns, he says, You have three choices. He explains that the last scene in the book is one of these:

A. Valentine and Martine are playing in the symphony, a Mostly Mozart performance on the Esplanade. He smiles broadly as he watches his pregnant wife play a solo.

Mireille smiles.

B. Valentine and Martine are in their Cambridge apartment teaching their three-year-old son to play any instrument except the French horn.

Mireille smiles.

C. Valentine and Martine huddle in a corner booth at L'Espalier on one of their clandestine trysts—his wife is in Switzerland, skiing with her family.

Mireille sleeps.

Olney holds Mireille's cold hand and puts it under the covers. He wishes he had known her when she was a waitress and new in town and he was a young, single crusading reporter, wishes he could have conducted a whirlwind courtship, wishes they could have planned a future, even if that future proved to be brief. It's the planning that counts. The dreaming.

That would have meant no Cully, of course. And that wouldn't do. He would have to have lived two lives, in the way he made another life for the man in the photo, the man he called Buck. And now he imagines Buck's passing. A massive stroke in the La-Z-Boy while binge-watching a British mystery, and the new puppy, Lady Di, is alone and whining, licking Buck's face, yipping, hopping up and down.

"Cully," Mireille says, and startles Olney. Her voice is a whisper. "Don't give up on him."

"I won't."

Now she's crying, and he kisses her cheek, wipes her tears with a tissue. She says, "He's your future." She closes her eyes.

IF I COULD START AGAIN

The phone plays "Doctor My Eyes" and startles Olney out of his dream, a dream he found fascinating but can't recall. Samir's on the phone with the news of Mireille's passing. He tells Olney it was peaceful. No pain. A deep and lasting sleep.

Olney calls Jack Tighe in Spencer, Mass., and speaks with Jack's sister Nora, with whom Jack lives. Nora thanks Olney for the call, tells him that Jack's quite incapacitated and won't be able to make the funeral. "Parkinson's," she says, "diabetes, prostate cancer, dementia with Lewy bodies, and rheumatoid arthritis, just to name the top five. He shakes like a dervish, can't walk, loses his balance from the Meniere's. While he's sitting."

"I'm so sorry to hear about Jack. You must be overwhelmed."

"God knows they're trying, but they just can't kill the son of a bitch."

Olney calls Kat to tell her the news and leaves a message on her voice mail. He heads to Merriment Manor and talks with what's left of Bill Tasher at the front desk. Bill offers his condolences and hands Olney a Publix grocery sack with some of Mireille's belongings. "She wanted you to have these. Well, I know she would have if she'd been aware."

In the sack is *The Appassionata*, Mireille's college-ruled spiral notebook, and a photograph of her and Olney standing next to a costumed pirate in Old Town. He opens the notebook to a random page, where she has written in her elegant script: *Sublime and abiding love makes the heart beat faster.* And below that: *Just because I'm looking at you doesn't mean I see you.*

Olney thanks Bill. Bill says he'll see to it that Mireille's belongings get carried over to the Goodwill on Plumeria. Her books they'll keep at the library here. And then he tells Olney how the world speeds up as death approaches. Bill says, "You don't know how fast the years fly by when you hit eighty."

Olney wants to cry, but he can't. That will take place in private at home. He'll play Johnny Cash, and he'll let go. He bites his lip and shakes Bill's hand. "We'll have a memorial service here in the chapel."

"I'll see you there," Bill says.

( )

MIREILLE WAS BURIED WITHOUT CEREMONY AT BAYSIDE RESURRECtion Cemetery. Olney and Auralee were there to witness the internment. They brought along two dozen yellow roses and tossed them onto the lowered casket. "Goodbye, sweetheart," Olney said. And then he waited while Auralee visited her daughter's grave and wondered what you could say to comfort a mother who has lost a child so young.

( )

"DON'T BE DISAPPOINTED AT THE TURNOUT," WHAT'S LEFT OF BILL Tasher says. He and Olney are welcoming guests at the doors of the chapel. "A lot of our residents shy away from these memorials. They're scared. Too close to home."

The Reverend Burgess surprises Olney by quoting Emily Dickinson and Shakespeare as well as the Bible. The sweeping up the house, the morning after death. To love that well which thou must leave ere long. They shall hunger no more, neither thirst anymore. "Death is the central fact of our existence, the sadness at our core," the Reverend says. "Everything we love vanishes. We can't hold on to anything." A frail woman in a wheelchair begins to sob, softly at first, and then uncontrollably. She's clutching a baby doll to her chest, and she is trembling. The man to her left pats her shoulder and whispers words of consolation. He's wearing suspenders over his aloha shirt, holding up his overlarge flannel slacks. On his feet, argyle socks and brown microsuede slippers. He stands and wheels the wailing woman out of the chapel.

This grieving woman is Octavia Desautels. She's ninety-one and quite fragile. Sixty-seven years ago, she lost her baby when his illness was misdiagnosed as "a little bug" that was going around Parkersburg. The bug turned out to be hemolytic uremic syndrome, and little Roland's kidneys shut down. Octavia's solicitous companion is Napoleon Lucier, a retired school bus driver and recovering alcoholic with a fondness for stories of the Old West, cowboys and Indians, Louis L'Amour, and the like—romance novels for men, Althea calls them.

"It is this tragedy," the reverend says, "that accounts as well for the beauty and nobility of our lives, because in the face of this knowledge, we go right on loving, trying to hold on to what we cherish, defying death with hubris, with stories, and with faith."

Yes, we go right on loving, Olney thinks. We must. And it's Cully whose face he sees.

( )

OLNEY HAS THE MOURNERS BACK TO HIS HOUSE FOR A RECEPTION. THE raucous blue jay in the live oak leans forward and eyes the Carolina anole on the screen in Olney's kitchen window. The anole lifts his head and flares his red dewlap, hoping a nearby eager female might gaze upon his splendor. A breeze ruffles the jay's contour feathers. He cocks his crested head, all the better to see the tantalizing green lizard. Tallulah Belle sweeps the anole up in her hand. When she opens her fist, the befuddled anole perches on her index finger and holds on tightly with his sticky feet. Julie looks out the window at her daughter. "Don't you bring that nasty creature inside."

"His name's Bieber."

"And you wash your hands before you eat, young lady."

Tallulah Belle strokes Bieber's smooth head and tucks him into her shirt pocket. The blue jay jeers.

Julie's standing the candied bacon strips in two highball glasses at the kitchen table. The oven timer buzzes. The sausage bites are ready. Auralee carries a platter of grape jelly meatballs—her aunt Jilda's recipe—into the dining room and sets it on the credenza next to the dish of deviled eggs. Dewey and Althea sit quietly at the dining room table. Dewey stirs his mint julep with a glass swizzle stick. Althea's promised herself that she will not read the book she has tucked in her purse while she's here, *The Red Love of White Hope*, but maybe, if she slips away to the bathroom for a bit, she could read a page. Better not. One page leads to another. It would be rude.

The sunlight through the dining room windows casts Samir's shadow on the hardwood floor. He's sitting, hunched forward, on the padded bench beneath the windows, his forehead in his hand, and he's speaking to his sister Lely, who is in London, where it's already evening, and she's leaving work at last and is off to dinner at Nando's with a Serbian fellow she met on Tinder. Auralee senses a dark disturbance radiating from Samir's body, waves of sadness, it feels like. And in the living room, Langley curtsies, hands the Reverend Burgess a red paper napkin, and offers him a corn fritter from the serving dish in her hand. He takes one and thanks her. He's looking through Olney's books. He sets the napkin and the toothpick on the bookcase shelf and pulls out a book on diagramming sentences. He wonders if diagramming sentences from scripture might lead to a more profound understanding of God's providence.

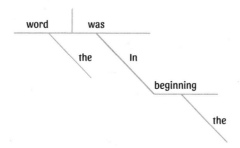

Yes, he could do an episode where he's helping Buddy with his English homework.

"What's a subjective complement, Buddy?"

"That's a fine-looking praying-hands lapel pin, Dad."

What's left of Bill Tasher eases himself down onto the couch beside his friend and driver, James Patrick Horan, and properly introduces James Patrick to Olney. Olney's standing beside the couch and has his eyes fixed on a cockroach on the floor behind the La-Z-Boy, waving its antennae. The roach catches the scent of a sausage crumb in its vicinity. It can see at once that said crumb is not behind, above, below, or in front of it. When Olney lifts his foot, he generates a smooth and subtle motion of air that drives the hairs on the roach's legs forward, and the roach, without a thought, dashes ahead to the safety beneath the La-Z-Boy.

Hedy is sound asleep in a laundry basket in the spare room. Julie kisses her baby's cheek and adjusts the blanket over her shoulders. Samir ends his call to Lely, looks up, and sees Auralee staring at him with squinted eyes and a furrowed brow. He asks her if she's all right.

She says, Are you? He smiles. She says, Would you like to talk about it? About what? he says.

Langley tells Olney that her mother Jen is out of bed today and is shampooing the carpets in her bathing suit with the music blasting. Nirvana. She thinks everything is funny today. She even liked your joke about the present, past, and future walking into a bar.

The hospital nurse Etta stops by in her scrubs on her way to work. Althea excuses herself and walks off toward the kitchen. Dewey watches Langley cross the dining room with a plate of baklava covered in plastic wrap, and he thinks how different his own life would have been with a child. Etta thanks Langley, tells Olney how happy the staff will be with this gift of such exquisite food. She tells him how sorry she is about Mireille.

Samir is across the street on Langley's front porch with Jen. They're sharing a bowl of mango kush and laughing up a storm. And then James Patrick Horan stands and sings "The Lass of Aughrim" a cappella and everyone goes quiet. "Another," Olney says, "please," and James Patrick sings "When You Were Sweet Sixteen."

> And even though we drifted far apart
> I never dreamt but what I dream of thee
> I love you as I loved you
> When you were sweet
> When you were sweet sixteen.

And Olney thinks of his accidental meeting with Mireille—her own misfortunate encounter with a vagrant trash bag, her wandering lost in the neighborhood, his own impulse to head to Publix for something he can't remember, his crossing the street, his heeding her summons. Whom we meet, where we live, what we do, it's all accidental, all a blessed fluke.

When Althea comes back from the bathroom, Dewey asks her if she's feeling all right. A little backed up, she tells him. Langley looks over at her mother and Samir on the porch and tells Olney that Samir must be funnier than she and Olney are. Samir tells Jen the one about the doctor who tells his patient she has cancer and Alzheimer's, and the patient says, "Whew, well, at least I don't have cancer." And Jen cracks up. He says, "Have you heard of Irish Alzheimer's?" She hasn't. He says, "You forget everything but the grudge."

Later, on Dewey's front porch, Olney and Dewey listen to the Brown Bats play the Melbourne Astros. The rookie Wyatt Tyler—Wy-Ty, Langley calls him—has gotten a hit in every game so far this season. "No one does that," Olney says. "Not even in Little League." And when Wyatt lines a double up the gap in right in his first at-bat, Dewey says, "There's a kid who takes advantage of every opportunity. "

"One and done," Olney says, and pours fresh whiskey into their tumblers.

"I'm sorry about Mireille. A damn shame," Dewey says. "The price of love is grief, and grief becomes remembrance, and remembrance restores the love. You don't lose what you keep in your heart."

( )

THERE IS NOTHING OLNEY CAN DO ABOUT THE LOSS OF MIREILLE, except, as Dewey said, keep her in his heart and in his mind. He talks to her still, and when she responds, he can hear her whispery voice, and he can see her clearly when he closes his eyes. Today her hair is pinned back the way it is in the picture on the fridge, and her nail polish matches her lipstick—Ruby Tuesday, she calls the shade. Olney has kept a heliotrope silk scarf she wore often, and when he holds it close to his face, he can inhale her scent.

I THINK I HEARD A MOAN

In 1904, Lasse Østergaard, at the behest of thirty-five of his fellow Danish settlers, wrote to U.S. Postmaster Henry L. Payne, requesting the establishment of a post office in their community close by the Everglades. Lasse confessed in his letter that he was having trouble choosing between *Aalborg* or *St. Canute* as a name for the new town and asked Mr. Payne for his advice. Lasse and his fellow immigrants had been without contact of any kind with family and friends back in Jutland for three years and were dispirited and tormented by their isolation. Oscar Jeppesen had stopped working altogether. He sat on the beach and stared out to sea. Aase Hansen lost her baby and then took to her bed. They all missed the cold and the snow. They cursed the heat and the sand flies. The Biscayne Stage Line delivered Postmaster Payne's letter of reply to Lasse three months later. The community could establish a post office indeed. As for the name, Mr. Payne's advice to Lasse was to "go with your feeling."

( )

THE MELANCHOLY MONKEYS—SEVERAL COLONIES OF AFRICAN vervets—escaped from a now-defunct roadside attraction called

Chimp World in the fifties and have been living in the mangroves in the Melancholy wetlands ever since. The Sans Souci is a derelict mom-and-pop motel surrounded by an easily breached cyclone fence on Melancholy Beach Boulevard at the end of the Melancholy Cut-off Canal, where once the Danish settlers had rowed their tomatoes from the fields down to Lake Mabel and then north to the New River. There's still a pay phone beside the Sans Souci office door, with a missing handset and a dangling metal cord. Cully often finds refuge here during afternoon thunderstorms. He rode out Hurricane Marlon in Room 10. Pulled an old mattress over himself and slept through sixteen hours of hell with pharmaceutical assistance. When he woke, he saw two monkeys holding hands on the patio. The mangroves had been stripped of their leaves. A queen palm in the yard had toppled onto the fence. The monkeys kept their dark eyes fixed on Cully and kept their distance. Cully calls the mother Marie and her child Bobby, and he has taken to raiding restaurant dumpsters nearby and bringing the food to the monkeys. A $500 fine, he knows, but worth it. Blood from a stone, and all that.

Whenever the monkeys see Cully slip through the tear in the fence, they scramble down from their perch in the trees and sit quietly on the apron of the empty swimming pool. Bobby's now Marie's size. Cully lays out the beggar's banquet and walks away. He watches them from the old BBQ pit by the rusted swing set as they devour the meal, and keeps up a one-way conversation with them. He talks about the deadening routine of life in Melancholy and about his desire to get out of this rut. At times, he thinks Marie and Bobby are his closest friends, and he thinks that's sad, but it's also pretty special because he must be a good person if these two trust him. "Listen to me, Marie; I'm losing it!" The monkeys are his secret. He can't tell any of his party buds about them. You never know what those sick fucks might do.

( )

OLNEY TELLS TALLULAH BELLE THAT HE'S NOT *GOING AWAY* GOING AWAY; he's just going away long enough to find his boy Cully and carry him back home where he belongs. Mireille's passing has stirred in him the desire to turn Cully around, to give it one last, or one more, try. They are sitting at a picnic table in Olney's backyard. "I'm tired of waiting for him. Time goes by so slowly when you wait."

Tallulah Belle says, "How long will it take?"

"A month should do it."

"Where is he?"

"I'm not quite sure."

"I love a mystery."

Olney's hosting a barbecue for friends, saying so long before he drives off to Melancholy. Tallulah Belle is trying to feed pulled pork to Hedy, and now Hedy's crying. Dewey's wearing Olney's spare house key on a lanyard around his neck. He'll be taking in the mail and whatnot, watering the flowers. Samir tells Olney to call if he needs assistance, and he'll come running. Olney's taken a leave from the mini-golf, gotten his Scion tuned up, had the tires rotated. Auralee takes the baby back ribs out of the smoker. Samir checks his text message and says he has to go to the hospital. Tiger Tivnan's taken a turn for the worse. Auralee sets the platter of ribs on the table beside a bowl of slaw and sits down beside Olney. She takes Olney's right hand in her hands, turns it over, and inspects his palm.

"The other one," she says.

Olney wipes his hand on the thigh of his jeans and holds it out to her. She inspects it, nods, and smiles.

Julie says, "Which sauce is the hot one?"

Olney nods at the bottle of sauce he made with scotch bonnet peppers, Dijon mustard, garlic, cayenne, onion, and brown sugar. "Easy does it."

Hedy has stopped fussing. She's sitting on Julie's lap drinking a box of juice through a straw. Althea's eating her ribs with latex gloves.

Dewey checks the Florida State League app on his phone and lets Olney know that the Brownies split a double-header with the Capital Panhandlers in Tallahassee. Wyatt Tyler got two hits in the opener and tripled to left center in the closer. The sun sets; the owl calls; Aura-lee, Julie, and the kids say goodbye and head for home with bowls of desserts. What's left of Bill Tasher and James the tenor head back to Merriment Manor. Althea, Dewey, and Olney begin the cleanup in the kitchen. Althea washes, Dewey dries, and Olney puts leftovers in Tupperware containers for the Lambs to bring home. He's already emptied the fridge. Althea asks how he's doing. Meaning without Mireille. He tells her he feels a little bit lost, a little untethered. She was never dying; she was always living.

( )

OLNEY HAS RESERVED A ROOM FOR A MONTH AT THE DIXIEWOOD, ground zero in the search for Cully in Melancholy. He spoke with the affable motel owner, Sister Robert, better known as Robbie. Given name, Roberta O'Malley. She explained how she had been a nun for twenty-three years.

Olney pictured Sister on the phone in her office at the Dixiewood in a tunic, full guimpe and wimple, starched coif, crucifix around her neck, and wooden rosary beads looped through the cincture at her waist, and he smiled.

"Firstable," she said, "you need to know we have no parking spaces at the motel because if you have a car, you don't need another place to sleep. You need gas."

"But I'll have a car."

"Park on Mango Court or Papaya Terrace."

"Will do."

"Second, this is not a bread-and-breakfast. You'll need to feed yourself."

"I'm used to doing that."

"No swimming pool."

"No problem."

"Let me ask you, Ollie—"

"Olney."

"Only."

"Olney."

"None of my business, but are you running from something or someone? Looking for a new leash on life?"

"Looking for my son. Running *to* someone, you might say."

"Check-in time is whenever you arrive."

"Thank you, Sister. I look forward to meeting you."

"Call me Robbie."

( )

OLNEY HAS TAPED TWO SNAPSHOTS TO THE DASHBOARD OF HIS CAR— one of Mireille in her splashy fishing outfit out at Bunny's Crappie House, and one of him and Cully when Cully was five. Kat had snapped the picture just as Cully was in midair, arms wide, eyes wider, Hollywood smile, leaping into his daddy's embrace. Olney's heading south on I-95, listening to WHY-AM's *Biscuits and Blues* morning show, and Barbecue Bob's singing about how all the womens got washed away. Making good time, his father used to say on every road trip. He remembers his father's ebony ring, his sky-blue eyes, the one jagged tooth in the front of his mouth. He remembers the smell of his father's cherry pipe tobacco and that mole on his chin. A beauty mark, his mother called it. When he's out of range of the station, Olney punches the scan button on the radio and hears the hiss of static like a distant rainstorm mixed with rumbles and clicks. Static . . . station . . . static . . . station . . .

Shhhh . . . *there may be a famine in Moab, but there is bread in Bethlehem* . . . .Shhhh . . . *say the police shot the unarmed black man* . . . Shhhh . . . *More immigrant-bashing from Florida Governor Ron DeSantis* . . . Shhhh . . . *gravity was weaker in those days, else them dinosaurs could not have been so nimble* . . . Shhhh . . . *was holding a cell phone and not a pistol, according to* . . . Shhhh . . . *peace means being able to blow your enemies to smithereens* . . . Shhhh . . . *Judge not that ye be not judged. For with* . . . Olney turns off the radio.

And now that he has space to think, Olney remembers teaching Cully how to hit a Wiffle ball in the backyard. And he was good at it but indifferent with it. Olney told him that one day he could play for the Brown Bats. Cully said he would if he could wear number two, because two was the only even prime number. He would wear number five in his dazzling but brief Splendora High baseball career because two was already taken and five is the first safe prime, the first good prime, and the first balanced prime. Math was something else Cully was good at. He never seemed excited by his talents or surprised by what he could do. When he was five and in kindergarten and the two of them were eating breakfast at True Grits, Cully asked, "What does a sold look like?"

"A sold?"

"The part of you that's not a body."

"Who told you about the soul?"

"Miss Johnson."

"In class?"

"Yes."

"What else did she say?'

"Her daddy was the seventh son of a seventh son."

"And what does that mean?"

"He sees things."

"What did she say about the soul?"

"That it's bigger than the body but fits inside."

"Like a folded winter jacket in a suitcase?"

"I told Miss Johnson you didn't believe in God."

"What did she say?"

"We all prayed for you."

Olney smiles and looks back at the photos on the dashboard. He thinks about what was and what never was and wonders if he ever leaped into his father's arms like that. Not that he remembers. He figures now he'll be crying by the time he reaches Melancholy.

( )

OLNEY PARKS ON PAPAYA TERRACE BESIDE THE DIXIEWOOD, LIFTS HIS suitcase out of the wayback, and does not see Cully and Pixie up the block crossing Papaya at Main, walking north to the bus stop at Cypress. They're headed for the beach, but they won't get there. Big party at the Pirate's Inn, Mikey Murray tells them, and off they go, picking up their pace and jabbering like crazy, talking about the poor saps at work there in the European Market. Pixie says she has news for Cully. Jasmine's been visiting Shane in jail, and she's filed an assault complaint against Cully with the police. "Probably nothing to worry about, but another reason you should leave town. And when I say *you*, I mean *we*."

Olney walks around the front, enters the motel office, and introduces himself to Robbie. She tells him she thought he'd be taller. She's wearing a navy-blue T-shirt with white lettering that reads LESS TALK. MORE SUCK. She hands Olney a tissue and a room key. She says, "I hope you're not suspicious. You've got Room Thirteen."

He shakes his head, wipes his eyes, blows his nose. "Allergies," he says.

"You keep your own room tidy. No chambermaids here. Laundromat up the street."

The sign above her head reads TOWEL EXCHANGE 7–10 A.M. "Follow me," she says. "So you're looking for your wayward son."

He shows her Cully's photo.

Open the door and you look straight back at the open closet. A hanging rod and a few wire hangers. To the left of the closet, a bathroom. Dark paneled walls, simulated wood laminate flooring, and overhead lighting on the ceiling fan. Along the right wall a small fridge. On top of the fridge, a microwave oven. Then a faux-leather comfy chair and a dresser. On the dresser, a TV and a coffee maker. To the left, a double bed and a bedside table with a lamp and a phone. The window looks out on the courtyard. In front of the window, a round table and two chairs. Above the door, an AC unit.

"I'll leave you to settle in." Robbie smiles. "Some of us gather around the firepit about dark-thirty. You're invited, of course."

Olney sits in the comfy chair, leans his head back, and kicks off his walking shoes. He wonders if he remembered to pack his knee sleeve. (He didn't.) He'll be doing a lot of walking, no doubt. He takes a framed black-and-white photo off the dresser and studies it. Taken, it looks like, at an RV tourist camp in the forties or fifties. In those days you dressed up to sit out on the Adirondack chairs beneath the palm trees. Or maybe you dressed up to get your picture taken, photography being an event in those days, not a given, as it is today. The gray-haired couple are smiling and waving, presumably to the family at the next RV site. Mister has a cigarette in his hand. Missus has a magazine in her lap. There is an empty chair beside her. The door to the Airstream is open. Who's inside? Olney wonders. *She* is. What's she doing?

Olney is often more interested in what is outside the frame, so now he looks across at the family at the next site, and he sees them in color. Mom's in a beach outfit: white shorts, green-and-white-striped sleeveless blouse, and a pink kerchief that matches her espadrilles. Dad's a redhead. He's at the grill cooking hot dogs, tongs in one hand, bottled beer in the other. He's wearing aviator sunglasses and a green apron. The little boy and little girl are tossing a beach ball back and forth.

Inside the Airstream, the couple's daughter, home for the holidays from college, is standing at the sink and crying. Her parents don't know her pain and anguish. No one knows. She thinks she can't keep this secret to herself any longer.

( )

OLNEY CALLS KAT TO LET HER KNOW HE'S HERE. NO CULLY SIGHTINGS on her part, she says.

"I'm at the Dixiewood."

"Hold on to your hat."

"What?"

"It'll be a bumpy ride."

"I'm here to bring Cully back home, get him into a program."

"What makes you think he'll go this time?"

"Maybe we can do an intervention here. You, me, Elbert. I can get Samir and Dewey to drive down. And Lip, Cully's sponsor."

"If we can get him to sit still and listen."

"Not to scare him or anything. To let him know some people care about him. To let him know there's a way out of this hell he's been living in."

"And then what? He won't go to rehab. Not without a court order."

"Maybe he'll go to a halfway house. There's one a mile from my

157

place. I talked to the guy who runs it. He'll get a bed, meals, meetings, therapy. They'll help him find a decent job."

"Don't get ahead of yourself."

"I think this could work."

Olney unpacks and then walks down Main to the Melancholy library. The library is one floor and reminds Olney of an airport terminal. There are lots of comfortable chairs arranged by the bright windows, several steel tables and chairs, a bin of DVDs, and a wall of magazines. The kids' section is set up with cushions, reading nooks, and wooden toys. The place, he thinks, is remarkably uncluttered with books. He takes a walk around the perimeter but does not spot Cully. There is a bank of computers in a windowed room, and all are in use. A sign at the door to the IdeaLab, as it's called, reminds the library's guests that there is a twenty-minute limit per session. There are a dozen people in a row of chairs outside the room waiting their turn at the computers. When one person exits, the person in the chair nearest the room stands and enters, and the rest all slide to the left. The person who exited takes the emptied last seat and begins his or her journey to the next session.

There are a handful of homeless-seeming men napping in the comfortable chairs. Olney picks up a book from the 7-Day shelf and takes a seat. He opens the novel—*Floater or Drain Fly?*—to a random page and reads: *Dr. Sochalski flicks his tongue before he asks James, "What do you think your mother did to your dog?"* Olney closes the book, turns it over, and studies Will Power's author photo. He's wearing a fedora, sports a graying beard, and is looking down so you can't see his eyes. So he is bald, and he would like you to believe he has a secret. He's being coy about it.

A woman enters the library carrying a half-dozen plastic Publix sacks in one hand and holding on to a leashed service dog with the other.

When she collapses onto a chair, drops the sacks, picks up the dog, and sits it on her lap, Olney walks over, smiles, and asks for the name of her charming dog. Yeti, she says. Yeti needs a bath, Olney thinks.

Olney says, "I was wondering if you might know my son Cully. I have his photo."

"Can you spare a dollar?"

"I can."

"Can you spare a five?"

Olney takes a five out of his wallet along with the picture of Cully and hands them to her. She tells him her name is Geraldine Schrab and, pointing to his book, says the psychiatrist did it.

Olney says, "That's a couple of years ago, that picture."

"I've seen him."

"In here?"

"Many times, but not in a while. Nice boy. Very polite." She hands Olney the photo. "You should talk to Preston." She points to the gentleman at the reception desk. Olney thanks her.

Preston is a tall, lanky fellow with dreadlocks down his back to his waist. He's wearing a lavender silk T-shirt, black slacks, and round tortoiseshell glasses. And, yes, he knows Cully. Fugue states and particle physics. He took me on a tour of the microcosmos. I got lost. Preston types Cully's name into his computer. "And he owes us money."

"How much?"

Preston taps a key. "Eighty-two bucks."

Olney pays the fine and asks Preston to tell Cully, if he sees him, that his dad is looking for him and is staying at the Dixiewood.

"I sure will. You say hi to Robbie for me."

Olney turns. He says, "I remember when libraries were full of books."

"Print books get moldy. They're expensive. They take up a lot of room. They're heavy. They get torn; they get stolen. E-books are forever."

( )

IT'S RAINING WHEN OLNEY GETS BACK TO THE DIXIEWOOD, AND A notice on the office door lets him know that the social hour at the firepit has been canceled. Robbie taps on the window and waves Olney in. She says, "What's your poison?" and walks behind the check-in desk and looks below the counter. "Rye, bourbon, vodka, gin, tequila . . . and, let's see, rum."

"Bourbon, please."

"Jim, Evan, Mark, Elijah, Basil, Ezra, or Redemption?"

"Redemption, please."

She pours four fingers of bourbon in two rocks glasses, adds a dash of water to each, stirs with her finger, licks the finger, and sets the glasses down on the coffee table. They sit on the divan and toast to a successful manhunt. Olney asks Robbie where she's from, and she tells him her story.

She runs her fingers through her spiky gray hair, clears her throat, sips the bourbon, and begins. She was a nun, Sisters of St. Joseph, taught sixth grade at Saint Damien the Leper Grammar School in Requiem, Mass. She was raped by Father John Buckley in the cloak-room adjoining her classroom. When she reported the crime, she was not believed by the monsignor, nor by Mother Superior, nor by the bishop, nor by the cops. Father Buckley was an admired man who had taken the vows of poverty, chastity, and obedience. And he was the brother of Requiem's district attorney, Blaise Buckley, who was also the Supreme Advocate and General Counsel of the Knights of Columbus and was also a somewhat careless but invulnerable pedophile.

"They took away my teaching assignment, had me cleaning the convent. I was so sick I couldn't eat. I got so thin I was skelatorial." She looks at her hands as she speaks. She tells Olney she finally got up the nerve to leave. Just walked out the door and hopped on the #5 bus. She took a job working behind the counter at Sibley's Jersey Bar, rented a room at the Aurora Hotel, and felt free for the first time in her life. But then she married an Irish bachelor fresh off the potato boat, and she moved in with him and his mother on the third floor of a triple-decker on Grafton Street. "When our second daughter followed her sister and went off to college at Salve Regina, I said, Liam, this is crazy. You're gay, and so am I. Let's call the whole thing off. Liam's mom, Rosemary, looked at him out the side of her eye and said out the side of her mouth, I told you so."

When Robbie's uncle Gene died, he left each of his nephews and nieces a bundle of money from the fortune he'd made from his construction business, and Robbie bought the Dixiewood sight unseen and moved out of the cold and gloom of New England.

She says, "Give me that photo of your boy, and I'll make up a wanted poster."

Olney hands her the photo. She puts the photo on the printer behind the desk and returns with the bottle of Redemption and a glass cruet of water.

(III)

Thunder in the Distance

AND HERE WE ARE IN HEAVEN

Eloy says it doesn't matter where we live—the past is our real home. Eloy is a man from the future, one of the many earthly futures, his an unextraordinary future as those things go, and he's quick to point out that he's not the smartest fellow from that future, but he *was* smart enough to get out. He came here to the twenty-first century, as we call it, to relax and collect his thoughts, and in doing so, he proved—or will have proven—the dismissive naysayers wrong, those who maintain that the past is theoretical, that it is a deception, a fantasy that can only exist in the present.

The future he comes from, as he describes it, is a chaos of conformity on the one hand and a holy mess of efficiency on the other. It is a docile, if not always agreeable, space and time. The citizens are relatively compliant and muzzled. This future is managed by robots. People welcomed the stillness and the serenity, and the anxiety that is its issue, which followed the catastrophe of the water wars, which followed the last of the glaciers melting, which followed the eruption of the Yellowstone super-volcano that blew away much of what we call in the twenty-first century the American West, which followed the Rupture—the explosion of methane gas released by the thawing permafrost.

So when carbon intelligence proved unequal to the task of running a civilization, silicon intelligence took over. It hasn't been easy for the robots. Precious few bees survived the tracheal mite assault provoked by severe climate change, so there are hardly any fruits or vegetables for the humans. Domesticated cattle can't get enough nutrients from the scant grasses growing in the scorched soil, so there's little meat, less milk, no cheese. Game animals were hunted to extinction, and when the iguana farms failed after the mouth-rot epidemic, there went the last reliable source of protein. Eating fish is suicidal due to the extraordinarily high levels of methylmercury in their bodies. Everyone's hungry; everyone's exhausted, but no one can sleep for the hunger pains. Still, no one complains. We'll all be okay, goes the thinking, because we are the AIs' means of making more AIs. We're indispensable.

There's a knock at Olney's door. He closes the book he's reading—Eloy Cole's *From There to Modernity*—and says, "Coming." He found the thin volume this morning under the Gideon Bible in the drawer of the bedside table.

The man at the door holds up the wanted poster of Cully and says, "I'm here to help." He's sandy-haired, fair-skinned, blue-eyed, tall and trim, and he's grooming his graying beard with a metal comb. He's wearing a white The Clash GUNS OF BRIXTON T-shirt, khaki cargo pants, and what Olney would describe as combat boots. The man holds out his hand and introduces himself. "Guy A. Boy."

"What's the *A* for?"

"Ahab."

"Thanks, I could use the help. I'm Olney Kartheizer."

"But first—breakfast. Ten minutes. Room Five. We'll make a plan."

When he was a kid, Guy's friends called him Maytag because he was so easily agitated. Guy is an affable fellow. He's sunny, garrulous, neighborly, but at the same time utterly paranoid and easily roused. Guy assumes that certain people are always coming for him. He's here at the Dixiewood hiding out. He suspects that even his wife, from whom he has escaped, has gone over to the dark side or may have always been there, like his father Ryan, who broke legs for the Rhode Island mob. Guy is never more than two feet away from a loaded weapon, even when he's in the shower with the bathroom door locked and bolted. He doesn't watch TV—that's how they corrode your brain. He doesn't own a cell phone—that's how they track you down. His motto is, *Prepare, Surveil, and Respond.* If you think everyone's after you, then you naturally have to protect yourself, so you build yourself a fortress, literally and figuratively. You don't think of it as a prison.

( )

A SHORT FELLOW WITH A MOP OF GRAY HAIR AND BAGGY EYES, WEAR-ing bib overalls, a blue work shirt, and a wooden cross on a length of rope around his neck, opens Guy's door. He says, "Reed Proust."

Olney says, "I tell people I do, but really just *Swann's Way.*"

"What are you talking about?"

"You asked me if—"

"I introduced myself. Reed Proust."

"Sorry, I thought . . . . Marcel Proust, the author."

"I don't know him, but we're probably kin. Where does he live?"

"He's dead."

Reed nods. "With the Father." He sweeps his arm and invites Olney in.

Guy sets a platter of food on the table set for three. He's soft-boiled six eggs in the coffee maker (three minutes) and nuked a half pound of bacon in the microwave. Coffee's in the carafe, toast, fried on the coffee maker's hot plate, is in a plastic container. Reed looks at the wanted poster and says he's seen Cully around plenty, and he shouldn't be hard to find.

The three of them talk a bit about their work. One might describe Olney's work these days as pursuance, Guy's as vigilance, and Reed's as reverence. Reed says his work—he doesn't have time for a job—is to think about the Sacred Heart. He goes to Mass and Communion every morning at St. Benedict's and performs the Corporal Works of Mercy at St. Agatha's Hospice. He's able to survive quite nicely on his disability checks. And then he excuses himself; he's off to the hospice where he volunteers. He cleans, he cooks, but mostly he prays for the souls in the agony of death.

Guy's plan is simple. Guy will search the beach, walk into every bar, restaurant, and souvenir shop on the Broadwalk with the poster. He'll scope out Boombox Park and the pier. He'll walk the trail through the sea grapes. Olney will search the area around Main. They'll meet back at the Dixiewood at, say, one, get some lunch.

Olney says, "I'll buy lunch. And who knows, maybe we'll be pleasantly surprised."

"I'll never be surprised," Guy says.

( )

OLNEY RECOGNIZES LIP O'BRIEN FROM HIS LAST VISIT AND TELLS HIM where he's staying and what he's up to. And would he help do an intervention for Cully. He would. Lip says Cully hasn't been attending meetings, and he lost his job at Katz Meow.

"What's that?"

"A kosher pet boarding facility. Told me he didn't like having to express the anal glands of dogs."

"Who would?"

When the Silpher twins walk by, Lip introduces them to Olney. "He's your new neighbor at the Dixiewood."

"Room Thirteen," Olney says.

"Room Eight," Agnes says.

Lip asks them if they've seen—in their way—Cully at all.

Agnes says they have. He was wrangling shopping carts at Buttonwood Plaza.

When Olney and Lip get to the plaza, they see a guy herding carts in the parking lot in front of Marshalls, but it's not Cully. His name is Isaac, he tells them, eager, it seems, for company. He lives with his mother in Lime City. She makes him egg salad sandwiches every day even though he's told her a million times he can't eat egg salad. He keeps the sandwich in his attaché case along with his counterfeit cell phone. He takes the #12 bus to work at the plaza. He leaves the sandwich on the bus for whoever needs it. He makes the pretend calls to his uncle Trayvon who doesn't exist or to his girlfriend, who is a real person named Tamika who works the registers in Marshalls, but who doesn't yet understand her significant role in Isaac's life. "Love you, too," he says, loud enough for other riders to hear.

Isaac says, "Who told you Cully was here?"

Lip says, "The Silpher sisters."

Isaac says, "Enough said. But it's your lucky day."

"How?" Olney says.

"Cully's working at the car wash on Main. The one by the Bahamian joint."

Olney says, "Thank you so much."

Lip says, "Who are you working for?"

"No one. I like it. I make friends—like you two—and I get tips. I save cars from being dented—like this Bronco—and I get satisfaction."

Olney hands Isaac a five and tells him he's a lifesaver.

( )

CULLY IS NOT WORKING AT THE HOLY WATER CAR WASH: *WE WASH THE hell out of your car.* Turnover here is pretty rapid, the manager, Gus DeFlavio, tells Olney and Lip. Cully was just not thorough enough to get the job done.

Olney and Lip walk to the corner of Main and Citrus. Olney says, "Shall we take a stroll around the block?"

Lip says, "This is where the accident happened."

"What accident was that?"

Lip tells Olney that his dad, Jamesy, an eighty-one-year-old alcoholic, was in Everglades General Hospital two years ago with pneumonia. He was given prednisone, and he went temporarily insane. Steroid psychosis. He imagined that the orderlies and nurses were operating a drug ring, and the guy in the other bed, who happened to be a childhood friend of his, Eddie Dumphy, was the hospital cartel's kingpin. So at three in the morning, Jamesy gets up, yanks out his various tubes, and attacks Eddie, battering his head with a steel bedpan until the nurses and security guards subdued and sedated him and got Eddie into emergency surgery. "With me so far?" Lip says.

"I'm listening."

"Eddie's grandson Dermid was marrying my cousin Mo's daughter, Mary Alice, that coming weekend. So around noon on the Wednesday that Jamesy clobbered Eddie, which I had not as yet heard about, I'm standing about where we are, under the awning, waiting for the rain to let up. A few minutes earlier, a few blocks thataway, my high school English teacher, Albert Harvey, another eighty-one-year-old alcoholic, is sitting in what he called his endowed chair at Ferrie's Tavern when he has a heart attack. Timmy Ferrie calls 911. Meanwhile, here comes Donna, mother of the groom, up the street. She's carrying this huge umbrella that almost pokes out my eye. She's on her way to the bakery to order the wedding cake. See you Saturday, I say, but she's hard of hearing and doesn't respond.

Lip looks at the intersection and points at the crosswalk. "The ambulance ran the red light just as Donna scooted across the street. Umbrella may have obscured her vision. I saw her get launched into the air and through the plate-glass window of the antique store across the street. The ambulance had swerved to avoid Donna and almost did. But it wound up wrapped around the light pole."

"Jesus."

"Albert died in the wrecked ambulance, Donna on the floor of Chic Antique, and Eddie lay in the hospital with the brain injuries."

"And your dad?"

"When he recovered and learned what he'd done, Jamesy checked himself out of the hospital, refused medication, stopped eating, and died sitting on the sofa with a drink in his hand. Sounds crazy, but shit like that happens all the time. There's not always someone there to connect the dots like I was. In the papers there was one story about a terrible accident, another story about a man assaulted in a hospital, one notice of a canceled wedding, and the obit I wrote for my old man."

Olney hears the honking of a horn, looks up, and sees Kat, who's pulling over to the curb on Citrus. Lip checks his watch, says he's got a meeting to go to, and heads off. Olney walks to Kat's car and leans in the window. Kat says, "Hop in."

"Where we going?"

"To look for Cully."

Olney gets in. Kat thinks a ride down Melancholy Beach Boulevard might be worth a try. "How's retirement treating you?"

He tells her about the mini-golf and about Julie and the kids. "I drive over to Spanish Blade once in a while and stare at our old house. They let the place go to shit."

"I loved that little house."

"Remember Cully sitting in the Florida room watching the blue jays knock the squirrels off the bird feeder?"

"We had that enamel-topped kitchen table."

"I even liked the stove with the two burners that wouldn't light."

"Every Sunday we read Peter Pan out loud together."

"And Cully would fly from the couch to the easy chair."

"I was sorry to hear about Mireille."

"Thank you."

Kat turns down the beach road, checks her watch, says they've got four minutes to beat the drawbridge. They drive pass the derelict Sans Souci, where Cully is napping by the empty pool, but they don't see him. She says, "Do you miss the reporting?"

"I do. I write for my own amusement these days. I'm going to write about this, too. About looking for Cully and about his recovery, I hope."

They drive down A1A along the beach for a mile and turn up Cypress. When they get back to Main, Kat says she has to meet Elbert in ten. It's her birthday and he's taking her to that wonderful fish restaurant she can't think of the name of in Poinciana. "Can I drop you somewhere?"

"Right here is good."

Kat pulls into the Pet Supermarket parking lot. She says, "If you find him, let me know how it goes."

"Happy twenty-ninth!"

Cully is not in Ace Hardware, and why would he be? He's not in the Peruvian sandwich shop or the Cuban restaurant or the waiting room at the urgent care facility. He's not in Smiley's Pub or in Little Bubbles Laundromat. Olney decides he'll buy Guy a Crock-Pot in the St. Vincent de Paul thrift shop. Cully's not in the thrift shop, either.

When Olney brings the Rival Crock-Pot to the register—a steal at $7—he shows Cully's picture to the cashier, and she knows him, but doesn't know his name.

"I'm his dad. I'm trying to find him."

"There he is." She points out the window, and sure enough, there's Cully sitting with his face in his hands on the bus-stop bench across the street.

Olney pays the young woman, tells her to keep the change, tucks the bagged Crock-Pot under his arm, and hurries out the door. He yells, but Cully doesn't hear him, and then the #2 bus pulls to the stop between Olney and his son, and when it pulls away, Cully is not there. Olney deflates. He walks back to the Peruvian sandwich shop and buys lunch-to-go for him and Guy. Two chicharrón and pork belly sandwiches with amarillo and fire sauces. Two toasted ears of corn, two cups of black beans.

( )

WHEN GUY CROSSES HIS LEGS AT LUNCH, OLNEY NOTICES THE PISTOL strapped to his ankle and asks him if it's real. It is. *Who would wear a fake one?* He asks Guy why he's wearing it. *Isaac might.*

Guy bites into his sandwich and fans his mouth with his hand. "Muy calor!" He wipes his forehead with the napkin. "Always be prepared," he says. "Daddy bought me my first handgun when I was seven and told me never to aim it at anyone or anything I was not willing to kill."

Guy also keeps a loaded Colt Cobra with a two-inch barrel and a fiber-optic front site under his pillow and a loaded FNS compact semiautomatic personal protection sidearm with a twelve-round magazine in the top drawer of the dresser beneath his shirts and slacks, and that loaded Iver Johnson Pocket Ace with four two-inch barrels in that ankle holster.

Guy reports the results of his morning's search, tells Olney that Cully was seen yesterday at Angelo's Pizza, last night at the Java Spot in the company of a young woman, and early this morning on a skateboard along Ocean Way. In fact, none of these sightings were accurate. Were the informants—a waiter, a barista, and a lifeguard—lying or mistaken or confused? In fact, Cully spent all of yesterday and most of today alone and crying. There's no dignity in blubbering in public. Keep it to yourself. He has, of course, cried publicly in his life, in front of his father when Anthony abandoned him, in front of the whole class when his girlfriend Clio Applewhite dumped him in the cafetorium, and in front of the vets when his cat Neo died. This time he cried because he felt disconnected, an object of pity, everybody's friendless friend, and because, though he has an abiding belief that he'll be okay, he doesn't quite have the strength to heal himself.

But right now he is at the beach, lying on his back in the sand with his shirt and shorts on and the surf lapping at his head. He's waiting for the wave that will wash over his face. He's here to meet Pixie, but Pixie has forgotten. She's with Jo Jo and Tracy in their room over Tattooine, a sketchy tattoo parlor on Main. They're getting high because Tracy's dad has died, and today is his funeral, which Tracy has missed. The death is being investigated. It looks like a suicide—bullet to the temple, Dad's prints on the revolver, and a suicide note expressing his despair. But who types a suicide note? Detective Whosee said. There's something fishy going on. Cully's soaked now. He gets up and walks to his towel and lies down beside it face-first in the sand and doesn't move. He won't move, he thinks, until Pixie rolls him over.

( )

OLNEY SITS AT HIS TABLE IN HIS ROOM WRITING A POSTCARD TO JULIE. It's a vintage linen card he picked up at a used bookstore at the Circle. An empty Melancholy beach at night: full amber moon, silver clouds, inky sky, glistening black water, sand, and palms. *Settled into the Dixiewood. Cully sighting but no encounter. Most of the guests are long-term residents. It's like a community of solitaries and freethinkers—disconcerting and refreshing. I met an orange cat outside my door when I returned this evening. I'm planning on feeding it. Making a friend. Hope you're well. Hugs to those babies.*

Olney decides he'll join Robbie and the gentleman he does not yet know out by the firepit. He pours himself a glass of Irish whiskey and heads out. Robbie welcomes him, slaps the chair beside her, holds up her Negroni for a toast, and introduces Olney to Dante Stone. She's wearing a black T-shirt with white letters that read: WHO TOLD YOU LUNCH WAS OVER? Dante asks Olney what he does for a living.

"Retired journalist. What about you?"

"I was an inventor's assistant, but I quit so I could devote all my time and energy to my research."

"What did your boss invent?"

"He was actually more of a reinventor."

"What did he reinvent?"

"The clock."

"The clock?"

"The spring-driven clock—from scratch. He was most proud of that one."

"How was it different from the original spring-driven clock?"

"Exactly the same."

Robbie refreshes her drink and asks Dante to tell Olney about his research. And she winks at Olney, flashes her eyebrows.

Dante suggests that his research might someday save the world. When Olney asks him for an explanation, Dante is at first hesitant, but then explains that there are only sixty people in the U.S. Congress who are human beings. "The others are solid holograms or clones."

Olney says he doesn't understand.

Robbie waves to a young woman walking by, tells Olney, "That's Tracy. Used to live here in number six with her boyfriend Jo Jo. Had to ask her to leave."

"Why?"

"She had a little itch down in her never regions, if you know what I mean. She had to scratch that itch something fierce. Peddled her wares up and down Main."

Dante says, "She could walk on her hands like nobody's business." He stares into the fire, kicks at a log, sending a plume of flame and ember skyward. He says, "Did you know that the king stepped down?"

"Charles, you mean?"

"Not because he's physically ill. He's immortal, of course. Prince William has been doing all the knighting, you may have noticed. One can be immortal, you see, without having all of one's royal marbles. Only the sovereign head of state can knight."

"Where do you do your research?"

"In my room on my laptop. Confidential, highly secure, and very dark websites."

"Maybe you should write a book about your research."

"The Secretary of State and the last Pope and a few Canadians are about to be arrested for as-yet-undisclosed offenses."

"By whom?"

"The Galactic Federation of Light."

"Who?"

"Palladians and others from a distant star system who live in the fifth dimension."

And then Lip O'Brien steps out of the darkness and into the flickering light of the fire and says, "I've got a message for you, Olney, from your son. He says he'll meet you for lunch tomorrow at noon at Koi Polloi."

"Koi Polloi?'

"Inexpensive freshwater sushi bar."

"What?"

"I'm kidding. He'll meet you at the Koffee Klatch on Mangrove."

Robbie invites Lip to join them here at the firepit.

"I don't drink, remember?"

"You haven't had a drink in eleven years. What harm can one drink do?"

( )

WHEN OLNEY ARRIVES BACK AT HIS ROOM, THE ORANGE CAT IS CURLED on his doormat. She stands, stretches, meows, and walks herself against and between his legs. Olney says, "Here's my friend. What's your name, baby?"

The cat makes a scratchy noise.

"Neutron it is."

BEFORE I TOOK UP SMILING

When he opens his door, Olney sees Reed Proust standing by the cold firepit, wearing a burlap smock and sandals, holding his bare, imploring arms above his head, and spreading his trembling fingers. Looking toward the pale blue sky, Reed says, "Ten candles of light." Looking over at Olney, Reed says, "You, too, can become a living flame."

Olney asks Reed if he'd like to grab a cup of coffee, and as if on cue, Guy steps out of his room with two cups of coffee and hands one to Olney. Reed says no coffee before the Eucharist. He's off to seven-thirty Mass. He makes the sign of the cross, turns, and walks away. Olney sets Neutron's saucer of wet food on the sidewalk. Neutron trills her thanks.

Guy turns to Olney. "The Koffee Klatch."

"How did you know?"

"They've got this Czech breakfast sandwich-type deal that's to die for. Get the sausage and egg kolache and thank me later."

"I will. What are your plans for the day?"

"Dante's being followed by some . . . some folks who want to get their mitts on his research." Guy takes a folded sheet of paper out of his shirt pocket. "Has he told you about the Archons?" Guy unfolds the paper and shows Olney the photo that Dante printed off his iPhone, the photo of a commercial van towing a trailer holding an industrial-sized pressure washer. You can read the company's name on the side of the van: OCD PRESSURE CLEANING; the company's services: HOMES, ROOFS, DECKS, DRIVEWAYS; and the company's motto: SOMETIMES IT'S OKAY TO BE A LITTLE OCD.

Guy says, "The van followed Dante down Mango and up Main, keeping a safe and unobtrusive distance, they thought. When Dante entered the library, the van parked out front. When Dante left the library, the van was parked in the same spot. Mr. OCD better hope I don't spot him today."

( )

CULLY IS NOT AT THE KOFFEE KLATCH WHEN OLNEY ARRIVES A FEW minutes early. Olney gets himself a colada and takes a seat at one of the four small tables, the one by the window. He wants a view of the street, so he can, maybe, see Cully approach. The only other customers in the shop are a couple sitting in the love seat with the window behind them and a coffee table before them. Their two pink smoothies are on the coffee table. Olney smiles at them and nods but gets no response. He wonders if they resent his sitting so close. He checks the clock—it's noon.

Both the man and the woman sit with their legs crossed at the knees and with their feet pointing at each other. They are both slim, pale, sandy-haired, and they're both wearing white Velcro walking shoes, white socks, light blue T-shirts, and dark blue cotton shorts, like they're on a competitive, sponsorless mall-walking team. They seem to have perfected a quiet way of conversing in public. They are speaking so quietly that Olney, just five feet away, can't hear them. He can see that their mouths are open, their lips are shaping syllables, and their eyes are fixed on each other, albeit in a sidelong manner.

Olney takes his memo pad and pen out of his shirt pocket, intending to jot down his observations of the couple. He now thinks of them as co-conspirators, as spies. And what are the secrets they keep from each other? No, not spies. Twins. They still live in the house they grew up in, still sleep in their respective childhood bedrooms. The parents are ensconced in some nearby assisted living facility. It's always been the twins against the world. They are two people with a single mind. They are brown-eyed. What else do they share? Olney makes his list: soft dental enamel, hammer toes, underactive thyroids, tinnitus, peanut allergies, and a devotion to Oprah Winfrey. They both carry EpiPens in their fanny packs. And what else? Tums. Nail clippers. Bus passes. Sunglasses and lens cleaner. He names them Paul and Paula Beauchemin. They're school-crossing guards. And now Paul raises his eyebrows— their conversation is becoming animated. Are they talking about him? When Paula sucks the last of her smoothie, and you would expect to hear the flatulent slurp of a straw disturbing air, you hear nothing.

"Mind if I join you?" a man holding a cup of coffee asks.

"Not at all," Olney says.

The man sits and introduces himself. "Brock."

"Olney."

Brock nods at Olney's pad and pen. "You're a writer?"

"I guess I am."

"Me, too."

"What do you write?"

Paul and Paula look at Brock and Olney and then at each other. They rise as one, deposit their plastic cups in the trash, and leave the Koffee Klatch.

Brock pulls a typed manuscript out of his shoulder bag and lays it on the table. "It's a novoir, part novel, part memoir. Could I read you a bit? Tell me what you think."

He reads a scene in which his central character, Brock, is hiking in the Grand Canyon with his pal Remy, and Remy slips on the scree and tumbles over the edge of the path and falls a thousand feet to the sandstone. Horrifying. Except that he stood up and walked away.

Olney says he's glad that was the fiction part, but Brock says, no, that part really happened.

"That doesn't seem possible."

"I know, right? Of course, he didn't walk far. Two steps and he fell flat. He had two broken feet, two broken legs, and two broken hips. He was in shock, of course. They airlifted him out. Spent six months in the hospital and a year in physical therapy."

"Is he okay now?"

"He owns a transmission shop up in Crystal River, but, no, he's not okay."

"But he can walk?"

"More like a hobble. He thinks I pushed him."

"Why do you say that?"

"He told me so." Brock taps his pen on the manuscript. "This is Part Ten. The book is already forty-five hundred pages long. It's like I'm Scandinavian."

"Where is the story headed?"

"Wherever my life leads me."

"Do you think the narrative needs a shape?"

"It has the organic shape of a life."

"Just one thing after another, you mean?"

"Maybe it should end right here in the Koffee Klatch in Melancholy, Florida, with Brock talking to a fellow writer." He makes a note on the top page of his manuscript.

When 12:40 arrives, but Cully does not, Olney leaves the Koffee Klatch without a breakfast kolache, wondering why Cully set up this luncheon date and then didn't show. Overslept? Overdosed? Overwrought? Overwhelmed? If Cully really doesn't want to see him or speak with him, then maybe Olney ought to respect his son's disregard, go back home, and give those little Fry babies a hug. He collapses onto a bus stop bench on Main. There's a metal armrest bisecting the bench intended to keep one from lying down to sleep, as if there were anything wrong or shameful about sleep.

Olney knows he has to at least speak with Cully before he surrenders his quest. He has to tell his son once again that he's loved, he's missed, that he deserves more in his life than indigence, insecurity, and instability. If Cully won't or can't have his father in his life, not now at any rate, and if Olney needs to live at some distance, then at least he'd like to know that his son has a tolerable place to live, a job, and a future that might include peace of mind.

Maybe they're better off apart, and maybe Cully knows that. The problem is that Cully once again has no phone and no mailing address and no computer. Olney thinks, I could buy him another phone. And then he thinks, Will he answer when I call? Will he pawn it?

Lip says, "Let's walk."

"Jesus, you scared the life out of me."

"Unless you're really waiting for a bus."

"He didn't show up."

Lip lights up a cigarette, waves the match in the air, and slips it into his pocket. "The power of addiction is physical." He holds up the cigarette. "Like me and my Camels. But also, it's mental, emotional, social, and spiritual." He exhales the smoke out the side of his mouth and away from Olney.

About Cully, Lip says, "I know he doesn't buy the spiritual side of things, but that's where he's hurting the most. He can get back to his old self if he'll let himself try, but we can't let him feel sorry for himself and blame everyone else for his troubles."

Olney hears the text-tone, excuses himself, and takes his phone out of his pocket. Lip points at his watch and sprints across the street. Tallulah Belle uses Olney's phone sometimes, knows his password, and downloads games. He gets a notice from her that his friends at the Happy Café Facebook group miss him. He sees this as a sign, and he calls Julie, but his call goes to voice mail. Julie can't answer because her phone's in the kitchen, and she's locked herself and her kids in the bathroom, so the kids won't have to see their daddy fire his pistol from the bedroom window at the gas pumps out front. When the shooting stops, when she hears the approaching sirens, Julie tells the kids that everything will be all right.

( )

"I HEARD YOU WERE LOOKING FOR ME," CULLY SAYS, AND OLNEY JUMPS, drops the phone. Cully has a tattoo of a snake coiled around his neck, swallowing its tail at his throat.

Olney says, "You are hard to find."

"A good man always is."

Olney smiles. "But easy to spot. Where were you at noon?"

"My life is complicated."

"It's so good to see your face."

Cully pulls a crooked cigarette out of his pocket, straightens it, and lights up. "What's new with you?"

"As you know I retired, and I'm friendly with a nine-year-old ventriloquist's doll named Buddy who has an acute sense of irony, and I had a girlfriend, whom you met, but she died, and I'm working at the mini-golf course we used to play at—"

"You sound like a busy man."

"I bought a lottery ticket when the payoff reached a billion dollars then I lost the ticket and I had three suspicious-looking moles removed from my back and had my first colonoscopy and was clean so that's good news for both of us I moved the TV out of the house and into the shed so if you want it if you find a place to settle you can have it by the way do you have an email address I learned a lot about dysphagia and Lutherans and crappies and romance novels and Wyatt Tyler who has a forty-seven-game hitting streak going and the Brownies are in Melancholy this weekend and I thought maybe I'd take you to the game—"

"You know I hate baseball."

"Let me take you to lunch."

"Deal."

"Why don't you smile?"

Cully explodes. "What am I, a fucking retail clerk at the cosmetics counter at Nordstrom's?"

Where's that anger coming from? He says, "Koffee Klatch?"

"Grampa's."

"Your tattoo."

"What about it?"

"Nothing."

( )

THE WAITRESS'S HAIR IS LIMP AND LAVENDER. HER NAME TAG READS DORSON. She sets a plate of sweet pastries on the table. Olney's teeth hurt just looking at the Danish and the tarts. Dorson says, "They're complimentary."

Olney says, "Will they tell me I look fabulous?"

Cully shakes his head. "Really?"

There are wooden bowls filled with sugar packets, with plastic cruets of creamer, and with foil-wrapped tablets of butter and margarine on the table. Cully orders bacon, scrambled eggs, and blueberry pancakes. Coffee and orange juice. Olney says he'll have grits and a side of bacon. Yes, coffee as well. Thanks. Cully juggles three cruets of creamer. Olney applauds.

There's an autographed, framed photo of a celebrity chef on the wall over the booth and beside it a starburst clock that must have come from someone's Levittown living room in the sixties. Dorson pours their coffees and leaves the carafe on the table. Cully pours in three French vanilla–flavored creamers into his coffee. No sugar. Splenda.

"I'm worried about you. You don't look healthy. Your pants are falling off your hips."

When the food arrives, Cully rolls a pancake around the scrambled eggs and eats it like a burrito.

Olney always has so much to say to Cully when he rehearses their conversations but has little of importance to say in his presence, and he doesn't know why. Out the window, Olney watches a man standing by a silver sedan, one foot on the ground behind the open door and the other on the car's foot sill. His right arm is resting on the roof. He's holding a cigarette. His left elbow is on the door. He holds a phone to his ear. He taps the roof at every stressed syllable of his emphatic speech. He's giving someone orders, Olney thinks. Black hair cut short, broad-lobed ears, cleft chin. He looks like a Steve. He might be in the debt-collection business.

Cully's finished with his breakfast, and Olney hasn't even buttered his grits. Cully's picking at a strawberry Danish. Olney says, "Lip wonders why you don't go to meetings anymore."

"I've got a strategy for sobriety that's proven more successful than AA."

"What is it?"

"Ketamine."

"Isn't that a party drug?"

"It's working miracles. You take it under a doctor's care. Nasal inhaler. Twice a week for a month."

"I'll ask Samir to look into it."

Cully puts his head in his hands. Olney reaches out and touches Cully's arm.

"I don't need to justify my emotions to you. Take it or leave it. I already hate myself. I don't need you to make it worse."

"What are you talking about?"

"I'm not letting you invalidate something I know is real just because you aren't inside my head."

"What does that even mean? None of us can be in another's head. That's why we talk."

"I'm out of here." Cully slides to the side of the booth.

"Come on. Sit."

He stands. "What?"

"Why don't you let me help you?"

"I don't want it. Help me what? Be like you?"

"You have a drug problem. I want to help you get clean. A problem is not a punishment. Problems can be overcome. It's not a condemnation. It's an obstacle I can help you get around."

He sits. "The drugs are a substitute for companionship."

"No, they're not."

"Adios."

Dorson asks Olney if he'd like to box the pastry.

"Just the check, please."

She clears the dishes.

He says, "The food was terrific, it's just . . ."

She nods. "I know," she says, "I've got two of my own."

Olney takes out his wallet and holds it in his lap. Dorson hands Olney the check and says, "Here's the damage."

( )

OLNEY WILL RESUME HIS EFFORTS TO FIND AND REASON WITH CULLY IN the morning, but for now he doesn't want to think any more about not being close to his son. He sees Robbie and Dante out at the firepit. He pours himself a glass of whiskey, grabs the bottle, and joins them. Dante tells him that Guy turned in early. "Did you know that he sleeps in forty-minute intervals? Don't know how he does it. Internal alarm clock, he says. Forty minutes down, ten minutes up. Tells me he never dreams."

Robbie says she saw a scarlet teenager in the oleander today. "One of those lovely red and black birds. Pretty rare down here." She asks Olney about Cully, and he fills them in on his disappointing encounter with his son. Robbie says he'll come around. They raise their glasses and toast to late-blooming sons. Olney thinks of the parable of the prodigal son and finds solace there. And hope. The prodigal comes home.

Robbie says, " 'For this son of mine was dead and he is alive again.'"

" 'He was lost and now is found,'" Dante says.

"Let's hope so," Olney says.

"It's hard to hold on to your kids," Robbie says. She has two. One daughter is an asshole like her daddy, and just as successful as he is. They're both financial advisers in Requiem. The other is a saint—a doctor without borders in Africa. "What your boy needs," Robbie says, "is some gameful employment."

Olney says. "Some stability and income. After some detox and rehab or a therapist maybe."

"A job with french benefits. He can start feeling better about himself."

Olney tells Dante that Guy mentioned Archons today. "He said these folks were giving you trouble."

"They are the bad guys in our universe. They're bipedal, bibrachial, carnivorous, interdimensional reptilian hybrids, and we are their food. They live beneath the oceans in the hollow core of the earth, and they feed on us, especially our children. We are their cattle, you might say. As long as they have food, they will stay beneath the sea."

"Who gets them their food?"

"Our military and the Babylonian Brotherhood that controls it and promotes the Archontic agenda. And that is why America is continuously at war all over the globe. Not for territory, not for the hearts and minds, not to defend our borders, but to provide the Archons with their protein."

"Are you putting me on, Dante?"

"Perhaps you've read that the earth's core had reversed its rotation?"

"I have."

"The Archons did it. They are arrogant and telepathic. They know your thoughts before you think them. They have viperous heads, dark unmoving eyes, teeth like machetes, and they can be up to twenty feet tall."

"That should make them easy to spot," Robbie says. "A bracer is called for." She holds out her empty glass and Olney fills it.

"How do you know all this, Dante?" Olney says.

"I've completed the coursework at the I AM University and Interplanetary Starseed School."

"Online classes?" Robbie says.

Olney says, "So where is this university?"

Dante points to his head and taps his temple three times. "Don't confuse space with time or matter with energy."

"I'm just trying to understand."

"Plus I've always been a tad psychic. When my ex-wife was screwing around with our Orkin man, I would get a headache every day at four."

Robbie says, "How did you know it was the exterminator she was schtupping?"

"Could smell the permethrin all over her."

"Maybe that accounts for the headaches."

Olney says, "So why don't most of us know about this? How is it kept secret?"

"Because all of your pineal glands—the Mind's Eye—have calcified."

"I think you've devised an intriguing mythology, Dante, but I'll admit to being skeptical. It's all so improbable."

Dante leans forward, elbows on his knees. "Is it any more improbable than light being *both* a wave and a particle? Any more improbable than entangled quarks at either end of the galaxy communicating instantaneously? Faster than the speed of light. This is the far-fetched mythology of physics. The present can affect the past. How about that?" Dante swallows the last of his whiskey. "There are a hundred billion galaxies in our universe. Think about that. And each one of them has ten million to one trillion stars. Hard to imagine, right?"

"You've done your homework."

"And our universe is only one of an infinite number of universes, and because the number is infinite, then every possible history must have played out. So, this conversation we're having right now must have happened an infinite number of times."

"And I don't remember any of them," Robbie says.

Dante says, "If you believe in your physics, then that's your reality. Archons would seem to be easier to comprehend."

( )

THEY'RE IN THE BATHROOM STANDING AT THEIR RESPECTIVE SINKS, staring into their respective mirrors. Taffi sprays her teased hair with

Aqua Net, the way her mother—God rest her soul—taught her. Rylan brushes his teeth for two minutes. Taffi wraps her hair in a toilet-paper turban to protect the shape of her bouffant when she sleeps. She turns left, then right, looks over her shoulder, and decides, Well, that's as good as it gets, I'm afraid. She's wearing her baby-blue babydolls with the flounced hem and the eyelet lace. Rylan flashes a smile and wonders how much it would be to get his teeth whitened at the kiosk at the mall up in Jax. He could write it off. He puts two earplugs in the breast pocket of his seersucker pajamas, short sleeves and short pants. He shuts the light, and they kneel beside their bed and pray for their congregants and for the seven babies slaughtered last week at the day-care center up in Georgia by a gun-wielding child-care aide.

They climb into bed. Rylan shuts off his bedside lamp. Taffi leaves hers on. She says, "Did Buddy seem unusually solemn to you? On the show, I mean?"

"He seemed fine, not so smart-alecky as usual."

"What he said about religion has me thinking."

"What was that?"

"When he said that belief was the least important part of religion. I think maybe he's on to something."

"Honey, he's nine."

"I liked his idea that what's important is that church is a place where we are embraced, accepted, and comforted. The idea that we matter—that's what it's all about, don't you think?"

"We live in a confusing world and an exhausting country."

"And death won't go away."

"'For the trumpet will sound and the dead will be raised imperishable.'"

"So death is like sleep?"

"Your faith is being tested."

"Not yours?"

"Jesus is our guide." Rylan takes Taffi's hand and kisses her palm.

"You write the scripts, Rylan. You put words into Buddy's mouth. You must be questioning some certitudes yourself."

"That's not how it works."

"It isn't?"

"Do you remember when we got Buddy?"

"As soon as we opened the box, he began talking, and he hasn't stopped since."

"I wrote it all down in my journal. We got to know him, and he started thinking for himself, saying what we did not expect him to say, doing what we did not know he would do. So now I let him tell me what he wants to say, and I say it for him. Even if I don't agree."

"That doesn't make sense."

"Shh! Did you hear that?" Rylan puts a finger to his lips. "Listen!"

"Mommy! Daddy!"

Rylan says, "He's up. I'll settle him down. Go to sleep." Rylan steps out of their bed and into his slippers.

( )

WHEN HE AWAKENS SUDDENLY, GUY IS ALERT. HE STEPS OUT OF BED, reaches under the open drawer of the bedside table, and grabs his spring-assisted folding pocketknife, spins as he slaps open the deeply serrated blade, and drives it deep into the belly of his imagined assailant. He checks the bolts on the door and the locks on the windows. He does ten push-ups with the right arm, ten with the left, ten on his fingertips. The incident with the OCD driver today is still bothering him. He does ten pull-ups on the bar in the bathroom doorframe. The driver smiled at Guy, made a gun with his fingers, aimed it at Dante, and "fired" while staring at Guy. He lost the smile when Guy lifted the cuff of his chinos, pulled out the Pocket Ace, and aimed it at the asshole. The driver put the truck in gear and sped off. Guy does ten squats. He'll need a plan to deal with these guys if they're now in the vicinity, and he'll make that plan in forty minutes. He sleeps thinking of the daughter he hardly knew who died at six months while he was deployed in Iraq. By the time he got stateside, his girlfriend, Alyssa's mom, was also gone. Suicide by automobile.

( )

PIXIE IS WORRIED YET AGAIN ABOUT CULLY, AND SHE'S SICK OF HAVING to worry about him, her pal, her beau, her boyfriend, her lover, whatever he is. They are sprawled on what's left of a musty double bed in what's left of Room 4 in what's left of the Sans Souci Motel. Cully's asleep on his back and drooling; Pixie's awake on her side and smoking. He told her before he swallowed the 40 that he thought he would always be like this, be sad and hopeless, that he would never be rid of the pain, and he didn't think he could cope with it much longer. And what would be the point? She called him an oxy moron. She calls him a misfit. Pixie likes to think that *she* might be the point. When Cully gasps for air and then stops breathing, Pixie sits up, yells his name, and punches his arm. When that doesn't work, she shouts his name into his ear and shakes him. When that doesn't rouse him, Pixie screams and grabs his shoulders and pounds his body into the mattress again and again. When she slaps his face, and he wakes, he's groggy, confused, and defiant. He wants to sleep. Pixie makes him stand. When he says he can't walk, says his legs won't do what his brain is telling them to do, she says, What brain? She stands behind him on the smoldering mattress, slips her arms under his, and kicks his heels, left-right, left-right. She pushes him along in front of her. She'll keep him moving until he can walk on his own. She has just saved Cully's life, but he'll never know it. The rest of his life, no matter how miserable or sublime or ordinary, no matter how long, days or decades, is her gift to him, the gift of time.

ALL THAT MATTERS

Pixie wonders how long she's been talking to this guy and what have they been talking about. She's forgotten his question. Her bones are throbbing, and her ears are buzzing. She closes her eyes, and he's still there kneeling in front of her, but his blue eyes are now orange, and his red hat is green. The man touches Pixie's icy hand and repeats his question. "Where is Cully?" Okay, now she gets it. She opens her eyes and drifts away for a bit until she hears the voice again. Pixie tells Lip who tells Robbie who tells Olney to check for Cully at the Sans Souci, only Robbie says "Santucci" (because Cookie Santucci is her best friend at St. Dominic Savio Grammar School), and so it is not until after dark when Olney and Guy find Cully curled on the ground in a clearing in the sea grapes beside the derelict motel. Someone has cut the lock on the now-opened chain-link security gate. They hear Cully's moans before they see him. Guy shines his flashlight toward the sound.

Cully's face is bloody and bruised. When Olney asks if he's okay, Cully rolls his eyes. When Olney asks who did this, Cully shakes his head. That's when Olney notices Cully's toothbrush and a broken lanyard on the ground beside Cully's head and the abrasion on his neck. That's when Guy notices two identical beetle-bodied goons with little pointy heads and narrow eyes leaning against a gray sedan in the motel's gravel parking lot. They seem amused. Guy pockets his flashlight and walks over to the pair. They look at each other and smile, fold their beefy arms across their thoraxes like they're synchronized swimmers.

"You two responsible for this?"

They flex their bloody fists and flare their pulpy nostrils.

"I'm Guy." He extends his open hand. "And you are?"

When he gets no response, Guy says, "All right, I baptize you AC and DC, the assault-and-battery brothers."

"Bite me, dickwad," DC says.

Guy takes a step toward them and gets shoved back and then kicked in the shin by AC. He steps back, pulls the pistol from the concealment holster on his belt, and shoots AC in the offending foot. AC screams and hops on the good foot twice and then drops.

Olney yells, "What the fuck are you doing?"

"Getting their attention."

"You can't just shoot people."

Guy turns back to AC and says, "Stop your blubbering, snowflake," and puts the muzzle of the pistol in DC's face.

DC says, "Are you insane?"

Guy tells DC to empty his pockets and then to empty his brother's: one tactical comb knife; two cans of pepper spray; one pair of zip-tie handcuffs; one 9mm Beretta Nano; one gator-head leather wallet with chain; one bifold trucker wallet with chain. He tells DC to open the trunk. There are five cardboard cartons of what looks like meth, oxy, coke, heroin, bath salts, and X, all packaged in two-by-three-inch Ziploc bags. Guy closes the trunk and smiles. "Get Dopey in the car."

DC says, "You'll pay for this, asshole."

Guy shoots him in the foot. DC screams, he falls, he threatens, he rages. It takes a few minutes for the pair to stumble into the car.

Guy says, "If I were you, I'd drive my sorry ass over to Everglades General pronto. You're both losing a lot of blood."

AC says, "Oh, God, it hurts!"

"You'll be wearing corrective shoes for a while." He peeks inside the car. "No clutch. Your lucky day, Hoppy," he tells DC.

DC starts the engine. Guy shoots out a headlight. "Hope you don't get stopped."

Olney leans into the opened window and says, "What you're doing doesn't make sense. If you kill Cully, you don't get your money back."

"We don't kill people that owe us money," AC says. "We make an example of them."

And off they go. Olney turns to Guy and says, "Was all that necessary?"

"If we hadn't stumbled onto the scene, he might be dead."

"How are we going to get him out of here?"

"I got a guy."

( )

REED'S TENDING TO CULLY'S WOUNDS IN OLNEY'S ROOM. NOTHING seems broken. Cully's lying on his back on the bed holding an ice pack over his swollen left eye. Robbie hands Reed a warm compress from the microwave. Olney's standing in the open doorway trying to reach Samir on the phone. Guy's pacing the walkway, talking out loud and indecipherably to someone Olney can't see. Reed says, "You've been kicked pretty bad in the ribs. It's going to hurt when you laugh." And that makes Cully laugh. And then grimace. "You're right," he tells

Reed. And then he moans. Reed helps Cully to sit up. Cully catches his breath.

Samir tells Olney to take Cully to the ER ASAP. "He could be bleeding internally."

"Will do. And how are you doing, Samir?"

"The knee's better. I'm spending a lot of time with Jen these days. She's taking her meds and feeling better. Up and about. And that Langley is a sweetie."

"Give them my love."

"Call me with the results."

Robbie tells Olney there's an urgent care center on Buttonwood. Olney calls Kat. Guy says, "We're on red alert."

( )

KAT MEETS CULLY AND OLNEY AT THE URGENT CARE CENTER AND breaks down in tears.

Cully says, "Look at us, one big happy family."

In the examining room, Dr. Twiss says, "What happened here?"

Cully says, "Things got a little out of hand in the schoolyard."

Dr. Twiss takes Cully's hands in his and turns his wrists. "I've seen you here before."

Cully says maybe that time he sliced his hand with a box cutter. By mistake.

In the waiting room, Kat and Olney agree that Cully can't go back out on the streets. Kat says she'll speak with Elbert. We've got a foldout in the den. Cully will stay with Olney tonight. "Of course, what he really needs is to get out of Dodge," Olney says.

"Maybe you can take him back to Anastasia."

"I would if he'd come. I'll ask." Olney watches a very pregnant woman grab her toddler and tug. She tells the boy if he sasses her one more time, she'll kick his ass.

The examining room door opens, and Dr. Twiss peeks out. Cully's putting on the Brown Bats T-shirt that Olney loaned him. Too big. Cully asks Dr. Twiss if he has anything for the pain.

"Ibuprofen will take care of the pain and the inflammation."

"But I won't be able to sleep."

"And find some new playmates."

( )

WHILE CULLY CHANGES INTO OLNEY'S LAUNDERED SWEATPANTS IN the bathroom, Olney makes a list of words in his notebook. *Illness, disease, addiction, cure, heal, pain, suffering, death, survival, depression.* He hears Cully curse, but Cully has said he doesn't want help getting dressed.

Guy knocks at the door, opens it, and pops his head inside. "I'm making ropa vieja in the Crock-Pot. Ready in a half hour out by the firepit."

"I'll ask Cully to join us."

Guy closes the door and raps on it twice when he does. Olney reaches for the computer and plays Mark Knopfler on Spotify, which he lowers when Cully joins him. He goes to Cully and takes his arm. Cully says he's okay. He eases himself into the chair at the table and sees the unwritten "Greetings from Melancholy" postcards and beside them on the table a pile of drug rehab program pamphlets. St. Jude's Treatment Center, New Beginnings Addiction Recovery, and Turning Points. He picks them up, waves them. "All of these—" he says, "bogus." He points to a photo of the elegant facilities at St. Jude's. "I've been here. You see this swimming pool—it's an algal swamp."

"How do you know they're all bogus?"

"They aren't in the recovery business. They're in the moneymaking business. And there's more money in relapse than in recovery."

"Some people get well."

"They bilk insurance companies and taxpayers out of millions. They charge five thousand for a urine test. A ten-dollar test! One buck at the Dollar Store. And they do the tests seven days a week."

"Maybe some of them do."

"Eighteen hundred bucks for a counseling session that doesn't take place. Reflections in west Everglades is run by a felon, a pimp who offers clients' sexual services on the website."

"How can a felon get a license to run a rehab center?"

"You put your wife's name on the application. Rehab doesn't work. Stop your dreaming, Dad."

Olney is caught off guard by that "Dad." He can't think straight, but he says, "You're not going to give up, are you?"

Cully drops into the upholstered chair. "No." He shuts his eyes and takes a long, slow breath. "I'm just so fucking sad."

"And we need to do something about it."

"Don't blame an addict for his addiction. That's what the Sackler family does. Blame the addict for taking the pill they addicted him to. These slimy fuckers started the epidemic, fed it, worsened it. The soulless Sackler scum killed hundreds of thousands of people, and they need to be in prison."

Olney sits at the edge of the bed and stares at his folded hands. "What do you want from life, Cully?"

Cully looks up at his father's face and sees his own. "To be happy like everyone else."

Olney knows that happiness can be hard to come by. It's a side effect of aspiration and struggle. "What's the first step in getting there?"

"Percocets always got me there."

"You're confusing happiness with euphoria."

"It'll do."

"Be serious."

"Sorry."

"You shouldn't be alone."

"I know that, but I can't connect." Cully slams his fist on the bed. "How do you think that makes me feel?"

Olney understands that depression comes naturally to Cully. Uninvited but inescapable. Mania, the equalizer, only comes pharmaceutically. There is no middle ground for Cully. Not yet. Olney hears Guy setting up the serving table. "Let's eat."

"I don't even know if I can stand."

Olney holds out his hand. "I'll help you."

( )

PIXIE'S WEARING RUSSIAN-RED LIPSTICK ON HER EYELIDS AND PERSIAN-blue eye shadow on her chapped lips. She's feeling very cosmopolitan. The espadrilles she stole from Goodwill this afternoon match both her eyes and her tie-dyed tube top. She's reading a book she checked out of the library, a popular novel called *Code Name Vermeer*, until she comes to this sentence: "The appalling squeal of the unoiled wheels of Stephen's mobility scooter set Nadine's frangible nerves on edge," and then she can't read one more word and drops the book off the Melancholy Beach Boulevard bridge, where she's standing, and into the Intracoastal, where the cops and the recovery vehicle are hauling a submerged car out of the murky waters near shore. You can see where the car careened through the parking lot of Jimbo's Sandbar and through the waterside patio dining area before hurtling over the seawall and into the drink.

( )

GUY APOLOGIZES FOR HIS ROPA VIEJA. "IT'S MISSING SOMETHING," he says.

Robbie says, "Needs more salt."

Olney says, "Are we still on red alert?"

"Until further notice," Guy says.

Cully says that no one knows he's here, so he should be safe.

Olney asks Cully if he remembers a time when they felt safe—back at Turpentine Park on their boys' nights out.

"Our what?"

"We'd get ice cream, sit on the bench, and talk. You'd chase pigeons and skim rocks across the pond."

"Doesn't ring a bell."

"What *do* you remember?"

"Sitting in my room listening to you and Mom fight."

"How old were you?"

"I don't know. Six?"

"Nothing before that?"

"I don't recognize this Cully you're talking about. That's not me. I think you made him up."

Guys says, "Cully can't remember what happened, and I can remember what *didn't* happen. I remember playing catch with my old man in the backyard, and that never happened. I remember bedtime stories. I remember snuggling with my mom on the sofa. I remember being listened to."

Kat walks into the courtyard and announces that Elbert is cool with Cully staying with them for now. Cully says his goodbyes. Olney asks for a hug and Cully steps into his arms but howls when Olney squeezes too hard. Olney apologizes and says he'll come by tomorrow, so they can all talk.

Robbie opens a bottle of Hennessy. She and Olney fill their snifters. Guy says he's not drinking until the danger is passed.

"Maybe we should call the cops."

"That can't happen. We are also felons, my friend." Guy sets out to walk the perimeter.

Robbie says to Olney, "Are you romanticizing Cully's childhood?"

"No."

"Neuralgia is a dangerous drug."

"Nostalgia?"

"It beautifies the past."

"It's what I remember."

"Or choose to remember. Could you be trying to absolve yourself of responsibility?"

Olney wonders now if Cully was really happy all the time. Did he love going to the park or was he being kind to his old man? Did I keep him to myself and away from his friends?

Robbie asks Olney if he's feeling guilty about what's become of Cully. "Another words, do you blame yourself?"

"I do."

Robbie says, "And you think you need his forgiveness, maybe."

( )

OLNEY'S BACK IN HIS ROOM, AT HIS TABLE, RELIEVED THAT CULLY HAS gone for now. He opens his notebook to the list of words that he hopes will lead him to some understanding of what his son is going through. He turns on the computer and clicks on the dictionary website. Cully's addiction is an illness. A good place to start. *Illness* is defined as a "disease," although there are, to be sure, some distinctions to be made between those two words. *Ill* means "not healthy," "sick," "not normal," and "resulting in suffering." As a noun, *ill* exposes its moral component, "a sin or an evil." Olney puts down his pen, stretches his hand, and hears Dante outside asking Guy what those hoodlums looked like. Like cockroaches, Guy says.

So Cully's addiction is an illness, but is it also a disease, a morbid physical condition? Disease is an affliction, and illness is your response to the affliction. Illness is the human experience of the disease. So you could say that Cully's illness is his body in conflict with itself. What might work that we haven't tried? Maybe a holistic approach would help—mind, body, spirit. And Cully needs a support system that he doesn't seem to get with AA. Olney will look into that Smart Recovery program Cully mentioned.

Cully is in pain and is suffering, Olney thinks. And Auden, that old master, was right as always—suffering goes on while someone else is mowing a lawn or slapping a line-drive single between short and third or biting into a breakfast kolache.

He opens Mireille's notebook to a random page and reads: *Just because you say something is true doesn't mean it is.* He thinks about Cully, who can't remember his past, not preschool, not Turpentine Park, not Spanish Blade, or so he says, and who has forsaken his future and is mired in the present.

( )

NO MATTER WHICH WAY HE TURNS ON THE FOLD-OUT BED, CULLY can't get comfortable. Every muscle aches; every joint throbs. This must be what it's like when you're eighty and you fall down a flight of stairs. He sits up carefully and pushes himself to his feet. He switches on the overhead light and browses through the books on the antique white bookcase. He finds his high school physics textbook, *Physics Principles and Problems*. He loved physics. Entanglement and nonlocality—he loved that spooky idea. And quantum consciousness. A universe built on paradox—what's not to like about that? He opens the book and sees his name written on the inside cover. Why had his mother kept the book? He wanted to talk about ideas in class; guys like Richard Dube and Foster Furcolo were doing the equations in their heads. Calculation paid off; speculation did not. He never took the Physics II class. He never did a lot of things. Imagine dying like he almost did and with so much left to do.

He takes a folded blank piece of foxed paper out of the book. Blank except for this formula written in faded peacock-blue ink: $e^{i\pi} + 1 = 0$, Euler's identity. And that makes him smile. Cully makes a list of what he's never done. *Never learned to play guitar. Never bowled. Never flown in a plane or ridden on a train. I never learned to poach an egg. Never had my eyes examined; never read the Bible; never went to a funeral, opened a bank account, owned a car, climbed a tree, bought a house, won a prize, shaved my head, milked a cow, played a video game, seen* Star Wars, *or eaten an oyster.* He titles his list *My Autobiography* and folds the paper back into the pages of the book. So much of nothing, he thinks.

PUT ON WRONG

Guy speaks to Olney through the closed door. "My name is Alex Marco. My new persona. I like the color red and the Barcelona football club. I love mac and cheese and thin-crust cheese pizza with orange slices on the side. My little brother's name is Theo. My baby sister is dead."

Guy steps back as he opens the door and invites Olney inside. Guy has dyed his hair deep-space-black. "What do you think of it?"

"It looks fake."

He's also shaved his beard. "Fake is the new real." He pulls out a chair and tells Olney to sit. "Breakfast is served." He's soft-boiled four eggs and nuked some bacon in the microwave. He sets a carafe of coffee, a carton of orange juice, and a cup of half-and-half on the table.

"What's all this?" Olney says, referring to the non-nutritional items on the table.

"All this," Guy says, pointing at each item in turn, "is a box of QuikClot clotting gauze, a tactical flashlight, a Taser, and a credit card knife."

"Preparing for combat?"

"We need to find those guys before they find Cully, because if they find Cully, they'll find us, and if they find us, there will be blood."

"Well, we know they're not on foot."

"Is that a joke? Because this isn't funny."

"Find them and then what?"

"You leave that to me." Guy stares at the table and furrows his brow like something is missing. "By the way, I would never sit with my back to a door."

"You told me to sit here."

"You always do what you're told?"

Guy cracks open his eggs and pours the yolks into his open mouth.

Olney says, "I guess we could check the hospitals."

"Walk up to the reception desk and say we're wondering if our friends have been admitted, a pair of repulsive-looking Neanderthals, who may or may not have been shot in one foot or the other?"

"I see your point. You've got yolk on your chin."

Guy wipes his chin with his hand.

"And hair dye right here on your ear."

"Why don't we buy the morning paper and see if there's something in there."

"Because it's not 1995. I'll get my laptop."

"You kids and your computers. How are the eggs?"

"A bit runny."

"The bacon?"

"Toothy."

"You're welcome."

"The coffee's decent."

"We need to keep Cully away from the Dixiewood, or we're all toast. Shit! I forgot the toast."

"I'll be right back."

To Olney's back and the open door, Guy says, "If those clowns went to the cops or to their handlers, someone might be on our trail right now."

When Olney steps back through the open door, he sees that Guy has a pistol pointed at him. "Jesus, Guy."

"Alex." He holsters his gun. "Always knock. Red alert, remember? Knock and announce. No surprises. No loud noises. No sudden moves. Constant vigilance."

Olney fires up the computer. And there on the *Everglades Journal-Gazette* web page is a photo of the car being hauled out of the water. The report notes that the two unidentified men in the submerged car did not survive the accident, and that the Eden Police found weapons in the car. Both men had gunshot wounds.

And one thing had led to another, as it happens. When DC couldn't take his brother's blubbering any longer, he reached over and dope-slapped the pussy, taking his eyes off the road and sending the car on a track toward the water. DC looked up, took the steering wheel in both hands, and slammed his injured foot on the brake with all his dead beef, sending a crushing pain exploding through his body. The foot, it turns out, was not up to the job. More a nudge than a slam.

"Weapons, but no drugs," Olney says. "Might the cops be the handlers?"

A knock at the door alerts Guy, who goes for his gun and stands in a shooting position.

"It's me," Robbie says. "Kat's here to see Olney. She's in his room. So are the cops."

( )

YOU KNOW ALREADY THAT GUY HAS LOST AN INFANT DAUGHTER AND that his double, Alex, lost his younger sister. And you know that Robbie's older, useless daughter is estranged from her. You should also know that Dante has twin sons, thirtyish now, to whom he has not spoken in fifteen years. The boys went with their mother after the divorce, after the affair, after their dad's discovery of our reptilian overlords. The twins, Jake and Esau, own an air-conditioning repair business, Stone Cold. You see their trucks all over town. They live a mile west of the Dixiewood in a duplex with their girlfriends, Misty and Crystal, and their dogs, Hulk and Rock. They may be, Dante suspects, working for the Archons. Reed has three daughters—Jo, an office manager for a sketchy law firm; Amy, a flight attendant for a no-frills airline, and Beth, a chiropodist. The sisters live together in Requiem, Mass., where they were born and will die, and where Reed also lived until he found Jesus and lost his family, and where he met Robbie. He prays for his daughters every day and for his deceased wife who fell through thin ice at Hurd Pond. There is the gravity of blood that holds families together, but there is also an undeniable repulsive force, a dark and mysterious energy that drives all families apart. We are all, it seems to Olney, hurtling away from each other at the speed of light, until that one day when we will be, every one of us, alone.

"He's gone," Kat says. "He may have had words with Elbert, I don't know. When I got out of the shower, they were both gone." She's talking with Jenkins and Smoke, two uniformed deputies with the Everglades County Sheriff's Department.

"You the father?" Jenkins says.

"I'm Cully's father, yes."

Smoke says, "As we told your wife—"

"Ex-wife," Kat says.

"We can't launch an official investigation until he's been missing for twenty-four hours. Usually they turn up, you know what I mean?"

"Understood," Olney says. "You do know he was assaulted last night?"

"Yes. By who?" Smoke says.

"He didn't say."

Jenkins says, "We also know he has a police record and has had issues with controlled substances. Sometimes the best thing for a guy like this is to get locked up for a spell. Three squares, roof over his head, no drugs, and counseling."

Kat says, "Jail is never the best thing for anybody ever. It's not even a good thing."

That makes Jenkins smile.

Olney thanks the officers and says he'll call them if he needs them. When Smoke and Jenkins leave, Kat collapses on the edge of the bed, covers her eyes with her hands, and shakes her head. "I just can't cry anymore about Cully," she says, "and how he doesn't love me or even like me. I don't know what to do."

"He loves you. He just doesn't love himself," Olney says.

Olney sits on the bed and wonders if Jenkins might be right, if prison would wake Cully up, but then he sees Cully trembling in a cell and weeping, and he tries not to think any more about it and takes Kat's hand. "Let's go find him."

"You can't help someone who doesn't want to be helped. You can't change someone who doesn't want to change," Kat says.

( )

LATER, AT HOME, WHEN KAT DISCOVERS HER PURVIS YOUNG, THE PUR-vis that was last night hanging on her kitchen wall over the gas range, leaning against a dumpster in the alley behind Pawnography, she aborts her search for Cully. "He's still a thief. He'll never change." Kat tells Olney she's not going on the search. "I'm not angry," she says. "I'm exhausted." He says goodbye and heads off to find his son and persuade him to either go back to Anastasia with him or to rehab. He'll begin his search at the scene of the crime—the Sans Souci. He'll, of course, be vigilant and prudent.

Olney does not see the pair of monkeys huddled together in the branches of the mangroves, but they see him, and they recognize him as one of the others that were here in the dark; at least, Marie does. Bobby's not so sure—they all look and smell alike. He sounds the leopard alarm because the danger is below. Marie grabs his arm and gives him a maternal shake. Don't make a scene, Bobby. They are both still rattled by the vivid memory of the three furious blasts of thunder that rang out in the dark, and they haven't been able to sleep soundly since. They watch Olney walk in widening circles, stop to pick up a shiny object and then another. He keeps looking over his shoulder. He turns and walks past the building with his head down until he's out of their sight.

Pixie thinks she's seen this guy walking toward her before. But where? She wonders if he'll smile back and guesses he will. Something about his getup suggests as much: the T-shirt with the amusing bat throwing a baseball, the baggy jeans, and the red kicks. Pixie smiles at everyone she passes. It's easy enough to do and results in a pleasant rush of endorphins when they smile back or give her the chin-lift eyebrow-flash. But when they don't return the smile, when they refuse to make eye contact, Pixie then feels an unpleasant rush of spite and derision, and she'll laugh loudly enough that the ignorant asshole will register her disdain, or she'll mutter a mocking and sarcastic remark like, *Isn't she charming?* Or, *No wonder he's alone.* Because the rebuff is a slap in her face, and it hurts.

So what about this red-kicks guy whose graying hair could use some product, whose eyes are puffy, and whose face is sunburned except for the bright white scar over his left eye? She smiles. He smiles back. She slips into one of her accents and says, "G'dye, mite." And now she remembers that she saw this guy talking to Lip O'Brien outside the Dixiewood. Australian, that's what the accent was, Olney thinks. And he smiles again. He fiddles with the bullet casings in his pocket and thinks it would probably be a good idea to get rid of them. He walks past the Intracoastal to the beach and finds an empty bench on the Broadwalk where he can sit and watch the walkers and runners, the Rollerbladers and skateboarders, the mothers pushing baby strollers, the caregivers walking the elderly clients, the kids on pogo sticks, the kids on tricycles, and the families pedaling their surrey bikes, watch them all go by. Here's a kid riding his bike with a scarlet macaw on his shoulder. Here's a thin young man with a pronounced widow's peak walking his gray toy poodle. They both seem to be limping. Olney thinks the dog is limping in sympathy with the man. The macaw says *hello* to Olney in an impressive baritone, but it sounds more like *hippo*. This grizzled graybeard has a slobbering Nile monitor lizard draped across his shoulders. A woman in a plumeria-print muumuu is walking her emerald-green iguana on a leash. A man feeds fried plantains to the diapered young sloth tucked into a BabyBjörn. A dozen or so helmeted Segway riders negotiate a path around a clutch of hefty French-Canadian couples in bikinis and Speedos, eating poutine from take-out boxes. But no Cully.

Olney spots a flashy green and yellow Cuban anole eyeing a cloudless sulphur butterfly that's feeding on a bougainvillea flower. The anole fans his red dewlap and takes a furtive step toward the monarch, and suddenly the monarch flies off and Olney is back in Turpentine Park in Spanish Blade. Cully is five or six. Olney's sitting on a bench, Cully in his red wagon. They are both eating strawberry ice cream in sugar cones. They have spent the last two hours indulging in their other sweet passion, catch-and-release butterfly hunting. Their nets are leaning against the wagon. They caught two zebra longwings, one monarch, a question mark, a Julia, and a pearly eye. The question mark perched on Cully's finger and opened and closed its wings for several seconds while Cully held his breath. One butterfly, the Julia, unfortunately, tore a wing when Cully tried to coax it out of the net and would not, they both knew, live beyond the day. They washed their sticky hands at the water fountain and then sat on the grass to watch the sun set over Palmetto Lake.

( )

THE BLOND GUY DRIVING THE STONE COLD AC SERVICE VAN WAVES Olney on, and Olney waves back as he scoots across Cypress Avenue. He stops at the foot of the bridge and looks down over the half-dozen boats anchored below in the cove. He takes a photo and sends it off to Samir (just then digitally examining a patient's enlarged prostate) and to Julie (reading *The 500 Hats of Bartholomew Cubbins* to the girls): *Thinking of sailing alone around the sheltered nook. Missing you. Touch and go with the boy.*

When Guy, as Alex, sees Olney up ahead, he stops. They shouldn't be seen together. Olney sees Guy, waves, and walks toward him, but just then the bridge's horn blasts, the red lights flash, the crossing gates lower, and the two drawbridge spans rise. Olney watches a handsome family lounging on the deck of a passing pleasure boat. The dad picks up a case of empty beer bottles and drops it into the water. Olney looks around. Apparently, no one else heard the splash or saw the violation. He yells to the people onboard. "What the fuck are you doing?" The shirtless blob in a Greek fisherman's cap, who is at the wheel, answers by gunning his engine and speeding off in a no-wake zone, while Mommy, Daddy, and the kiddies all blow kisses at Olney. When the bridge spans are lowered, Olney sees that Guy is no longer there.

( )

OLNEY STOPS AT PUBLIX FOR STRAWBERRY ICE CREAM, DROPS THE BUL-let casings in the trash barrel by the door, and sees Dante on the bench up front. He sits. Dante's drizzling lemon juice on his sardines.

Dante says, "Would you like one?"

"No, thanks."

"Heavenly. And good for you, too. Decrease insulin resistance. Better than carrots for your eyes."

"I prefer them deep-fried."

"Anything deep-fried. Am I right? In lard."

"Deep-fried, beer-battered tofu burgers."

"You just missed Guy. Went home to cook supper."

"I'll get dessert. Strawberry ice cream."

"Enough for six."

On the walk up Cypress, Dante says, "Another mass shooting at a pickleball tournament in Lantana. You know and I know our government will never do anything about gun control. Well, the Spiritual Hierarchy of Ascended Masters has just about had it. Up to here."

"And they are?"

"Spiritually enlightened beings who, in their past lives, were ordinary humans. When the time is right, they will see to it that all weapons will not fire, discharge, blast, explode, report, shoot, salvo, shower, or volley. Nada. And that's when we become the Planet of Love."

( )

CULLY'S RIGHT SHOULDER THROBS. HE CAN HARDLY LIFT HIS ARM. HIS lower back, where he was kicked, is sore and tender. And something inside, a kidney maybe or his spleen, hurts like hell. But his legs work fine, and those boats moored in the cove are not more than thirty or forty yards offshore. He sees that one small sailboat is half-submerged, nose-down in the shallow water. One fishing boat is draped with a brown tarp. The sailboat with the thirty-foot mast would be too hard to climb up onto.

With the bridge spans up and no traffic passing for the moment, Cully decides to chance it. He stands at the water's edge and strips down. He stuffs his clothes in a plastic Publix sack and wades into the water. He lies on his back, sets the sack on his belly, like he's an otter and it's a sea urchin, and he kicks his way to the anchored powerboat. He steps onto the swim platform and hauls himself up and into the cockpit of the *NautiLady*. He can't stay on deck and risk being seen by people driving over the Cypress Avenue Bridge. He unlatches and opens the cabin door and steps down into the cabin, where he finds two cushioned benches, on one of which he'll sleep. He finds towels in the john and dries off. He finds a T-shirt and shorts in a drawer and puts them on. He pokes around the galley and finds canned vegetables and meat, should he get hungry. He opens the bottle of Pappy Van Winkle bourbon that he finds in the cabinet over the stove. He takes a sip and enjoys the immediate buzz. He tells himself he'll need to be off the boat before dawn. He lies down for a nap on a bench. His dreams begin as they always do—with a computer screen and a list of document files. He scrolls down until he sees the faces of his beetled assailants, clicks the mouse. and then he is underwater inside that car, and he can breathe somehow, but they cannot. His window is open, and he swims to the surface.

( )

AT THE DOOR, ROBBIE'S DATE SAYS, "I'M MARY. WE SPOKE ON THE phone. Pleased to meet you."

Robbie says, "How long ago did you leave the convent?"

"Six months."

"What have you been doing for work since you left?"

"I'm in the health care business. Online. I sell negative-ion sanitary pads, Ultrathistle, wellness balls, and other stuff."

Robbie leads Mary through the motel office to her room. She pours Mary a glass of California burgundy and herself a bit of Anastasia Distillery rum. They toast their new friendship. Robbie hooks a Do Not Disturb sign over the office doorknob and shuts and locks the door. She turns over the sign in the office window so it reads Office Is Closed.

Back in the room, Robbie says, "You'll have to excuse me, Mary, if I seem a bit scattered. Too much excitement around here lately, and I haven't had a proper date in ages." She lights the several candles in the room and douses the desk lamps. She tells Alexa to play Gregorian chants. They sit at the table, where Robbie has set out a platter of rosemary flatbread and a wheel of Saint André cheese. She smiles and says, "Tell me about yourself."

"Well, I believe in love," Mary says. "And in the healing power of touch."

Robbie takes Mary's hand and leans in for a kiss. Their lips meet.

"I believe in the forgiveness of sins and the community of saints."

Robbie snaps off a piece of flatbread and brings it to Mary's mouth. Mary shuts her eyes, opens her mouth, and receives the gift on her tongue. The Benedictine monks sing Thomas Aquinas's words: "Newer rites of grace prevail."

Robbie says, "Come." She takes Mary's hand and leads her across the room to the bed.

( )

REED IS LYING ON HIS BED AND LEAFING THROUGH OLD ISSUES OF *Treasure Chest* comics, currently the one where Chuck White is at his own birthday party, catered by Mom. Chuck is an affable, studious, and athletically gifted student at Steeltown's Catholic high school, and a cub reporter at the *Steeltown News*. He's the child of a problematic mixed marriage. The high school boys wear sports coats and ties to the party. Everyone was white in those days, Reed remembers, not just Chuck. Chuck's dad, an Episcopalian, wears a suit and tie and glasses, and peeks in on the party from the hallway. Chuck's friend Al tells a joke. " 'Johnny, use the word *fascinate* in a sentence,' the teacher says. Johnny says, 'I have nine buttons on my shirt, but I only fasten eight.' "

Reed remembers that *Treasure Chest* arrived on Friday afternoons at St. Damien the Leper Grammar School. He took it home and read it Saturday mornings while eating Wheaties. He thinks he hears "Tantum Ergo" being chanted. The music brings him back to the choir loft at St. Damien's, where Mr. Gallipeau conducted the choir and where he, Reed, was asked not to sing but to mouth the words because he was tone-deaf. Mr. Gallipeau, the fastidious bachelor, given to foot-stomping and fixed glares, who lived with his mother on Caroline Terrace, the whispered-about Mr. Gallipeau, whom Reed once saw sitting alone and crying in a pew beneath a stained-glass window depicting a barefoot Saint Jude, cradling a miniature sailboat in his left arm.

( )

OLNEY AND DANTE RUN INTO LIP OUTSIDE FERRIE'S TAVERN. DANTE says he'll carry the ice cream home and stuff it in his freezer. Olney thanks him, and he and Lip walk inside. Two solemn gentlemen stare into their pints at the end of the bar. Lip fist-bumps Larry Sullivan, the bartender, and introduces him to Olney. Lip orders a club soda with a twist, Olney a shot of Paddy's. Lip says, no, he hasn't seen Cully today. "But I've seen Pixie."

"Who?"

"His girlfriend. She was on her way to see him. And I told her to tell him what you said. You'd take him home or you'd rent him a room. Told her to tell Cully he'd have to show up at the Dixiewood to talk with you first."

"You're the man, Lip."

They toast Wyatt Tyler, who extended his hitting streak last night to forty-eight games. Olney says, "What do you know about those guys they fished out of the Intracoastal?"

"A couple of enforcers. Thugs with drugs."

"How did you find out?"

"All my sibs are cops."

"So did they find drugs in the car?"

"They never find drugs in a car."

"What are you implying?"

"Those two guys are expendables. Brutes in suits."

"We found Cully last night. Lost him again this morning."

"Say a prayer to Saint Anthony."

"He can't seem to stay in one place for long."

"He's alive. He has you. He has hope. That's more than we can say for some people."

"Like our friends at the end of the bar, you mean?"

"My uncles. Marty and Eamon McCarthy."

"You're not on speaking terms?"

"Right now they're beyond speaking. Marty's deaf. Retired fire-fighter. Eamon's an ex-Jesuit with Parkinson's. And they both have advanced liver disease. The family's running a dead pool. I've got

Eamon in November. I'll order them drinks, ones-and-dones, go to my meeting, come back here, and call them a cab for the ride home."

( )

AS THE *NAUTILADY* ROLLS WITH THE RISE AND FALL OF THE GENTLE swells, Cully sits back on the cushioned bench with his feet up on the small dining table, shuts his eyes, and imagines himself on the high seas. He's sailing alone around the world, pulling into port in remote tropical islands, fishing for his supper, catching rainwater in a barrel on deck, sleeping soundly beneath the stars. He thinks maybe he could learn to sail, get his captain's license like Pixie's brother Gerald, and embark on a life of adventure. Maybe invite Pixie along, or is that a coals-to-Newcastle situation? Tomorrow he'll get a book on sailing at the library.

But he already suspects that he'll do no such thing. His sweet tooth keeps him from wandering too far from the sugar bowl. He hears the whistle of a freight train from the tracks a mile and a half west of here, and then a siren and the whoop-whoop of an ambulance. And then it's quiet enough to hear the splash of lapping waves against the hull and then the throb of his own pulse in his ears.

Who knew that, after that first glorious ignition, that initial blast of ecstasy, life as an addict would be one of profound boredom, so profound that even a beating now and then or an excruciating parental intervention or a spell in rehab or a night in jail would serve to break the incapacitating monotony, and so these intrusions are not entirely unwelcomed.

Cully counts the Ativan he took from his mother's coffee canister. Nine. One should do for now. He swallows a pill with a shot of bourbon, lies back, and watches the sun sink behind the Australian pines.

He thinks about his dad, who would be bearable if he weren't so intolerant. The pill is kicking in nicely. He knows what he has lost, knows that he should be sweeter to his parents—they do love him—but he just can't. And anyway, how is love going to solve anything? He'll go to the Dixiewood after a snooze. Talk to his dad about the offer of a room. Mollify the old man. Get a meal, if nothing else.

ACCIDENTS WILL HAPPEN

"If you don't eat your placenta, something else will," Larry Sullivan tells Olney. He looks up from his steno pad and bites the barrel of his pen. "How does that sound?"

"You have my attention."

"Good, I'll lead with that." Larry's writing his prebituary. He has no plans to die soon, but you can't leave your legacy in the hands of people who don't know the truth from the facts, from the lies, from the rumors. Olney takes no offense. Larry tells Olney that his mother Margaret (Peggy) Mary (née O'Sullivan) Sullivan, God rest her soul, believed that whoever or whatever devoured your placenta would control your life.

"Did she?"

"She did. And because she was not about to ingest an expelled vascular organ no matter how well it was prepared, not even in a beef-and-Guinness stew, she carried the afterbirth home from the hospital and chose to bury it just up the road here, up off Main. There's an FP&L substation on the very spot now."

"By the canal?"

"Yes, and whenever there's a power surge, I can feel it in my teeth."

"How do you think you'll die, Larry?"

"Texting and driving, like everyone else."

"Maybe you could pencil that in, in the opening paragraph."

Olney orders a round for the McCarthy brothers and a double shot of Irish for himself. What would he include in his own obit? The wife, the child, the jobs, the facts. All his life Olney has never really been sure if his memories are factual and the recalled events actually happened to him, or if he read about them or saw them at the movies, or if they were lies he made up or stories he told or if he dreamed them or imagined them. Maybe Robbie was right about his nostalgia. Memories that you imagine. They are all real, if not all factual. And does it matter?

Abandonment is a recurring theme in Olney's life. He can't be the last person to leave a meeting or a social gathering. He doesn't mind solitude. He minds being left behind. He panics. He traces this fear to a traumatic day when he was six and his dad dropped him at the Palace to see a movie that he no longer remembers. But his dad forgot to pick him up when the movie ended, and his mother was visiting her sister, Aunt Teddy, in Cross City. Olney stood there downtown, not knowing his way home, not having a dime to make a phone call. Stood there for three hours. Day turned to night. Dismay turned to alarm. But he did not relinquish hope.

Dad showed up. He'd fallen asleep. What's the big deal? You knew I'd be here. But did any of this—the movie, the wait, the panic—really happen? Does the recollection of the event explain the dread or does the dread explain the memory? Did Olney, in fact, become aware of this inexplicable and illogical fear and then create a narrative that would explain it? A possibility that has not occurred to Olney. What has occurred to him, a lesson learned, call it, is that to live without hope is to die.

Olney sets his empty glass on top of his five-dollar bill and says so long to Larry Sullivan. He waves goodbye to the oblivious McCarthys and heads off for the Dixiewood. As he walks, he looks ahead but doesn't see what's in front of his eyes. His mind is elsewhere. He's watching Cully, a few years from now, in a high school classroom teaching American History. Cully writes, *Ocoee Massacre, 1920*, on the whiteboard. Cully's a father of two, a boy and a girl, Holden and Esme, and he understands how fathers are helplessly spellbound by their kids. Cully tells the class that this event is "the bloodiest day in American political history."

And then Cully's telling his students that a rabid mob of white citizens murdered at least sixty black citizens of Ocoee because a few of them had the temerity to try to vote in the national election. The mob lynched July Perry, a prominent black farmer, and left his bullet-riddled body hanging from a telephone pole. The mob then burned down every African American's home they could, burned down the black churches, the black school, and every black business in town. That's how great American was.

When Olney arrives back at the Dixiewood, Neutron is curled on the plastic lawn chair outside Olney's room. Olney scratches Neutron's orange noggin, and Neutron hops down and rubs herself along and between Olney's legs. "Shall we dance?" Olney says, and he thinks about Mireille wanting tap pants, and he smiles. He opens the door, and Neutron scoots inside and leaps on the bed for a belly rub during which she bites Olney's hand. Because that's the way it's done. After the rub, Olney fills Neutron's Tupperware bowl with wet food and sets it on the floor by the wastebasket.

He calls Julie in Anastasia, tells her he's feeling homesick. She tells him the girls miss him and send baskets of kisses. "It's Hedy's birthday. I'll have her call you when I get home. And guess what? Pigs fly. Since he somehow got probation and a court-ordered therapy and community service, Lonnie's spending more time with his loving family and less with his ratbag brothers. The girls need their daddy, so we're working things out." She and Auralee have joined the Anastasia Women's Chorale. "We meet every Thursday evening at the Methodist church and raise a joyful noise. We do a cappella ballads and sacred music." And when Olney asks, Julie sings a bit of "Barbara Allen" into the phone. She does. "There's no *practical* reason to get together with a dozen other ladies and sing these old songs in an empty church. And that's why I love it."

Olney calls Samir, who is in his office recovering from his last therapeutic encounter. After treating a four-year-old for an ear infection, Samir looked at the boy's chart and told the parents the boy was due for his second dose of measles, mumps, and rubella vaccine at his next scheduled visit. Mom and Dad said that wouldn't be happening. They've learned that the vaccine is derived from monkey brains, and they don't want Gordito picking up food with his feet, baring his teeth, and throwing his feces at them.

Samir reports that he has Jen on the right mood stabilizers, and they are enjoying each other's company. He and Langley have a date for miniature golf this evening. "Your friend Taffi Burgess from the TV show is gravely ill, but she's not seeking medical help. She's waiting for God to heal her."

Olney recalls that he had a premonition of Taffi's illness a few days ago, a foreboding that he dismissed as fanciful because how can *his* present know anything about *her* future? In fact, it is Olney's recollection that is fanciful. He had no presentiment of misfortune, but now he has subconsciously changed his past because having the premonition connects him more closely to Taffi, to the Burgesses, and to his life in Anastasia with Mireille.

Olney calls Althea and asks her what she's reading. Right now she's reading *The Ticket That Imploded.* "It's my first Man-slash-Man." She reads him the jacket copy. "When Trevor Beaty's shih tzu, Mr. Blue, is swept away by a rip current at Dog Beach, he is rescued by Niall Gooch, a reference librarian in Buttonwood Bay. Trevor is overwhelmed with gratitude and embraces Niall, and they both understand instantly that something electric and undeniable just happened. Soon they are sharing lunch, drinks after work, and eventually steamy weekends at the Gays Inn in Key West.

"When Trevor throws a birthday party for Niall, Niall arrives with his longtime companion, Andrew White, owner of Ticket to Ride, a law firm specializing in traffic violations. Trevor is crestfallen. Niall takes him aside and says, 'I thought you knew. Everyone knows. We *do* have something special, you and I, but we're continual, not continuous.' Trevor is devastated, but decides he'll do whatever is necessary to win the heart of his beloved. First, he'll get himself stopped for speeding on A1A."

Dewey takes the phone from Althea and walks out to the front porch. He asks how Cully is doing, says he has a good feeling about the outcome. He reminds Olney that today Wyatt Tyler goes after the record in a double-header against the Melancholy Danes. The longest hitting streak in league history. "And I've got a good feeling about that, too." Olney says his search for Cully will keep him from going to the game. Dewey tells Olney he's keeping the AC at seventy-eight in his house if that's okay. Perfect, Olney says.

Olney sits at his table and opens his notebook. He draws a picture of Neutron eating. He says, "Well, Neutie Kazootie, will you be coming with me back to Anastasia?" Neutron looks at Olney, blinks once, and turns back to her food. Olney looks out the window and sees Reed standing at the firepit praying the rosary.

Olney makes a note to send a get-well card to Taffi and a check to Rylan. Taffi will never again be in that TV kitchen with her husband and her nine-year-old boy. And Olney will never again be in that small kitchen in Spanish Blade with his wife and nine-year-old son. The simple kitchen with the Hotpoint fridge, the Florence gas range, the pine double-drop-leaf table, and the framed Clementine Hunter print by the door of a baptism on the Cane River with the white church at the top of the hill. He remembers the day that Cully made supper for the family on his mother's birthday. Planned the menu, did the shopping with Olney, and did the cooking with Kat's help. Pineapple-and-banana salad, scrambled eggs, sweet corn, and lemon sherbet for dessert. And Olney and Cully sang "Happy Birthday," and then they all sang "Mockingbird," and then they put on a Michael Jackson CD and bopped until they dropped. And every Sunday morning they cooked and ate breakfast together, and it was always the same meal—grits, cheddar and bacon crumbles, topped with a sunny side egg. Cully's favorite. And every Sunday afternoon, Culley and Olney built an improvised Hot Wheels track that snaked from the living room, through the kitchen, and into the den, and they raced their favorite cars. Cully's favorite was a magenta '55 Chevy Bel Air with a yellow roof that he called the Big Deal; Olney's was a '60 Ford Econoline pickup, orange with black flames, that he called the Burner. First car to win eleven races was the champ. The champ was always the Big Deal.

Olney takes notes for a story he wants to write about loving parents and their exemplary child. The boy's a cello prodigy who could play Bach's Sixth Cello Suite flawlessly when he was ten and who is a recent summa cum laude graduate of the state university with a double major in music and information technology. Olney names the parents Mozelle and Frank for now, the Alldays. Frank's a pharmacist and hiking enthusiast. Mozelle's a nurse practitioner and the volunteer director of the community food bank. The son? Call him Richard, Richard Kyle, goes by Ricky. At the end of the summer, Ricky's off to his Ph.D. program at an Ivy League school on a full ride. Mozelle and Frank are probably more excited than Ricky is.

Ricky has a long-distance girlfriend he met online, the way kids do these days. She lives in Ohio and plays the oboe. Early in the summer, Ricky spends most of his time in his room, on his computer, texting Unni or FaceTiming with her. They've never met in person but seem over the moon with their romance. When Mozelle offers to buy him a plane ticket to Columbus, Ricky flinches, squints, holds up his palm, and says, I got this. When he's not talking to Unni, Ricky's surfing the dark web, as he calls it, looking for God knows what. Ricky takes his lunch to his room and skips supper until Frank and Mozelle have gone to bed. He takes a pass on heading to the beach for a week with his parents and opts out of the annual July 4 Allday family reunion in the mountains. "Allday and All of the Night" is the theme. Your cousins will miss you, Mozelle says. He's anxious about school, Frank tells the disappointed aunts and uncles.

And then one day, Mozelle and Frank get home from work with Chinese take-out to find a note from Ricky on the kitchen counter. *You will never see me again. We have no relationship.* Mozelle calls Ricky's cell. No longer in service. He left with his technology, his skateboard, and a duffel bag stuffed with clothes, from what they can tell. He did not take his cello. Frank calls the police. An officer arrives and reads the note, inspects the bedroom, and tells the Alldays that Ricky is an adult and is free to live where he wants. He's missing from your life, but he's not officially missing, in the foul play sense of the word. They hire a PI, tell him about Ohio and the dark web. Ricky does not register for school, and Olney has the trouble he was looking for.

Frank and Mozelle try to get on with their lives. At first they don't tell anyone in their families; then they tell everyone. At first they throw themselves into their jobs; then Mozelle takes a leave so she can try to track down her boy. For a while they hear nothing from the PI, and then he calls with news. Their son is alive and well and married and living in one of those open-carry states out West. He has a website which they can visit. He's changed his name, legally, to Johnny Pascal, calls himself a philosopher on his website, but he's a philosopher in the same delusional sense that Ayn Rand is a philosopher. You'll see that he espouses such traditional American values as white supremacy, misogyny, and xenophobia. And there's other disturbing news. *You two, as his family of origin, have been disowned, disacknowledged, disavowed, DeFOOed they call it, the clever bastards. Yours was an involuntary relationship that Ricky has severed.* So he wrote on the website. *And you probably miss having a victim around the house to abuse*, he also wrote. The PI gives the Alldays what he thinks might be Johnny's street address.

So that's what they know when they sit down at the kitchen table to discuss what they'll need to do. What they don't know is that Ricky will soon be famous, at least in the burgeoning world of conspiracy theorists, and will soon be as filthy rich as a faith-healing televangelist and just as arrogant. And they don't know that soon they will have three beguiling granddaughters whom they will never see, never hold, and never get a chance love. Olney pulls up a chair to the table and watches his couple.

And what *will* they do? Olney knows that if he looks closely and slowly at his characters, they will do something. Simply wait. Simply watch. Looks like Frank's got Dupuytren's contracture, from the look of the right ring finger. Olney turns to Mozelle and is startled to see that she looks exactly like Mireille. Startled and then delighted. When Mozelle asks Frank to make her a drink and make it a double, Olney hears that voice and realizes this is not a Mireille look-alike;

this is Mireille. When Frank leaves the kitchen, she looks at Olney and smiles. "I didn't expect to see you so soon." She touches his hand, and he gets a chill. She says, "We've got to get our boys back, don't we?" And now Olney can't wait to write the story, to hang out with Mireille. She's going to eat well. She's going to become an Internet sleuth. She's going to find that boy, and that's when everything will intensify.

( )

GUY AND DANTE ARE IN GUY'S ROOM GETTING THE EVENING'S COM-munal meal together. Burgers and hot dogs. Guy's on edge. The hot dogs are actually Big John's bright red pickled sausages. They come in a half-gallon jar and keep without refrigeration—perfect for motel living. The burgers are ground horsemeat, which no one needs to know about, from a slaughterhouse in Andytown. Guy did a felonious solid for the butcher and was paid in product. It's a crime to possess horse-meat in Everglades County, but it would be a crime to let it go to waste. So let it go to waist.

"Redundancy and situation awareness," Guy says. "That's how we stay alive. You need to know the meaning of your surroundings regard-ing time and space."

"Aren't they the same thing?"

"Observe, orient, decide, act. You need to check your six and be aware of anomalies: something that should happen, but doesn't; some-thing that should not happen, but does."

"Do you have buns for these babies?"

"Bottom dresser drawer." Guy puts down a mound of meat on the counter, wipes his hands on his apron, and says, "And you need backup." He dips his hand into the Crock-Pot and pulls out a handgun. He opens the small fridge. "Shit!"

"What?"

"We're out of mustard."

"I've got some. I'll get it," Dante says.

Guy says, "Leave the door unlocked. I'll be up to my elbows in ground Seabiscuit."

"What?"

"Just knock and announce before you enter."

( )

NEUTRON'S SPRAWLED ACROSS THE TABLE AND FLICKING HER TAIL IN Olney's notebook. Olney puts down his pen. Neutron swats it off the table. "I'll get you some milk," Olney says. But he has no milk. "I'll be right back," he says. He picks up the cat's ceramic bowl and leaves the door cracked in case Neutron wants to roam. He heads to Guy's.

Guy doesn't hear a knock, but he does hear the groan of the slowly opening door. He slaps a burger patty on the table and reaches into the Crock-Pot for his SW22 Victory. He grips it in both hands and says, "Dante?" When Olney shoulders the door open and holds out the empty bowl, he sees an earsplitting flash of blinding light. Guy sees a puff of white smoke exit the wound in Olney's gut. When the puff clears, he sees the burned shirt and black hole from which no escape is possible. He sees his friend stiffen, slump, and fall into the room, knees first and then face. Dante's at the door wanting to know what happened. He says, "What have you done?"

Robbie peeks around Dante and sees what Guy has done. "Jesus, Mary, and Joseph!" She calls 911 and almost immediately hears the sirens from the fire station two blocks south. Guy lowers his gun and backs away, then walks to the bathroom and locks the door. Reed squeezes past Dante and bends over Olney. He sees the laceration on Olney's forehead from when he fell. He tells Robbie to fetch some fresh linens, sheets, pillowcases, something. He checks Olney's pulse. The sirens stop and Robbie is back with laundered towels, and Reed begins to sop up the gurgling blood.

Robbie says, "Is he going to be okay?"

"He's not going to be okay, but he might survive." Reed murmurs a prayer. He stands and backs away from Olney when the two paramedics enter. He rubs his arthritic left knee.

The first paramedic slips on purple nitrile gloves, kneels, and sees that Olney is breathing, if faintly. He slips the Ambu bag over Olney's face. The second paramedic lifts the sopping towel from Olney's abdomen and says, "We don't have time for intubation. Scoop and run."

The first paramedic says, "Board and collar this guy. I'll call the hospital. They'll be waiting for us." He calls in a trauma alert, code red. GSW to abdomen.

Olney is, he realizes, at a gathering of friends, but doesn't know how he got here or where *here* is. His father's whispering in his ear. "We need to go."

Olney says, "I knew you'd come."

Outside, a pair of Everglades County deputies arrive, two officers named Schaefer, a young man and an older woman. Robbie thinks they could be mother and son, and they are. Rachel and Elliot Schaefer. They step away from the door as the paramedics wheel Olney out on a gurney. "Easy does it," the second paramedic says. They lift Olney into the ambulance, and in a moment they head off, blue lights flashing, sirens wailing.

The Deputies Schaefer enter the room and step around the puddle of blood. Dante follows them. Deputy Rachel says, "What happened here?"

"Got shot," Dante says.

"By whom?"

"By Alex," Dante says.

"By Guy," Reed says.

"Same difference," Dante says.

"How so?" Deputy Elliot says.

"An alias," Reed says.

A flash of lightning is followed by what sounds like an explosion. They jump. Wait. Breathe again. Lightning has struck the FP&L substation. The AC unit over the door rumbles to a stop, and the lit bulb on the bedside table lamp pops and goes dark.

At Ferrie's Tavern, Larry Sullivan grips the bar and steels himself against the drilling pain in his teeth. When it passes, he shakes his head and rubs his mouth.

Deputy Rachel says, "Why would this guy Alex shoot . . ."

"Olney," Reed says.

Dante says, "Shot because he was working with the Archons."

"The who?" Deputy Elliot says.

Robbie says, "Stop it with the Archon nonsense."

Dante says, "The Doom Thirty-three agenda is in operation."

Deputy Elliot says, "What's your name, partner?"

"Dante."

"I'll need to see some ID."

"In my room. I'll get it." Dante steps outside, walks past his room, past the storage shed, around the corner of the motel, picks up his pace up Mango Court, and does not return to the scene of the crime.

Deputy Rachel says, "So is it Guy or Alex?"

Reed says, "Guy A. Boy."

"He's a boy?"

And that's when Guy, the man, steps out of the bathroom, crying, holding the stainless-steel Victory to his temple, and fires a bullet into his own brain before Deputy Elliot can say, "Put the weapon down, sir. We can work this out." The bullet punches out an oval wound in his skull, driving fragments of bone into the brain. The bullet's intercranial journey is brief but catastrophic. It pierces the corpus callosum, ricochets off the skull opposite the entry, and buries itself in the occipital lobe.

Deputy Rachel calls for backup.

In the ambulance, with the monitor and sinus tach attached, the attending paramedic checks Olney's vitals. Heart rate 130. Blood pressure eighty-four over sixty. He says, "He's headed for the eternal care unit, I'm afraid."

When the Kia Soul ahead does not pull to the curb, the ambulance driver shifts the siren from *wail* to *piercer*, and that gets the Kia's attention and the attention of Brock, who's sitting at the window in the Koffee Klatch, working on his novoir. He looks up from the passage he's writing about the young man with the neck tattoo who came into the Koffee Klatch yesterday.

The driver asks the ambulance attendant about his date last night with the cute little nursing student.

"We had a great time. Pizza and a movie at her place."

"How old is she?"

"Eighteen." And off the driver's amused look, he adds, "I check IDs."

Olney's wallet is missing, and he can't remember where he could have left it. Seems like he's spent his life losing things. He can't fly home without his driver's license. Where am I? Who's holding my hand? Dad?

The driver takes a call on his radio. "Roger that. ETA two minutes." Just then another ambulance blows through the red right at Heliconia in front of them. "What the hell!"

The driver turns right and follows the ambulance that is carrying an unconscious Wyatt Tyler, who was struck in the left eye by a fastball at River Bank Field, which ended his evening, his quest for the hitting record, and, he will learn, his baseball career.

The driver says, "We thought this was our last job, but we've got another blue call."

"Where?"

"Back at the Dixiewood."

Pixie thinks maybe the guy with the NOT TODAY, SATAN T-shirt didn't hear her say hi over the shriek of the sirens, so she turns, and taps him on the shoulder, and when he looks at her, she smiles and waves. He nods. He's got a heart-shaped face, and Pixie thinks he'd look good in a pair of rectangular-framed glasses. Black with rose-tinted lenses.

Cully opens his eyes, and when he doesn't recognize where he is, he shuts them again. This darkness he does know. Ah yes, the *NautiLady*. He sits up and sees that the clock on the microwave reads 5:59. Nice to wake before dark. He reaches for the bourbon and drinks. He'll go to the Dixiewood. He'll consider Anastasia but probably opt for the rent.

Olney's ambulance is given priority and pulls around the ambulance that had been in front of it. They're met by two trauma surgeons and two nurses. Olney's placed on a stretcher, and they all head for the ER. The attender says, We're fifteen minutes out from the event. The driver tells the docs he thinks it was a small-caliber bullet. And he tells them they'll be back shortly with another victim.

The nurse, Mark, slaps a stopwatch on the wall of the ER. His partner, Lucy, cuts the clothing off Olney and bags it for the cops. Dr. Bullens says, "We need a lateral neck X-ray and a flat plate abdomen. And have OR stand by."

Dr. Gwilliam says she's made two large-bore IVs. "Run normal saline wide open," she tells Mark.

Olney thinks, You finally fall asleep and then the racket starts. He can hear voices outside but can't hear what they're saying. He's at the kitchen table going through a set of index cards with Glorietta's prescriptions for leading a well-ordered life of addiction.

- Head off the table.
- Stop before you start.
- No hand-me-down needles.
- No open flames in your bedroom.

Tiger is in the living room because he's dead. Is that Bunny from the Crappie House with him? Olney's girlfriend must be in there with him. He can't remember her name. Begins with an *M*. Names are the first to go. He'll remember it later when he's not thinking about it. Names and then nouns.

In Anastasia, Julie calls Olney so Hedy can say hi and when are you coming home. But Julie can't reach him. His voice-mail box is full. She calls Samir. He's at the miniature golf course with Langley. She's beating me like an old Persian carpet. Jen's sitting on a bench eating pine nuts and reading Alice Munro's "Carried Away." Samir says when he reaches Olney, he'll have him call Hedy with a birthday greeting.

Out his kitchen window, Olney sees a luminescent woman in a blue bathing suit walking on her hands toward Althea's window. Althea must be reading a Werner Herzog romance novel. When he turns back, Buddy's sitting across from him at the table. White shirt, plaid suspenders, red bow tie. Buddy says, "Mireille."

But Buddy's not there. Olney looks around, hears Buddy say, "The name you were trying to remember." And then Buddy asks after Cully, and Olney says he's good. And he sees Buddy sitting across from him and Buddy says, Is he? and lifts his disarming eyebrows, and then he's not there. He's at Olney's side. Olney tells Buddy that Cully teaches high school now. Buddy says, Oh, does he? Those eyebrows again. He shifts his eyes, and Olney asks him who he's looking at. The audience at home, he says.

Dr. Bullens says that the entry wound is over the liver. The bullet's path is unclear. The gall bladder might be involved and the small intestine. No exit wound identified. "Call the lab," he says, "for emergency blood." The Foley catheter and the NG tube are in place.

Cully's in the head grabbing a bottle of diazepam and a slightly used blue Oral B toothbrush when he notices the domed camera on the ceiling with a 360-degree view of the cabin. Someone's watching him right now on a home computer. And someone else must already be on his way to nab him. He drops his gear onto the swim platform. He steps down and reaches for the dinghy tied up to the *NautiLady*. He unties the knot and pushes off. He rows himself to shore. He ties the dinghy to a tree—no sense being an asshole—and heads for the Sans Souci to stash his stuff. He settles into Room 17, figures he has time for an appetizer and a drink before heading off to see his dad. He sits on the crumbling mattress. He opens a slightly stale box of Kellogg's Town House Flatbread Crisps, drinks some bourbon, and chills. He uses what's left of a dresser as a table. He's trying to save the Ativan, so he swallows a diazepam and washes it down with the Pappy.

A nap, like the one he just took on the boat, should have refreshed him, but he's feeling tired. His body feels heavy, like they just turned the gravity up to eleven. One more drink and he'll hit the road. Now he has a rash on his arms. He's allergic to pomegranate, but he hasn't had any. His throat is scratchy, his tongue and face are swollen. He's having to catch his breath. He lies down, lies still. It'll pass.

Olney lifts his head from the table when he hears his name and sees Cully across from him. He wants to know what happened to Buddy. Cully apologizes for forgetting to bring the tomatoes from his garden. They hear the call of the barred owl and the chime of the honeysuckle. Olney sees himself on a gurney being wheeled along a hospital corridor by the Silpher twins. They're humming that song about Ezekiel and the wheels. Cully asks him what it was like getting shot. Olney says,

Is that what it was? Well, at first you feel nothing. And then you feel everything. And then you feel nothing again. He tells Cully he's dying, but I'm glad I got to see you safe and happy.

The crime-scene tape is still up around Guy's room. The Schaefers have gone, but other deputies and the forensic investigators are still collecting evidence. The TV crews are getting it all on video. More thunder; still no rain. Robbie pokes at the logs in the fire with a golf club and pours another drink for her and Reed.

Reed shuts his eyes and lets the warmth of the whiskey flow to his stomach. "I'm praying that Olney makes it." He flexes his knee.

Neutron shows herself and rubs her length along Robbie's leg. She chatters and squeaks. Sounds like a seagull, Reed thinks.

Robbie says, "Poor baby." She rubs Neutron's ears and scratches beneath her chin. Neutron sits for more of the same, stares into the crackling fire.

Deputies Rachel and Elliot Schaefer sit in their squad car in the parking lot of Se Llama Peru eating lomo saltado.

"Elliot, you need to visit your father tomorrow."

"He doesn't know who I am."

"He knows. He just can't respond."

"Doesn't it break your heart to see him like that?"

"Yes. Now eat your supper. We've got reports to write."

The radio crackles.

Lucy lifts Olney's eyelid and shines a light on his pupil. "Fully dilated, nonreactive. Fisheye."

Mark says, "We're losing him. Heart one-forty-five. BP sixty." He stares at the monitor, says, "Escape beats."

Meanwhile, Cully has passed from awareness—as vague as it was—to oblivion and is now beyond thought, beyond dreams, and beyond sentience. His breathing is labored, halting, and is punctuated with snorts and gasps. He's been in this altered state before, but, of course, can't remember that time when his father found him unresponsive, naked and face down in the bathtub, and lifted him up, yelled his name, pounded his chest, grabbed him by the shoulders, and hauled him out of the water and onto the tile and shook him until Cully woke and said he was just overtired, that's all, and the warm bath was so relaxing. Marie pokes Cully's face and Bobby howls. That usually works.

Olney sits up and says, "I need to get dressed."

The woman in the mint-green scrubs says, "You're not going anywhere."

"I'm going home."

"You've been shot."

Olney's eyes close and he collapses back on the surgical table.

The heart monitor beats more and more rapidly until it settles into a single continuous note that sets off Mark's tinnitus. He looks over at the body lying on the table under the spotlight as the monitor's rhythm line goes flat.

On his front porch in Anastasia, Dewey sings:

Sheep, sheep, don't you know the road?
Yes, my Lord, I know the road.
And don't you know the road leads home?
Yes, sweet Lord, I cry for home.

I WONDER WHERE YOU ARE TONIGHT

Olney wants to tell the dead ones in the living room about his dire status, but he no longer has the words, just pictures and sounds and smells. He's home, but he doesn't know how he got here.

( )

MARIE AND BOBBY FINISH THE LAST OF THE FLATBREAD CRISPS. MARIE reaches into Cully's shirt pocket and pulls out a bottle of pills. She shakes it, flips the cap off, and sniffs. She dumps the pills on the ground, picks one up, and examines it. She drops the pill, turns, and walks away from Cully. Bobby follows her out of Room 17. They groom each other by the empty pool before climbing a red mangrove and vanishing into the branches.

( )

THE S'MOORES, ROSE, TULIP, AND IRIS, EACH ASLEEP IN HER OWN BED, each wearing identical purple-and-white-striped Sleep Squad jammies and Starburst candy-wrapper bracelets on their left wrists, each clutching identical plush bunnies—Honey, Sunny, and Funny—share a dream inspired by a book they were reading before lights-out, a dream about Nancy Drew, detective, and a blue wheel of fire deep in the woods.

( )

DEWEY LIES ON HIS COT BESIDE THE CRIB WHERE HE PILES HIS FOLDED clothes. He's listening to the Brown Bats Radio Network for breaking news on Wyatt's condition and praying for Wyatt to recover, return to the team, and begin another hitting streak. He should get up now and reheat the chicken and dumplings. He turns off the radio and sings, "Why do I still live on?" He hums, slides his feet into his slippers. He stares at the stenciled message he once painted on the wall above the crib: WELCOME, LITTLE ONE. "While the young, the fair have vanished from the day before their sorrows had begun."

( )

DR. GWILLIAM BEGINS HER HEART MASSAGE ON OLNEY.

( )

ALTHEA READS *THE MADE-MAN AND THE MAIDEN,* A MAFIA ROMANCE SET in Providence, Rhode Island. Carlo "Elvis" Castiello, enforcer for the Buffone crime family, has made the mistake of falling head over heels in love with Lydia Battista, an unassuming beauty who loves coffee milk, quahogs, and Carlo. He doesn't know how he could live without her. She even thinks his jokes are funny. He's handsome, thoughtful, and breathtaking in bed. He's also been ordered to whack Lydia's dad, Tony "Ziti" Battista. Carlo wonders if their love is strong enough to survive her grief and the overwhelming loss. And then Dewey's standing by Althea's chair. He says, "Can we talk?"

( )

ELBERT ARRIVES AT THE ER WITH COFFEE AND A GUAVA-AND-CHEESE empanada for Kat. No, she says, they haven't told me anything, and the golden hour is almost up. They have an hour to stop the bleeding. He says, I can stay with you, or I can go look for Cully. Look, she says. He should be here with his dad. Elbert notices the TV is on to Fox News. At least he can't hear whoever it is defending white supremacy from this far away.

( )

ALL THREE ARE IN THE BED HOLDING HANDS, RYLAN TO TAFFI'S LEFT, Buddy to her right; all their eyes are closed. The lights are off, the curtains drawn. Rylan says, "Yea, though I walk through the valley of the shadow of death, I will fear no evil; for thou art with me." Buddy clears his throat and quotes Auden. "Death is the sound of distant thunder at a picnic."

( )

JULIE AND THE KIDS ARE IN DONNY BURKE'S LINE AT KMART—THE kids love Donny; he gives them lollipops—when she recognizes the couple in front of her. She taps the man on the shoulder. "Girls," she says, "I want you to meet Grandmother and Grandfather Ljungborg." Tallulah Belle puts on her Broadway smile and says hi. Gwen makes the sign of the cross and says, "Let's go, Russ." And they hurry off before they've even paid for the scented trash bags and Fiji water they leave behind. Donny shrugs, sneezes into his hanky, smiles, looks at Julie, and says, "My three favorite ladies."

( )

WHAT'S LEFT OF BILL TASHER AND JAMES PATRICK HORAN ARE EATING oysters and smoked mullet at Edith's Raw Bar on the beach and shooting the breeze with Fleet Lentz, their shucker. Fleet shows the men a dry, withered, cloudy oyster that he just opened. He says, If I gave you this one, you'd be dead tomorrow. What's left of Bill Tasher says, Promises, promises.

( )

DR. GWILLIAM COMPRESSES OLNEY'S HEART, AND THE MONITOR BEEPS, and the rhythm line ascends. Mark, eyes on the monitor and fingers on Olney's femoral artery, says, "He's back. We've got a pulse."

Dr. Gwilliam says, "Give him an amp of epi and hang a dopamine. Lucy, tell the trauma OR he's on his way." And then she walks to the waiting room, sits down beside Kat, and tells her what's going on. "In the trauma OR the doctors will do an abdominal explore and begin to put Olney back together. They'll replace his blood with ten units of O negative, and, hopefully, transfer him to the trauma ICU. And then we wait."

Kat tells Dr. Gwilliam that the man who shot her ex-husband was wheeled straight to the morgue. Dr. Gwilliam sits up. They both see the flashing lights of an ambulance through the waiting room windows. Dr. Gwilliam slaps her knees, squeezes Kat's hand, and says, "Back to work."

Elbert walks through the doors. Kat stands and says, "Did you find Cully?"

"They're taking him into the ER right now. He's hanging in there."

Kat collapses into her chair and cries into her hands. Elbert sits beside her and puts his arm around her shoulders. He kisses her head. When she catches her breath and can speak, Kat says, "Where was he?"

"The Sans Souci."

Kat says, "Drugs?"

"They found pills on the floor. So they know what he probably swallowed, but not how much."

"Was he conscious?"

"Yes, and then no. He was flat on his back when I got to him. That's when I called 911. And then he threw up, and then he passed out."

Olney is five-ish, and he's watching the reflection of the Independence Day fireworks in his father's glasses, the aviator glasses with the missing nose pad and the cracked bridge. He hears the *pop-pop-pop* of the grand finale and smells the sulfur wafting over the river. When his father looks down at him, his eyes are red, white, and blue.

Olney holds the swaddled baby in the crook of his arm and sniffs the intoxicating scent of the baby's pointy head. The baby's eyes are squeezed shut against the delivery room lights.

Jesus sits on the Mount of Olives, from where he will, in time, ascend to heaven, looks down upon the city of Jerusalem, and weeps. His hands are folded on his knees. He's thinking about fathers and filicide and Abraham and incest and Lot and Ahaz, and he's thinking about his own biological father, Joseph—same cleft chin, same attached earlobes, same Nubian nose, same unibrow, no genetic doubt about it, friends—who vanished when Jesus was twelve. Went on an errand to Sepphoris and never came back. Walked out on his chilly marriage and his adoring son. A full moon shines behind dark but scattered clouds. And then Olney's standing beside Jesus's rock. Jesus turns to the intruder. Jesus's eyes are on fire. Olney steps away and falls, and as he tumbles through the firmament, he accelerates until he's traveling at billions of light-years per second, past the stars, past the galaxies, and beyond our universe, beyond the multiverses, and into Hell, all the while screaming for mercy and understanding. Please! He stops. Or doesn't. Hard to tell. Time has been obliterated. He's the only one there, and *there* is nowhere. Nothing to see, nothing to touch, nothing to hear except for this low hum, and so the hum becomes his center of meaning.

Mireille is wearing her peach tap pants with the lilac hem and a matching flowy blouse. She's onstage at Olney's house under the bright lights doing a song-and-dance number about simple gifts.

Flap HEEL heel SPANK heel TOE heel
To turn, turn will be our delight,
Spank HEEL shuffle HEEL step
Till by turning, turning we come round right.
Hop BRUSH SPANK

Olney's in the trauma ICU, a ventilator doing his breathing for him. He's in an induced coma. He can hear people speaking but can't hear what they say, and he doesn't know who they are. He's hooked up to blood and saline IVs and has a nasogastric tube up his nose and down his throat and a Foley catheter inserted into his penis. His words are coming back, but he can't use them yet. What was that screaming flash of light? Where is his son?

Cully was given the Romazicon, prescribed by the Poison Control Center, and was then sent with a sitter to the medical surgery unit. He is on suicide watch. When he recovers and is cleared for release, he will be Baker-Acted and will spend the following seventy-two hours in the psych unit. It's likely he will be referred to detox and to rehab after that, but his participation will be voluntary. Right now everything he hears has an echo-ho-ho-ho. Everything smells like kerosene. He was definitely going to Anastasia with his dad, start over, get it right this time. But now he's screwed that pooch.

Olney's breathing on his own now. How long have I been here? He sees Kat across the room speaking to a nurse. Everything in the room is white, including the wires and tubes. Everything is on wheels, the tables, the monitor, the sleek machines. Sunlight slants through the blinds. All the white machines are trimmed in light blue to match the nurses' scrubs. They must have hired a stylist. Olney closes his eyes, and he can still see. That's a good sign. His throat is sore, too sore to speak. He'll try telepathy. He asks Kat if she's seen Cully. She doesn't answer. She doesn't move. He'll whisper. Kat puts her ear by Olney's mouth. She smiles and says, As a matter of fact, he's on his way to see you right now.

Cully's on his way to the psych unit for his three-day, three-squares-and-a-bed vacay, and he's been allowed a brief escorted visit to see his dad. He arrives with an orderly. He holds Olney's hand, and they both cry. And so does Kat. Cully apologizes for everything, the whole ten-year shit show. He says, "When you get out of here, we're going home, you and me, to Anastasia."

After two weeks in rehab, Cully signs himself out. He tells Olney his counselor urged him to stay longer, but when he explained how eager he was to get his new life with his old man started, they wished him well. "I'm good to go. I told you'd I'd be back for you, and here I am, clean and sober."

With Samir's help, Olney will be admitted to a rehabilitation center in Anastasia, and Samir will check on him every other day. The doctors at Everglades General were not happy with Olney's decision, but he signed an AMA, a release against medical advice. He was cautioned to go slow. Dr. Virgin told him he had a truck driver in the midst of a heart attack sign an AMA two nights ago. Died in the parking lot before he got to his car. "Your leaving now might result in serious injury or even death."

"I'll be careful."

He was offered an ambulance to take him to the center, but he tells them his son will drive. He wonders if Cully has a driver's license. "We're going home."

Dr. Virgin says, "You're going to have trouble getting up and down."

"I'll stay put."

"This isn't a joke. If the pain becomes too intense, stop at the first ER you see."

"I will."

"We're giving you this large abdo dressing. Don't change it. Don't touch it. Don't get it wet. There's a trauma dressing in the bag with your meds. Use it over the large dressing if it leaks. Got it?"

"Got it."

"You're going to be in pain."

"Already am."

"Here are your pain meds. Very strong. Take one as needed but be judicious. Don't drink alcohol. These here are stool softeners. You can't be straining yourself and bursting stiches. And these are antibiotics should the wound get infected."

"Thank you."

"Are you sure you won't change your mind?"

"Sure."

"Have Dr. Abdelnour call me after he's examined you."

Cully drives Olney to the Dixiewood to say his goodbyes. Robbie has Olney's suitcase packed and waiting, and she's put all his notebooks, pens, and pencils in a messenger bag. The Silpher twins walk out hand in hand and tell Olney, "Safe home." The twins head off for the bus stop to catch the #11 to the Senior Center. Reed joins the group, and they all sit by the firepit. Olney says he can't believe Guy shot him.

Robbie says, "His hypervigilance got the best of him."

Olney asks about Dante.

Robbie says, "Well, he lit out of here after the shooting, and he hasn't been back. I cleared out his room. He had a metal box full of cash. I stopped counting at seven thousand dollars. You'd think he'd come back for that."

Lip says hi to everyone and takes Cully aside. He tells Cully he needs to get to at least one meeting a day, every day, including today. Cully tells him he went this morning at St. Luke's. "I'm going to be okay. I know the next relapse will be my last relapse."

Lip claps him on the shoulder. They bump fists.

"Anyone seen Neutron?" Olney says. "I was hoping she might want to come along with us."

Robbie says, "Your sweetie pie is pregnant."

"Get out!"

"She's looking for a safe place to birth those babies. I may end up giving her the bottom drawer of my dresser."

"I'm a little sad."

"Well, we expect you to come visit, and then you'll see Neutron and the kitties."

Kat arrives with Elbert. They've brought a box of avocado-and-cheese arepas for the travelers and a gallon jug of water. Olney whispers in her ear. "We did it, Kat, we saved our boy." She smiles and they embrace.

Reed asks them all to hold hands and observe a moment of silence for Guy, for Olney's recovery, for their mutual friendships. And they do. And then Elbert helps Cully settle Olney into the front seat of the Scion.

Cully starts the engine, turns to Olney, and says, "You're going to be proud of me, Dad."

Cully drives up 95, drinking Red Bulls and eating arepas. He's fooling with the radio, trying to find a podcast about serial killers that he likes. Olney tells him he's got AM and FM and nothing else. And then Olney dozes off and dreams that Cully tells him that he has been betrayed and misinterpreted. Olney asks him to explain, but Cully goes quiet and curls up into a little ball on the floor of wherever it is they are. "Answer me." Olney pokes Cully in the side with his foot. "You deaf?" Olney squats beside his son. He wants to shake some sense into the little jerk, but that's when he wakes up, and there's Cully behind the wheel, and he's whistling, of all things.

Cully says, "Welcome back."

"Where are we?"

"Near Vero."

"Let's stop soon."

They stop at the Halfway Inn near Palm Bay, a single-story motel with the office up front and the ten units in single file behind. Room #7, a smoking room, has two rumpled double beds, two lamps on two bedside tables, one metal folding chair, one TV, three shelves beneath the TV counter, no drawers, a noisy AC unit below the window, a drab dark brown carpet, beige walls, and floral polyester bedspreads that Cully strips off the beds and piles in a corner. There is a small square table by the window and an amber glass ashtray on the table. Cully pulls a pack of American Spirits from his pocket.

"Really?" Olney says.

"I have to have one vice."

"Can you take it outside?"

Cully picks up Olney's iPhone. "What's your passcode?"

"Your birthday."

Cully grabs the chair, steps outside the room, sits, and lights up. He downloads a sobriety app and learns there's an early-riser AA meeting at seven-thirty at the Russian Orthodox church.

Back inside, Olney's lying on the bed. Cully tells him about the meeting. He'll be back by eight-thirty and they can hit the road. Olney texts Samir with a noonish ETA. Cully turns on the TV but lowers the sound. An old episode of *Dog the Bounty Hunter*. He flops on the bed.

Olney tries rolling to his side, but the spasm of pain stops him.

Cully says, "You okay?"

"What went wrong with us, Cully? We drifted apart."

"We were never really that close."

Olney is stunned. He pictures himself with Cully bouncing on his knee at Turpentine Park, and the two of them singing "B-I-N-G-O."

"I thought we were."

"We never had the kind of relationship where we were honest with each other. You were always so judgmental. I was never good enough. But let's not get off on the wrong foot. We're starting over."

"I love you more than you know. I almost got myself killed trying to save you."

"You almost got yourself killed by hanging out with a psychopath."

"Who saved your life."

"He didn't have to shoot those guys."

"Could you bring me my meds? In the bag there."

Olney is going to put them under his pillow for safekeeping.

On TV, Dog and Leland are staking out an apartment complex on the Big Island, where a pedophile-on-the-lam was spotted. Cully opens the bag and removes the plastic prescription vials.

"One of each," Olney says.

Cully hands Olney the plastic cup of water and taps out two pills.

Olney swallows the pills. Cully sits on the edge of his bed. The mattress is so thin, he can feel the supporting slat on his butt. He changes the channel on the TV to local news and turns up the volume a bit. A woman from Jensen Beach was arrested at her home today for the murder of her three-year-old son thirty-two years ago at a swap meet in Las Vegas, where she then lived with the child and the child's stepfather. She and her husband had already been arrested for physically abusing the boy and were facing trial when the boy vanished. A week after his disappearance, the grieving couple held a garage sale at their home where they sold the missing child's toys. New but undisclosed evidence has led to the arrest.

Olney says, "Did you finish that play you were working on?"

"Not yet, but I've finished a screenplay and I'm working on the pitch." He pulls a notebook out of his suitcase, sits on the bed. "Want to hear it?"

"I do."

"I'm calling it *Uncertain, Texas*. An actual place. It's a psychological drama-slash-mystery. The logline is, 'He can't remember his past, but his past has not forgotten him.'"

Olney says, "The past has a mind of its own."

Cully reads. "One bright morning before his wife and daughter awake, Felix Rowan packs his suitcase, gets in his car, and drives away from his home in Rochester, New York. He doesn't know where he's going; he doesn't know who he is. Five years later—it seems like five days—Felix wakes up in bed at the Dreamland Inn on Caddo Lake in Uncertain, Texas, with no idea how he got there. He calls his wife. He drives to Rochester. Back home he's a stranger in the house. He has a sense of déjà vu—he's been here, and he knows what will happen, but feels unbalanced. He has to relearn his marketing job at Xerox. He sees a psychiatrist and learns that he's experienced a fugue state brought on by something he experienced as a child, which he cannot accept, and when the memory was triggered by the return of someone or something into his life, he fled. Through hypnosis, and reluctantly at first, Felix begins to search for the source of the trauma. He also wonders who he was for five years and what his life was like. He explores Uncertain on the Web and intuitively feels that he was happy there, content. And then he finds a photo online of himself sitting with a woman on a bench at the Dreamland Inn. He's determined now to uncover the mystery of his past. He goes to Texas despite his wife's protests. And soon his worlds collide."

"I like the name Felix."

"Happy."

"Irony."

"The wife has remarried."

"I love it. And you've written it?"

"Some of it. Most of Act 1. And outlined the rest."

"What was the childhood trauma that set Felix off?"

"I know, but he doesn't. That's the part I'm working on now. Was. I'll get back to it. Felix and his shrink. And, who knows, I might find out I'm wrong."

"What do you think happened?"

"He was teased and bullied and beaten by older boys. They tied him to the flagpole outside of school and left him."

"Anything like this ever happen to you?"

"No, not that I remember. And I would remember. Felix has buried his memory, but the shrink, Dr. Florin, tells him he needs to uncover to recover."

Olney yawns and apologizes. Cully stretches his arms over his head. "Let's get some sleep."

( )

OLNEY CLOSES HIS EYES AND WAITS FOR A FACE TO APPEAR, A FACE HE can watch, a face that will lead him to dreamland. But when no sleep-inducing face materializes (or immaterializes), he imagines instead his life with Cully in Anastasia. They'll fix up the spare room for Cully's bedroom. He sees Cully waiting tables at Captain Cook's Chowder House—lunch shift—and taking education classes at Anastasia College. Olney will have supper waiting for Cully when he gets home.

Cully can't sleep. He takes Olney's phone and types the address of the AA meeting into the map app. Right on East Florida, then left at the light then first right. Nine-minute drive. He grabs his cigarettes and the chair and steps outside to sit and smoke and think. The night is clear and breezy. He lights up, inhales, and rehearses what he'll say at the meeting. Hi, I'm Cully and I'm twenty-three days clean and sober. What a ride it's been. He walks to the Popeyes down the street and orders Cajun rice. He sits by the window. Hi, I'm Cully, and I'm an . . . . should he say "addict" or "alcoholic"? Some of these drunks look down on junkies as second-class reprobates. He realizes the meeting can't start too soon. He keeps thinking of his dad's pain meds.

Olney stirs and wakes. He sits up gingerly. No Cully in the room. He goes to the door, opens it, sees the chair and a cigarette butt on the sidewalk. He needs to buy gifts for Hedy and Tallulah Belle. They'll stop at that souvenir shop outside Daytona. Langley, too. He gets back in bed, shuts his eyes, wonders why the meds are not putting him to sleep. He decides that he'll go back for Neutron when he's on his feet again.

Cully wakes at six. He showers quickly, gets dressed as he watches his father's fitful sleep. He checks the time—7:10. He packs his suitcase and sets it by the door. He realizes he won't be able to lock the room when he leaves, figures nothing will happen. His dad will be up in a matter of minutes. He claps his pockets and looks around the room. What else should he pack in the car?

Olney hears the car start up and back away from the room. He sits up gingerly and reaches for his phone but can't find it. The pain inside is so severe he needs to take a breath. Cully must have taken the phone. He opens the door, sees the empty chair and the cigarette butts on the sidewalk. He heads for the bathroom.

Cully stops for coffee at the 7-Eleven and drives with the windows down. He's listening to Warren Zevon sing about lawyers, guns, and money, and he's singing along. The shit has hit the fan. He feels exhilarated. Mornings sure are better here in Soberville! He calls Pixie. No answer. Probably just as well. He leaves a message: It's Ishmael. Call me. Will she get the joke? Yes, she will. Left at the light. The phone rings.

After his sponge bath, Olney pulls on his sweatpants and decides to just wear the same Superman T-shirt they gave him at the hospital. He lifts the blinds and peeks out the window. It's eight forty-five and Olney thinks maybe the meeting went long. Some of those horror stories must be fascinating, after all. Maybe Cully stopped to buy cigarettes. Maybe he got stuck behind a funeral. Took a wrong turn. That could happen to anyone, GPS or not. Olney thinks he should maybe take a painkiller, but the bag is not where it was by the TV. He doesn't see it anywhere. Cully must have packed it. At nine, Olney fears that Cully might have gotten into an accident. (He hopes that he's wrong; he hopes that he's right.) Has he died dreaming? Is he in that dream now? he wonders. If so, is he dreaming from his hospital bed? He looks around. He stamps his feet. He knocks on the door. No, he's here in Palm Bay, all right. It's matter over mind, not mind over matter. That's the message he gets from the lacerating pain in his gut.

He listens for sirens. Where is Cully? He walks to the motel office, stopping every few feet to take a restorative and analgesic breath. He enters the office and asks to use the phone. The clerk can see that he's in bad shape, and she has him sit, slowly, on the leatherette easy chair. She introduces herself. "Bolivia Regalado. I'll call 911 for you."

"I don't know if this is an emergency or not."

"It's an emergency for me."

"My son has been in an accident."

"You're in pain, aren't you?"

"He has my meds."

"I'll get you something. Tylenol, Aleve, Motrin, Percocet."

When Olney looks confused, Bolivia says, "You would not believe what people leave behind. Our Lost & Found is a pharmacy."

"Tylenol," he says, and then says, "No. I'm not sure I should take it." He gives Bolivia a description of his car—a salsa lunchbox—to which Bolivia asks for more specific info. "It's a 2006 Scion xB, maroonish."

"Gracias." She calls the police. No accidents reported. And then she calls Samir and hands the phone to Olney, who leaves a message on voice mail. "Exit . . . . what exit, Bolivia?"

"Exit One-forty-one."

"One-four-one. Halfway Inn. Room Seven." He hands Bolivia her phone. "Do you have children, Bolivia?"

"Only six." She smiles.

"You have your hands full."

"And my heart. My husband and me, we manage."

"How old?" Olney says.

"The oldest two, the twins, David and Patricia, are in Gainesville in college. Michael, Cali, and Juan in high school, and the baby, Maria, in middle school." She tells Olney that Samir just texted that he's on the way. "He will help you find your son."

Olney's back in his room, standing by the window because it hurts to sit. He's trying not to think about this exhausting and flashing pain, radiating from what's left of his internal organs. Maybe he *should* ask Bolivia to call the ambulance. She could direct Samir to the ER when he arrives. He sits carefully, knowing he will not be able to stand again without help. He opens his notebook and writes his son's full name. Cully Franklin Kartheizer. He writes it again. He underlines it. He writes, *Olney loves Cully.* He draws a heart. Draws an arrow through the heart. Draws blood dripping from the wound. He's gone too far. He smiles and puts down his pen. He looks out the window and sees Cully hurrying up the drive, not the twenty-seven-year-old Cully but little Cully and his red wagon. There's a black cat in the wagon. A sweet feral cat. What was that cat's name? Smokey? Olney watches and waits and cries. Sometimes waiting can make things happen. That's what he believes. Believing is more important than knowing. You can't live without hope, and you wouldn't want to. But then he thinks hope contradicts the future, doesn't it? He thinks of all the people who have come and gone in his life, and how once they start going, they don't stop.

IF I KNEW THE WAY

Olney's sitting at the kitchen table by the open window on an early spring evening, inhaling the lustrous scent of petrichor after a brief rain shower. He's sipping cognac and once again writing down memories of Cully to keep Cully in the here and now—Cully the Halloween pirate, Cully weeping in Santa's lap, Cully with the missing front teeth—and listening to Slim Gaillard on the Wednesday night jazz program on WHY-AM. Neutron's sprawled out on the table, chewing her catnip mouse and flicking her tail at the page as Olney writes. Cowboy Cully on his rocking horse. Olney wonders if Neutron remembers her kittens, gone to good homes, every one. He listens to Slim sing about a puddle o-vooty, and he smiles. Cully in a safety helmet riding his bike with the training wheels and crashing into the magnolia out front. He gets up laughing, brushing the dirt from his dungarees.

Olney's pretty much back to normal, although normal is different than it used to be. Refurbished and presentable, is what he thinks of himself. He hasn't seen Cully in nine months and hasn't stopped searching the Internet for him—arrest records, mug-shot sights, social media, Google searches. Olney's Scion was found three months ago, in

Timothy, Georgia, abandoned in the parking lot of a closed and shuttered barbecue joint. No damage. No gas. The guy from the impoundment lot who called Olney said the interior stank of spoiled food and cheap wine and was littered with empty prescription bottles. Olney paid Craig Dillon to fetch the car back for him.

Taffi Burgess died. "Went on ahead," was how Rylan put it. Rylan and Buddy carry on at the Wellspring of Joy Ministry with a small but devoted congregation but without *The House of Burgess*. The emptiness in that kitchen set would be too hard for either of them to bear. Mr. Nick, Mrs. Woodbine's dad, also passed. Olney hears the barred owl call, *who-cooks-for-you?* and so does Neutron. She gets up, walks to Olney, and knocks her head against his nose.

Julie's dream came true. Lonnie sold the gas station and moved his wife and kids to Orlando, where he took a job working at the BibleLand Theme Park. He plays Judas Iscariot in the Passion Play and Lot in the story of Sodom and Gomorrah. If Lonnie can be redeemed, so can Cully.

Althea waited too long to get her failing eyesight checked. By the time she saw the retina specialist, her macular degeneration was too advanced to make any improvement. It's hard for her to read anymore, so she sits in her chair in the dark and listens to her five Harlequin romance novels a day on her tablet, or Dewey reads them to her. When he does, he gives Olney a one-sentence recap of what he's read: "She's afraid of the water, and he's a merman"; "The president had intimacy issues until he met the Queen of Bohemia"; "He's a rebel in leather pants, and she's a debutante in lace." He tells Olney that the lives lived in romance novels might not be credible, but they might be desirable. And Olney thinks that Althea would not have enjoyed *The Appassionata*.

This morning, Dewey came by for his coffee and bacon, and Olney said, "So now that you're an expert on the genre, what's your verdict?"

"Romance or freedom—you can't have them both." And then he asked Olney when they were going to bring back that boy of his.

"When we find out where he is."

"You ain't in this alone, okay?"

Olney smiles and nods.

"You found him once, we can find him again." Dewey raises his coffee cup.

"So what book are you reading her today?"

"Long Healing Prayer." Dewey pulls the book out of his back pocket and reads from the jacket. "On the night of their senior prom, Cade Stinson and Mona Connelly are in a car accident that leaves Mona with only a broken wrist but Cade in the hospital in a coma. Instead of going off to Liberty University together, Mona sits by Cade's hospital bed day after day for months praying for his recovery. She is stunned to find herself falling in love with Dr. Dick Rappenecker, Cade's physician. Mona wonders if Cade's 'vegetative state' is concealing his consciousness. Can he, in fact, hear everything that she and Dick are whispering?"

"The plot thickens."

"I say we make a road trip to Timothy, Georgia."

"Maybe so."

"That's our only clue."

"So far."

After Dewey leaves, Olney slides Neutron off his book. She slaps her paw on the back of his offending hand with claws in place, but not penetrating the skin. She looks into his eyes. How do we want to play this, Olney? He calls her a goon and opens *The Appassionata* and reads a few pages. Valentine's marriage to Ms. French Horn, the Boston Brahmin, is going on as planned, a destination wedding at the Sandals Resort in St. Lucia. But Valentine and Martine can't stay away from each other. If Valentine calls off the wedding, he'll have to leave town,

Olney thinks. He shuts the book. Valentine will be lucky to find a chair in the Texarkana Philharmonic if Ms. French Horn's daddy has anything to say about it. There certainly won't be room for the three of them in the Boston Symphony Orchestra. Neutron walks a circle on the braided rug, curls herself into a ball, nose to tail, and sleeps.

( )

OLNEY SETS THE MAUVE AND YELLOW TULIPS ON MIREILLE'S GRAVE, steps back, and admires the simple granite headstone. Her name, her dates, and the epitaph: END OF STORY. He tells her that Jack Tighe has also passed away, quietly, in his sleep. Ran out of gas, his sister said. He sees Auralee at Zoë's grave and joins her. They embrace and smile. After a moment of silence, they walk toward Old Town. The pink is gone from her silver hair. She asks about Cully.

"MIA, but he's out there, and I'll find him." He tells her that Julie called. "Tallulah Belle is in school and Hedy in day care. Julie's working at BibleLand with Lonnie, waiting tables at the Last Supper."

"We should visit."

"I would love that."

"Soon."

He asks her what she sees in his future. She takes his hand, looks at his palm, asks for the other hand. "I see you and me having cocktails at George's Majestic Lounge with Samir and Jen."

What if this hunt for Cully were a novel? Olney wonders. How would it end? Not with a vanished Cully. Leave the state—okay. Leave the planet—unbearable. Maybe it ends with Cully out of detox, out of rehab, and into AA. He's found a power greater than himself that he can believe in—Time. You can't stop it. He's at Step #9, making amends, and he is writing a letter to his dad, expressing his sorrow and his love. He can't promise when he'll be back or if he'll be back, but he is sound and stable, and he is grateful. Olney could live with that. But then he remembers the future he's already devised for Cully—the college professor living in Anastasia with his wife and son, Sky, the light of Olney's life. He sees himself and Sky on their boys' night out, sitting on a bench at the miniature golf course, eating strawberry ice cream and watching the S'Moores, wearing their identical high school uniforms, over at the windmill hole. Sky says he can tell them apart.

( )

CULLY SAYS, "YOU USED TO GLOW IN THE DARK."

Pixie says, "You used to have a future."

They are in their room at the Royal Inn Motor Court in Pond City, Florida. They've been here two days, and Pixie has had enough. When they checked in late Tuesday night, Pixie found a used tampon in a dresser drawer and a soiled diaper on the bathroom floor. No microwave, no coffee maker, no remote, no soap, no shampoo, no washcloth, one towel. Black mold on the pink bathroom tile, blood on the bedspread, glass shards under the sheets, and bedbugs in and on the mattress. The AC unit makes a racket.

Pixie's packing her foldable nylon shopping bag with her few clothes, fewer cosmetics, and her travel umbrella. Cully's sprawled on the bed in his briefs and his socks. He opens his eyes and says, "Where are we, again?"

"At the end of the road."

"What's that supposed to mean?"

"I'm done living like this."

"Like free, you mean?"

"Free?"

Cully props himself up on his elbow. "We can go anywhere and do anything we want. Free!"

"Well, I want to go to Paris and stay in a five-star hotel. In a suite with a fireplace."

"When?"

"Now. If we're free to go anywhere, why are we here in a roach motel in East Whipshit? Why am I working my ass off in dollar stores while you sit on your flat ass?"

"I do my part."

"You can't keep showing up at pain clinics with self-inflicted wounds forever."

"I do it because the meds make you happy."

"Don't confuse *high* with *happy*, Cully."

"Where are you going to go?"

"I have family."

Cully swings his feet off the bed and onto the floor. "Maybe they can help us out."

"Call your father."

"With what?"

"Pay phone." She turns her ear to his face. "Pull some change out of the air."

"What's going to happen to me?"

"I suppose you'll realize eventually that you have betrayed yourself for nothing, and you will implode."

Cully walks to Pixie and takes her hand. "It won't always be like this. I'm almost clean. I'm a survivor."

"I'm out the door in ten minutes with you or without you. I've got a bus to catch."

Cully collapses on the bed and cries. "Don't you love me anymore?"

Pixie shoulders her bag, looks around the room for anything she might be leaving behind. She walks to the bed and pats Cully's head. "You're like an abused puppy, Cully, and I love you. But I can't unchain you."

( )

OLNEY'S BACK WRITING DOWN MEMORIES. CULLY IN SWIM GOGGLES, rubber boots, and a diaper, stomping through puddles in the yard. Cully as George Gibbs in the Splendora High School production of *Our Town*. One-year-old Cully with his face buried in his chocolate birthday cake. Cully crying at the window, waiting for Anthony to come over to play. This memory still breaks Olney's heart. He puts down his pen. He sees the elaborate Hot Wheels track set up on the living room floor. He sees Cully bereft at the living room window. Cully's kneeling against the back pillow of the leather sofa, weeping, his head against the windowpane, his shoulders trembling. He's wailing and gasping to catch his breath. Olney sits beside him and rubs his back.

"It's okay, Cully." He holds Cully, who at first resists but then collapses into Olney's embrace. Olney rocks Cully in his arms, kisses his head, tells him everything's going to be all right.

"Why doesn't Anthony love me?"

"Anthony does love you. He just can't be with you today." Olney remembers now, in his kitchen, how irrationally angry he felt then, in the living room, at Anthony's parents for taking Anthony away.

"I have no one to play with."

"I'll play with you."

"It's not the same."

"Friends are forever," Olney lies, "but they can't always be together."

"I'll never be happy."

"You will. I promise."

"Never ever."

Cully puts his arms around Olney's neck and his head on Olney's shoulder. Olney holds his boy and sings.

> Hush, little Cully, don't say a word
> Daddy's gonna buy you a mockingbird
> And if that mockingbird won't sing
> Daddy's gonna build you a front-porch swing
>
> And if that front-porch swing won't rise
> Daddy's gonna get you a big surprise
> The big surprise is long and black
> Daddy's gonna buy you a Cadillac
>
> And when one day we say goodbye
> Daddy's gonna squeeze you and we'll both cry
> And if by chance you should get lost
> Daddy's gonna find you at any cost
>
> No matter when, no matter where
> When you look up, I'll be there.

(IV)

Stay the Distance

I WOULD TAKE YOU HOME

Olney and Dewey are belted in, coffee'd up, and ready to roll. Olney adjusts the rearview mirror. "Pond City, here we come!" The Scion has a full tank, a fully inflated spare tire, and new windshield wipers. They're off to rescue Cully from his demons.

Olney says, "Bottled water?"

Dewey says, "Check."

"First-aid kit?"

"Check."

"Sandwiches?"

"Cuban and reuben."

"Photo of Cully?"

"On my phone."

"Changes of clothing?"

"Check, check. Check." Last night late, Olney got a call from Unknown Caller, who introduced herself as Pixie, Cully's former squeeze, and told Olney that he and she met in Melancholy. Olney didn't remember. She told Olney that she left Cully at the Royal Inn Motor Court in PC and that he asked her to call him.

Olney said, "PC? Is it spelled like it sounds?"

She said, "Pond City."

"I'll go fetch him."

She tells Olney that Cully is ready to come home. He could not have gotten far from the motel in his condition. And then, out of nowhere, she asked him if he'd read *Skylark*. He has not. "You'll love it," she said. "Sad as shit."

Langley will feed Neutron and play indoor soccer with her in the kitchen with the little sponge ball. Auralee will check on Althea, read to her, and set up the Audible. Jen will cook Althea's meals and carry them over. Olney types the motor court's address into his map app. "Should take about three hours," Olney tells Dewey. Dewey says he'll likely need to pee before then. In fact, Dewey sleeps. They'll be gone two nights. If they can't locate Cully by then, they'll come home and wait for the next clue. He'll call Pixie to see if Cully checked in with her. Assuming she called from her own phone. What they won't do is give up the search. Olney's not stopping till he finds his son. Right now Cully is all that matters.

Dewey wakes when Olney brakes, slows the car, and says, "We're here." He pulls over in front of the WELCOME TO POND CITY, HOME OF THE MARSH SLUG sign. Below the welcome, this: *COME AS YOU ARE.* They drive the main drag past the Lincoln Temple Church of God in Christ, past the People's Choice market, past the Friendship Baptist Church, and past a sagging wood-frame house with a collapsed front porch. "There it is," Dewey says. Olney turns into the empty motor court parking lot. The tall marquee sign out front reads from top to bottom:

R YAL MO OR C R T

AMERICAN OWNED

PETS WELCOME

Vacancy ("No surprise there," Dewey says.)

Lowest Rates in Town ("Only rates in town," Olney says.)

A sandwich board on the sidewalk points to the office.

Two adhesive signs are pasted to the front of the simple pine reception desk: Cash Only and Ring Bell. Olney taps the call bell. A small state flag is tacked to the wall behind the desk, and below it is a corkboard with ten room keys on hooks. A heavyset Black woman with box braids, snaggled teeth, and turquoise cat-eye glasses, walks out of the bathroom wiping her hands with a paper towel. "Can I do for you gentlemen?" She sits in her swivel chair.

Dewey shows her the photo of Cully on his phone. She looks at it over the top of her glasses and nods.

Olney says, "We're here to find my son and think he may have stayed here this week. I'm Olney by the way, and this is Dewey."

"Destiny."

Dewey says, "Pleased to meet you."

"He was here with a young lady, but now he's gone. Lady left first. Got something back here that might belong to him."

Dewey says, "Not many guests today."

Destiny says, "We don't get many tourists here. We're mostly a spare bedroom, you might say, for the locals. You know what I'm saying?"

"I do," Dewey says.

Destiny takes a metal box out from below the counter and lifts the lid. "Your boy looked like he was back from the brink of something."

"He's had a long struggle."

"Here you go." Destiny hands Olney a Hot Wheel toy car with a yellow roof that he recognizes as a magenta '55 Chevy Bel Air.

Olney smiles and says, "Big Deal."

"Something wrong?" Dewey says.

"Big Deal's the name of the car. Cully's car. When he was a kid."

Destiny says, "Got you a sentimental boy."

"Do you happen to know where he went?"

She points to her right. "Last I saw, he was headed west on Main. Thing of it is, about three miles yonder the road forks, and who's to say which road he took? One way to Whynot, the other to Gracious."

"We'll ride around town just to check before we head west," Olney says. "Where is the library?"

"Don't have one."

"Got a coffee shop?"

"I can make you some coffee."

"A place where someone might sit and sip and read."

"Nothing like that."

"Thank you so much," Olney says.

( )

"THAT'S FOUR," DEWEY SAYS.

"Four what?"

"Rebel flags. Five."

They turn off Main and drive along a winding, nameless, unpeopled dirt road, littered on both sides with discarded furniture, mattresses, sinks, appliances, lawn mowers, and tires.

"What the fuck?" Olney says.

The road brings them to the town cemetery. Olney points out that so many—most—of the graves are painted a light blue. "Wonder what that's about."

"Haint-blue," Dewey says. "Keeps the bad spirits away."

They circle the cemetery, checking to see if Cully might be snoozing in the shade of a headstone. He's not. When they exit the cemetery and turn left, they pass a closed gas station painted beige. Over the two bay doors, someone has printed JAIL in black paint. And over the office window SHERIFF'S DEPT.

"Must be a joke, right?" Olney says.

"Or conceptual art," Dewey says. They see lots of men and boys standing around, leaning against walls. There are cars in every front yard. Vacant lots have become parking lots. Rusted-out cars and trucks. Some of the others, washed and waxed, look like they might run fine. The bed of one vintage F-150 with four flat tires has become a flourishing garden of ten-foot-high weeds. Some folks have parked their backhoes beside their campers. Other folks have left some room in their front yards for trampolines or kiddie pools. Lots of folding lawn chairs in front of the double-wides.

Back on Main, they pass Pond City High School, the Home of the Rattlers. There's a taco place beside the Dollar Store, so they stop. Dewey shows Cully's photo to the woman, Giovanna, taking their order. "¿Reconoces a este hombre?"

She studies the photo like she might, but then shakes her head. "No."

While they wait for the food, Olney talks about ignoring Cully when he was a boy. "I'd say, Cully, Daddy's working on a feature story for the paper. We'll play when I'm done. I'd hold him off with one hand and type with the other. I was a bit of a monster."

"Don't start!"

"It's just—"

"Stop!"

When they finish eating, they gas up at the Citgo and hit the road west. Dewey says he has a good feeling about this rescue mission. "We'll find Cully today. He left that Hot Wheel for you to find."

"I don't know . . ."

"I do." Dewey takes the Chevy Bel Air out of the ashtray and puts it on the dashboard facing the road. They see the road sign for Gracious with an arrow pointing right and 1Mile.

Olney says, "How will we know which road to take?"

Dewey hums a tune and then sings his version of the old spiritual: "We'll know the road by the singing of the song. Yes, sweet Lord, we know the road." He claps his hands. "We'll know the road by the clapping of the hands, by the sharing of a smile, by the loving in your heart." As they approach the fork, Dewey looks at Olney, raises his eyebrows, and sings, "Sheep, sheep, don't you know the road?" And they both sing, "Yes, sweet Lord, we know the road." Olney veers left toward Whynot.

ACKNOWLEDGMENTS

It takes a village to build a novel. Thanks to those who helped me build: Jill Bialosky, Bill Clegg, Teddy Jones, Jim Bob Jones, Lisa Gouveia, Jill Coupe, Garry Kravit, Karen Kravit, David Norman, Cully Perlman, Helena Rho, Liz Trupin-Pulli, Peggy McGovern, Peter Stravlo, Kim Bradley, Sandra Jones, Scott Jones, Zack Strait, Penn Elliott, Lauren Rivera, Maureen Welch, Jean Dowdy, Stephanie Josey, Lisa Mahoney, Mark Dufresne, Peter Mladinic, Chet Jakubiak, Carolyn Jakubiak, Theodore Harrison-Rowan, Debra Monroe, Jeffrey Knapp, Phoebe Barzo, Paula Sullivan, Cyndi Wondolowski, Jason Zelesky, Alyssa Zelesky, David Beaty, Marilyn and Donny, Maureen Powers, the Friday Night Writers, Louis K. Lowy, Tristan, Jean Campbell, Tom DeMarchi, Bruce Harvey, Julie Marie Wade, Denise Duhamel, Howard Khani, Leo Stouder, Kimberly Harrison, Jeremy Rowan, Joe Walpole, Evan Wondolowski, Leo "Wolfie" Wondolowski, and these two: Django and Zoë. We did it!